THE DREAMCHASERS

Eda de Moise

Table of Contents

2024

This book is dedicated to all who are dream chasers.

To the individual who has the fortitude to follow their heart and the conviction to succeed in their chosen paths.

CHAPTER 1

It was a glorious day in July of 1974. The sun shone brightly overhead, casting a warm, golden glow that reflected off the ocean's surface, and a gentle, cool breeze whispered through the air. It was a perfect day, the kind that lifted spirits and promised unforgettable moments.

Maria had never seen the Pacific Ocean before, and she was radiant with excitement, the sun illuminating her long black hair as it flowed behind her in the breeze. She walked alongside her younger sisters, Emily and Edith, on the pristine white sandy beach that stretched endlessly before them. Emily had curious eyes and a wide-brimmed hat shielding her from the sun. Edith had her infectious laughter and boundless energy.

Maria had always dreamed of seeing the ocean and could hardly believe she was finally there. The temperature was perfect, with a refreshing light breeze that caressed her face and fluttered her dress. Her family had embarked on a trip to Northern California to visit relatives, and Maria had successfully persuaded her parents to take a scenic detour to the beach.

As Maria stepped closer to the water's edge, her heart felt an overwhelming sense of peace wash over her. The vast, open expanse of the ocean, with its shades of deep blue and turquoise, filled her with a sense of excitement and happiness she hadn't known she was missing.

The temperature that day was in the eighties, with a light breeze. This was the first time Maria's family had ever taken a road trip. Her parents could never afford to take a vacation, but when Maria's mother, Ethel, found out that her mother, Elizabeth, was sick, she packed the station wagon, and the five of them set out on the road.

Ethel told the three girls, "You can stay at the beach the rest of the day, and we will leave when it gets dark." They were all excited and anticipated all the fun the day would bring.

Maria and her sisters were enjoying a spirited game of frisbee on the sun-drenched beach, their laughter carrying on the ocean breeze. Their parents sat contentedly on a bench perched above the cliff, keeping a watchful eye over the girls with smiles that mirrored their daughters' joy. Suddenly, as Emily threw the frisbee toward Maria, a golden retriever darted across the sand, catching it deftly in its mouth. The dog's owner, a handsome young man with tousled dark hair and striking blue eyes, jogged over to retrieve it.

"My dog, Ginger, can't resist joining in. She loves frisbee almost as much as she loves the beach," he said, chuckling as he approached. He extended the frisbee back to Maria with a friendly grin. "Hi, my name is Alberto."

Maria, slightly startled but amused, replied, "I'm Maria. It's really nice to meet you and your enthusiastic frisbee thief there." She gestured playfully towards Ginger, who was now wagging her tail expectantly.

As Ginger nudged the frisbee into Maria's hand, Alberto laughed. "She's always been the icebreaker. I think she likes making friends more than I do."

The sun cast a golden glow around them, and the rhythmic sound of the waves provided a soothing background to their conversation. Maria and Alberto stood just a few feet from the lapping waves, the fine sand cool beneath their feet.

Maria shared a bit about herself, the breeze catching her words. "I'm 18 and just finished high school. We're from a small town in Iowa—this is actually our first time out here. It's a different world from the fields and farms back home." She glanced around at the expansive ocean, her eyes reflecting the vastness before her. "My dad works in agriculture, and my mom's a housekeeper for a family in Cedar Rapids. It's just us and my two sisters," she added, nodding back toward Emily and Edith, who were watching them curiously.

Alberto nodded thoughtfully. "Iowa, that's quite a shift from here to there. I grew up around these parts. I graduated with a degree in science this June, but I'm still figuring things out. Maybe I will head into my dad's construction business come fall." He paused, looking out at the horizon. "This beach, it's always been a place to think, to dream about what's next. What about you? Any dreams you're chasing?"

Maria smiled, the question stirring a flicker of aspiration within her. "I'm not sure yet. I've always been fascinated by the stories in books and the places they describe. Maybe I'll find a way to see some of them myself one day."

Their conversation flowed easily, the initial encounter growing into a genuine connection as they shared laughs and dreams under the sunlit sky. Neither of them noticed how quickly time was passing, the afternoon shadows growing longer across the sand.

Maria had always heard about the sunshine of California and always dreamt that one day she might go there. Maria explained to Alberto that her grandmother, Elizabeth, had been sick, and they were going to Northern California to visit her grandparents. "I have not seen my grandparents since I was seven years old. I am really looking forward to seeing them, but I am worried about my grandmother," Maria said the words with a worried look on her face.

Maria and Alberto continued talking. They were both enthralled with their conversation as if they had known each other forever. Their conversations flew swiftly, filling their hearts with a special connection. Maria had never met anyone like Alberto before. Her two younger sisters continued to play frisbee with Alberto's dog Ginger.

The moment Alberto laid his eyes on Maria, he was captured by her beauty. He thought that Maria was a beautiful, sweet girl with gorgeous eyes. Alberto told Maria, "I am 23 years old and just graduated from college this June with a bachelor's in science."

He then continued to share his thoughts about his career with Maria since he felt like she could understand him completely. "I love science, but just not sure what I want to do with my degree. I have considered being a doctor, but I am unsure if that is how I want to go. I've decided to work with my Father in his construction business starting in September. I am not working this summer so I come to the beach every afternoon to let my dog run. The beach is my favorite place on earth."

Maria listen to Alberto carefully. She gave him nods to assure that she understood what he was saying. Then she told him about herself, "This is the first time I have ever seen the ocean, and you are so lucky to be able to come here every day."

Listening to Maria's perspective raised a realization in Alberto, "I had never thought of that, but you are absolutely right." They kept talking on and on and felt the warmth of the sunshine on their backs. Maria had never connected with anyone the way she did with Alberto.

"How long are you going to be here?" Alberto asked.

"We are going to leave in the morning. It will be dark soon, and my parents would say that it is time to go." Alberto felt he could talk to Maria forever. Neither one wanted to leave. They had connected on such a deep level in such a short period of time.

It was a matter of time when they heard Maria's parents yelling, "Girls, it is getting dark. We must leave."

But Alberto was just not yet ready to let Maria go. "Can I meet you here at this spot in the morning before you leave?" Alberto enthusiastically asked.

"I would love to meet you in the morning. Meet me at this exact spot at nine." They kissed, and both said, "I can't wait till I see you in the morning."

The Hernandez family left the beach and found a motel room about 10 miles away. They ate dinner at the family restaurant next door. The whole family was curious to hear more about Alberto. "Maria, what about the young man you were talking to on the beach," Ethel asked.

Maria's heart was flattered with Alberto's words, she told her mother, "Alberto was such a nice young man, and we had so much in common. I can't wait to see him again."

"We are leaving in the morning, Maria," Ethel responded.

"Mom, I know that, but I told Alberto that I would meet him tomorrow at nine in the morning at the beach."

Maria was very convincing, and thus Raymond said to her, "That is fine, but we need to leave by nine-thirty." Maria went to bed and couldn't sleep at all that night. All she could think about was Alberto and how he made her feel. She couldn't wait until nine in the morning to see him again.

Alberto drove home, which was about 15 miles inland from the beach. He had gone home to live with his parents after college. He kept thinking about Maria and that he had never met anyone like her before. He asked himself why she had to live so far away. If only she lived close, I could ask Maria for a date. He thought very seriously that maybe he had met the one. He was so excited to see her in the morning that he hardly slept at all that night.

The next day, Maria was the first one to wake up. It was seven in the morning, and Maria struggled to pick a dress that she should wear to the beach. She was so excited and couldn't wait to see Alberto. All five of the Hernandez family got dressed, packed their belongings, and checked out of the motel. They went to the restaurant next door and had breakfast. The whole family had a very hearty breakfast, but Maria couldn't even eat as she was on cloud nine.

The Hernandez family finished breakfast and headed to their car. It was eight thirty, and Maria thought it was perfect timing, just enough time to get to the beach before nine. Raymond tried starting the car, but the battery was dead. "This can't be happening," Maria shouted.

"Don't worry, Maria. We will call a tow truck, and they will come, give us a charge, and we will be on our way," Ethel responded.

Raymond went to the restaurant and used their phone. He came back and told the family, "The tow truck should be here in one to two hours. They are very busy and have many calls. I tried to have them come sooner, but it is not possible."

"We will still go to the beach after they come, and hopefully, you will still be able to see Alberto," Ethel tried to console Maria. But Maria was very anxious. She thought that she had no way to contact him. She kept thinking that this could not be happening.

On the other hand, Alberto was at the designated spot at the beach at nine with his dog. He thought Maria and her family were running late. He stayed at the beach till eleven in the morning and decided that she must not be coming. He was completely heartbroken and thought to himself; I spent a few hours with Maria yesterday, and how can I be feeling the way I do now? He left the beach and drove back to his parent's house. He felt depressed and couldn't get Maria out of his mind. He kept regretting that he should have asked her for her phone number at least. But he also questioned why Maria had not shown up. Did something happen, or did her parents say no, or did she decide she did not want to see me? Alberto thought that he might never be able to find the answer to this question, yet he decided that he would go to the beach every morning at nine for the rest of the summer in hopes that Maria would be there.

The tow truck finally showed up after 11 am. Their car battery was charged, and then they drove approximately 10 miles to the beach. Maria flew out of the car and ran down to the designated spot on the beach, but her heart shattered when she found out that Alberto was not there. She ran up and down the beach, but Alberto was nowhere to be found. There was nothing she could do, and her heart sank.

"It is now 11:45 a.m., Maria. We need to leave; I am sorry," Ethel proclaimed. Maria wondered if Alberto had been there and left or just not shown up. She was so upset and kept asking herself why this had to happen today. Maria felt heartbroken and felt she had met and lost the man of her dreams.

CHAPTER 2

The Hernandez family reveled in their drive up the California coast, marveling at the sprawling beaches and stunning scenery. For them, having never ventured out of Iowa before, each mile brought a burst of excitement about their new adventure. As the lush landscapes of California unfolded before them, Maria sat silently, her thoughts adrift in memories of Alberto.

"Look at those waves!" Emily exclaimed, her face pressed against the car window, her voice filled with wonder. Edith, clutching a deck of cards, chimed in, "Maria, come play 'I Spy' with us! It's your turn to guess!"

Maria smiled faintly, shaking her head. "You two go ahead," she murmured, her gaze lost to the passing scenery.

As the family drove past the towering Redwood trees, their father, Raymond, couldn't help but express his awe. "Can you believe how tall these trees are?" he asked, steering the car through the verdant landscape.

"Yeah, it's like entering a giant's garden," Ethel, their mother, added with a laugh. "Everything here is so different from back home."

Maria nodded, her mind weaving through her dreams and aspirations. "I think I'd like to move to California someday," she confessed softly, more to herself than to anyone else. "There's so much of the world to see."

Emily overheard and turned to her sister, "That would be amazing, wouldn't it? Maybe you could find Alberto again!"

Maria's heart skipped a beat at the mention of his name. She turned to look at her sister, a gentle smile spreading across her face. "Maybe," she said, her voice a whisper of hope. "Maybe one day."

After seven days in the car, the Hernandez family finally made it to the girl's grandparent's house. They live in a small town in Northern California with a population of about 9,500, which reminded everyone of Iowa. Grandma Elizabeth and Grandpa Joe were so excited to see the family. It had been eleven years since they all had been together. Emily was a baby, and this will be Edith's first time meeting her Grandparents. The girls were so thrilled to be here. Grandpa Joe had so much personality and was so funny that the girls were constantly laughing. Grandma Elizabeth was less talkative than Maria had remembered her to be and seemed more distant but still very sweet.

Grandpa Joe made a delicious dinner, and the family enjoyed the food and conversing with each other. They had so much to catch up on. Maria remembered Grandpa as an excellent cook, and he would cook you anything you wanted. Grandpa seemed to cheer up Maria and finally she was laughing and acting more like herself.

Emily and Edith went to bed after dinner, but Maria was going to stay up and visit. Elizabeth had gone to bed, and Maria, her parents, and Grandpa Joe sat around the dining room table and talked for hours. "What is going on with Mom," Ethel asked her dad.

"Well, you know her heart problems and diabetes are pretty stable, but she is acting very unusual. She is having difficulty remembering things, forgets to do daily tasks, and sometimes has a blank stare. I don't feel like I can leave her alone. I am feeling overwhelmed and not sure what to do for Mom," Grandpa replied sadly.

"Now that we are here, we are going to find an answer for this situation. Dad, we won't leave till you are feeling comfortable with the plan. What do the doctors say about Mom?" Replied Ethel, giving some hope to her Dad.

"She has dementia, and they put her on some meds to help control her symptoms," said Grandpa with a heavy heart.

Maria's heart broke at this; she said to her Grandfather, "I am so sorry, Grandpa, but I will help you care for Grandma." He was so appreciative of Maria's thoughtfulness that you could see the relieved look on his face. They all said goodnight and went to sleep as it was after 1 am.

The next morning, Maria asked her Grandpa, "Where is the library? I want to get a book and read up on Grandma's condition."

"It is just down the street on the corner," Grandpa answered, pointing in that direction. Maria left for the library and came back with three books about dementia.

The family had been there for 3 weeks. They were having lunch, and everyone interacted around the table except Grandma, who just stayed quiet. Over the ensuing time, Maria and her grandparents developed an exceptionally close bond. Each morning, she would assist her grandmother, Elizabeth, with the careful ritual of dressing, ensuring each button was fastened and every scarf was gently tied. They would venture out for leisurely shopping trips, where Maria learned to choose items that brought a twinkle to Elizabeth's eye, and they would spend quiet afternoons watching old movies together, during which Maria would listen intently as Elizabeth shared tales from her youth—stories of a time that seemed like a different world.

Maria also became her Grandfather's apprentice in the kitchen, where he taught her the secrets to his famous beef stew and how to perfectly season homemade pasta sauce. As they cooked, Joe would recount anecdotes from his early days as a young man in the bustling heart of San Francisco, infusing the kitchen with laughter and history. Together, they tackled the household chores; Maria diligently followed her Grandfather's methodical ways of keeping the home tidy and warm.

Despite the fullness of her days and the joy she found in her grandparent's company, thoughts of Alberto would often drift through Maria's mind, casting a shadow of wistfulness over her smile. She cherished her time helping at her grandparents' home, feeling a profound sense of purpose in caring for them. Yet, in quiet moments, while her sisters played games in the yard and her parents assisted with the more strenuous tasks, Maria's thoughts would wander to the sandy beaches of California and the connections left behind.

Her heart held onto the hope that perhaps, someday, paths might cross again. Each night, as she lay in the small spare room listening to the gentle snores of the house, she dreamed of Alberto—his laugh, his thoughtful gaze—and wondered about the myriad possibilities that life might still hold for them both.

Over lunch they were discussing that Elizabeth has a doctor's appointment in the morning. "Can I go with you to Grandma's doctor's appointment," Maria asked her Grandpa.

"Of course, honey, your Mom is coming too."

Maria had read all three books that she had checked out from the library. Maria had questions for the doctor. The whole family went to bed early that night since the appointment was early in the morning.

The next morning, Grandpa Joe, Grandma Elizabeth, Maria, Ethel, and Raymond set off to the doctor's appointment. Samantha from next door came over and stayed with Emily and Edith. Grandma Elizabeth's doctor was a sympathetic female physician, and everyone really liked her. She examined Elizabeth and asked her several questions. Elizabeth would answer with a no or yes. The doctor stated, "Everything seems stable and looks good."

On the way out, Maria asked, "May we speak with you in private."

"Of course, we can go to my office." Grandma went with Raymond and waited in the waiting room. Ethel, Maria, and Grandpa went into the office.

"We are Elizabeth's daughter and granddaughter, and we are trying to get a handle on the situation. We have some questions: Does she need full-time care? What else can we do to help her? Does her diet need to be modified?" Both Maria and Ethel blurted many questions, which were all answered by the doctor as she understood the concern. After getting the answers, Maria and Ethel felt that they have a better grip on the situation.

Another week passed, and the Hernandez family had been away from Iowa for 4 weeks. Both Maria's mother and father had taken a leave of absence from their respective jobs for six weeks. The time was getting close, and they would have to leave and return to Iowa. They wanted to see if the state would pay for a caregiver to help Grandpa Joe. Maria had a wonderful idea and said, "I can stay here and help Grandpa take care of Grandma." I am going to college, but I don't know what I want to study. This is the answer to this situation." Grandpa couldn't believe that Maria would do something like this, and he started crying. The family talked it out and they decided that Maria would stay, and the rest of the family would leave for Iowa in about five days. Emily and Edith wanted to stay too, but their Mom explained, "You both need to go back to Iowa and go to school."

The Hernandez family's departure from Northern California was bittersweet. As the car pulled away, it carried only four of its original five passengers. Maria had chosen to stay behind, her heart anchored by a deep sense of duty and affection. She would remain to assist her Grandpa Joe in caring for her Grandma Elizabeth.

In the quiet moments before their departure, Maria hugged each family member tightly, her emotions a mix of determination and sadness. "Take care of each other," she whispered, her voice steady despite the tears that glistened in her eyes. Her father, Raymond, gave her a long, reassuring hug, his pride in her decision clear despite his own reluctance to leave her behind.

"We're just a phone call away, always remember that," Ethel, her mother, added, her voice thick with emotion. Emily and Edith, too young to fully grasp the gravity of the situation, promised to send letters and drawings to keep Maria updated on their lives back in Iowa.

As the car faded into the distance, Maria turned back to the house, feeling the weight of her choice settle around her. She walked up the steps, her resolve strengthening with each step. Inside, Grandpa Joe waited, his expression a mixture of gratitude and concern.

"Don't worry, Grandpa. We'll manage together," Maria assured him as they settled into the new routine that would define their days ahead. The house, once filled with the noise and chaos of her entire family, now echoed with a quieter, more somber tone. Yet, Maria felt a profound connection to her grandparents and the life she was choosing to build with them. She knew the days wouldn't be easy, but the thought of making a real difference in her grandparents' lives gave her a sense of purpose she had never felt before.

CHAPTER 3-

Maria waved to her family as they departed for their trip back to Iowa. As the car disappeared down the road, a mix of emotions swirled inside her. She felt a surge of excitement about the precious time ahead with her grandparents, but this was tinged with sadness at the thought of being separated from her parents, sisters, and friends for an indefinite period. Drawing a deep, steadying breath, Maria resolved to channel her feelings into action.

The first thing she did was to carefully organize a care schedule for her grandmother and a list of household chores to assist her grandfather. She spread out her notes on the kitchen table, detailing medication times, dietary needs, and daily activities. Each medication was carefully researched; she noted down their purposes and side effects, ensuring she understood how to manage her grandmother's diabetes and high blood pressure, both of which were thankfully well-controlled. Maria also learned how to perform finger sticks to monitor her grandmother's blood sugar, which typically ranged between 90-110, and she took up the responsibility of measuring her blood pressure daily, usually finding it around 110/70.

With a slight tremor of uncertainty, she turned to her grandfather, who was watching her with a mix of concern and admiration. "Grandpa, do you think this schedule is a good idea? Will this help us keep everything under control?" she asked, her voice revealing her underlying anxiety about taking on such significant responsibilities.

Her grandfather, Joe, moved closer, his eyes scanning the detailed schedule before resting back on Maria. He placed a reassuring hand on her shoulder. "Maria, this is more than a good idea—it's a fantastic one," he affirmed warmly, squeezing her shoulder. "You're doing something wonderful here, not just for your grandma but for all of us. I'm proud of you."

Maria felt a swell of relief mixed with pride. Her grandfather's words bolstered her confidence, reassuring her that she was on the right path. "Thank you, Grandpa. I just want to make sure I'm doing everything right," she admitted, allowing herself a small smile as she felt the weight of her new role melding with a newfound resolve.

"Go for it," he answered.

"Grandpa, I learned from reading those books from the library that routine is a good thing in these types of situations." Maria made a schedule for Grandma's care, such as dressing, bathing, meals, medications, outings, and time for relaxation and watching television. She also made a schedule for the different tasks to help Grandpa clean the house.

Grandpa Joe was so happy with Maria's schedule that he felt they had some control back in their lives. Maria was a blessing in their lives, but they also wanted her to have her own life. "You need to go out with friends and take care of yourself, too," Grandpa exclaimed.

"Grandpa, I don't know anybody here."

Maria would cook meals with Grandpa, and she learned to be an excellent cook. Grandpa was half Italian and half

Mexican. He cooked the best Italian food and sometimes Mexican food. Maria loved Italian food. Grandpa was so funny, and she was always laughing. He would tell her stories about her Mom when she was young. Maria would ask Grandpa numerous questions about their relatives. Maria learned a lot about her Grandpa's side of the family. Maria found the family history so fascinating and wanted to start making a family tree. She would try to ask her Grandma some questions about her side of the family, but she was more on the quiet side. Grandma was also usually quiet during her care, but Maria would get smiles from her, and she would always say, "Thank you, darling."

Maria's parents were proud of her and would call frequently for updates. Maria would speak with her parents and sisters, and they would catch up about what was new in their lives. Things were going well, and after a while, life in Northern California seemed to be routine. Grandpa introduced Maria to the granddaughter of the neighbor next door, Samantha, who was also visiting her grandparents. The two girls decided they would go to the movies on Friday night.

Friday night arrived, bringing a rare opportunity for respite. With Grandma Elizabeth soundly asleep and Grandpa Joe settled in front of the television, Maria and Samantha seized the chance to escape into the world of cinema. The two 18-year-olds, who shared so much in common, reveled in the simple joy of watching a movie outside the confines of daily responsibilities. For Maria, stepping out of the house felt liberating—a much-needed breath of fresh air.

Back at home, the tranquility was abruptly shattered. Grandma Elizabeth awoke in a state of confusion, her eyes searching the room frantically. "Elizabeth, honey, what can I do to help you?" Joe asked, his voice laced with concern as he approached her cautiously.

"I want Maria," she demanded, her voice rising in panic. Suddenly, she began throwing things within her reach, her agitation mounting rapidly. Joe, overwhelmed and unsure how to soothe his wife's distress, attempted to reassure her. "Maria just stepped out for a little while; she'll be back very soon," he said, his voice steady but his heart sinking as he realized his words did little to calm her.

Feeling helpless and torn, Joe decided it might be safer to give Elizabeth some space. He retreated from the room, closing the door behind him with a heavy heart. From the hallway, he could hear the continued sounds of her distress. "My wife needs me, and I don't know what to do," he whispered to himself, the feeling of helplessness gnawing at him.

At that moment, the front door creaked open, and Maria stepped inside. The sounds of chaos reached her ears immediately. "Grandpa, what happened?" she called out, her voice filled with alarm as she dropped her purse and rushed toward the sound.

Joe looked up, his face a portrait of distress, as he met Maria in the hallway. "She woke up very confused and got upset. I tried to calm her, but nothing seemed to work," he explained, his voice cracking with emotion. Maria nodded, her own anxiety spiked by the sounds of her grandmother's cries echoing through the house.

"Grandma woke up and didn't know who I was. She was screaming and throwing things at me, and I thought it was best I leave the room." Grandpa was crying as he felt so helpless. Maria felt terrible as she had left the house for about two hours, and poor Grandma and Grandpa had quite a night. Maria goes into Grandma's room and immediately turns on the night light. The light being off probably confused her, Maria thought. Grandma seemed to be more alert and said," Honey, I am glad you are home. Can you fluff my pillows?"

"Of course," Maria fluffed her pillows and said, "I love you, Grandma. Go back to sleep. If you need anything, I will be in the room next door."

"Thank you. Love you too, honey. Sleep well." Maria left the night light on.

Grandpa was sitting on the couch crying and seemed very upset. "Grandpa, everything is okay; Grandma is fine. I read in the book that it is a good idea to keep a night line on; otherwise, they may get confused. "

"You sure are a sharp girl. I can't thank you enough for all that you do. I love you so much, Maria. "

"I love you too very much. Don't worry, Grandpa, everything will be fine."

The next day, after lunch, Maria went back to the library to get a new supply of books and return the books that she had already read. She wanted to find a book on Grandma's medications, diabetes, high blood pressure, and maybe another book or two on dementia, which would help her understand the progression of the disease. Every night, when she went to her room, she would read for at least one hour before going to sleep. Maria felt that by educating herself, she would be a much better caregiver.

Maria realized that she would need to help Grandpa understand how dementia progresses and that the things occurring were a normal progression of the disease. Grandma's physician had tried to explain these things to Grandpa, but Maria thought that Grandpa was very stressed while in the office and didn't hear what the doctor was saying. She thought that she would need to step up to the plate and be more responsible in this area.

Maria learned that the confusion and outbursts may be more prevalent with Grandma one day. She hoped that things would remain calm but knew this was very unlikely. Maria was having more difficulty during mealtime with Grandma. Elizabeth said, "I don't like the food around here." Grandpa heard his wife and got very upset.

"Grandpa, there are stages of this disease, and we have to remain calm and do our best; that is all we can expect. I am going to talk to Grandma and see what food she would like to eat. One of my books says that it is normal for persons with dementia that one day they will eat very well, and the next day they will close their mouth and refuse food altogether. It is day by day. We must make sure that she is getting adequate nutrition, but we should let her have some control over this situation. I have done a lot of reading and believe I understand that everything will be fine. I bet by dinner, Grandma will be hungry and ready to eat." At dinner that night, Grandma was hungry and ate very well. Grandpa felt very reassured by Maria and felt that she had the situation under control.

Things were getting more difficult with Grandma. It was now the beginning of November, and Maria had been in California for 3.5 months. She was thinking about the holiday season and what she could do to make it more cheerful for her Grandparents. She also thought about Alberto and was daydreaming that he had found her Grandparents' house and appeared at the front door.

It was now Thanksgiving morning, and Maria and her Grandparents were on the phone with her Parents and Sisters. They all wished each other a "Happy Thanksgiving." Maria had told her Grandpa a week ago, "Grandpa, I am doing the Thanksgiving dinner, including shopping, cooking, setting the table, and cleaning. All I want you to do that day is watch football." Grandpa was continuously amazed at Maria's generosity and maturity and was so proud of her. Grandpa had invited the neighbors next door and their granddaughter, Samantha, to Thanksgiving, too. Maria was very happy to hear this.

Maria had set the table carefully, arranging her grandparents' finest dishes and sparkling glasses with care. Each placement was a reflection of her dedication and attention to detail. As Grandpa Joe walked into the dining room, his eyes immediately welled up with tears upon seeing the beautifully set table. It was not just the elegance of the arrangement that moved him, but the profound love and effort Maria had poured into preparing for the evening. He paused, taking in the sight, his voice thick with emotion as he spoke. "The table is absolutely stunning. You are so amazing, Maria," he exclaimed, his voice catching slightly. "To think, all this creativity and depth from someone only eighteen years of age—it's just remarkable." He reached out to grasp her hand, squeezing it gently, overwhelmed with gratitude and pride for the young woman she was becoming.

"Thank you, Grandpa. I am so glad that you like it."

The neighbors came over at 4 pm. They had a variety of appetizers prior to dinner. Maria had cooked a fabulous dinner of turkey, mashed potatoes, sweet potatoes, Cornbread, peas, creamed corn, asparagus, and pumpkin pie for dessert. Even Grandma ate a little bit of everything and complimented Maria "Everything was absolutely delicious." Everyone talked and laughed, and they all had a wonderful evening. Maria was so, so happy that evening had turned out so well.

It is the first week of December 1974. Maria looked out the window and saw it was snowing. It reminded her of Iowa. Maria loved the snow and would go tobogganing down the hill by her house. She had always wanted to learn how to ski as there were several ski resorts near where they lived, but her family couldn't afford it, and she understood. Maria thought when I went to college, I was going to pick a career where I could afford the good things in life and provide my parents and sisters with a better life, too. Maria was so giving and thought about everyone else. She also realized at a young age that I had better do well in school so I would be able to receive a scholarship to college. She knew her parents would not be able to afford college. Maria studied very hard and came out of her high school Valedictorian with an A average.

"Where are your Christmas decorations," Maria asked.

"They are in the corner of the storage shed."

"I am going to decorate the house and make it look magical." She knew her Grandparents were on a somewhat fixed income, so she didn't mention about getting a tree.

"Maria, you never cease to amaze me. Go for it. This will make me and your Grandma very happy."

Maria went to the storage shed and saw an Artificial Christmas tree and was so excited. She looked through all the decorations and realized they had an abundance of them. Maria worked on the decorations for more than a week. She would work on it when Grandma would take her naps. Maria was very content doing the tree and all the Christmas decorations. She did such an outstanding job that her Grandparents said, "Maria, this house with the amazing Christmas decorations and tree could be in the Sunset Magazine Christmas issue." Maria never heard of Sunset magazine, but she knew they were happy and proud.

Grandpa loved to talk on his phone and would tell all his friends, "You have to come over and see how our Granddaughter decorated our house. You would be amazed." In the two weeks before Christmas, many neighbors and friends would stop by the house. Her Grandparents had many friends who were so concerned about their well-being. This made Maria happy to see all their friends. Maria missed her family and friends back home but knew she was doing the right thing. Her Grandparents needed her, and when she looks back on this experience in the future, she can be proud that she stepped up to the plate.

Maria had another idea: she needed to bake Christmas cookies. Her family and Grandparents weren't planning on exchanging gifts.

"I need to go to the grocery store," Maria says.

"That is fine," Grandpa Joe responds.

Maria had saved quite a bit of money while in high school, doing babysitting, odd jobs, housecleaning, and errands for neighbors. She brought all her money with her when she came to see her Grandparents. She is so happy that she has the money with her.

Maria made a list, and she was going to make six types of Christmas cookies. She planned to get Christmas tins so she could place the cookies in decorated tins. While Grandma Elizabeth took her afternoon nap, Maria took off to the grocery store. She found everything she was looking for and more. She came home with three full shopping bags full of ingredients. It was already four in the afternoon when she got home, and she thought it would be best if she woke up early the next morning to start baking.

Maria got up at six in the morning and went into the kitchen. She got her recipes from Grandma Elizabeth's cookbooks. Around eight in the morning, Elizabeth awoke and said, "Something smells really good."

"Grandma, I am baking cookies," Maria responds.

She had spent the entire day helping her grandmother with daily care, making sure she was comfortable in the living room with the television on before she resumed her marathon baking session. Maria baked tirelessly all day, filling the kitchen with the sweet aroma of cookies. "Maria, who is going to eat all of these cookies?" Grandpa exclaimed, peering over at the growing piles of treats.

"We will, Grandpa, and we're also going to take some to the homeless shelter down the street," Maria replied, her voice cheerful despite the fatigue setting in. By 10 pm, she had finished baking. The counters were covered with dozens and dozens of cookies, each looking more delicious than the last. Once the cookies had cooled, she filled the festive Christmas tins with a selection of each type. After cleaning up the kitchen, it was well past midnight. Exhausted, Maria headed straight to bed, skipping her usual night-time reading. Sleep claimed her the moment her head hit the pillow.

With Christmas only a week away, Grandpa brought up the holiday plans one morning. "Maria, I'm taking over the cooking and cleaning for Christmas. I want it to be a day of rest for you. You just help Grandma as usual, and I'll handle the rest," he declared.

"That's really sweet of you, Grandpa, but I still want to help. It's a lot of work, and I can't let you do it all by yourself," Maria responded, her voice laden with appreciation and a firm resolve to contribute.

"We'll see how the day goes," Grandpa replied, his tone soft but firm, leaving a little room for negotiation.

The next day, Maria and Samantha went down to the homeless organization down the street and came with tins of cookies with bows on them. This is an organization that collects items for the homeless throughout the year. The organization was so thrilled with their donation of cookies. They were collecting turkeys and donated food items so they could cook the homeless Christmas dinner. The plan was to hand out a tin of cookies to each family member or individual who showed up for the Christmas dinner. "Can we volunteer to help serve the food on Christmas," Maria and Samantha asked.

"We can use help between 1 to 4 p.m. on Christmas. Thank you so much for the cookies; these will be the hit of the whole event," the manager, Stacey, responded.

"We will be here at 1 pm. See you then."

Maria and Samantha went home and informed their Grandparents of their plans. Both families were planning their Christmas dinner for 5 p.m., so the timing worked out great. The plan for Christmas was to go to church in the morning, help with the Christmas dinner at the homeless center in the afternoon, and then come home to Christmas dinner with their respected family.

It was Christmas morning. Maria was going to morning Mass with the neighbors next door, the Logan's (Samantha's grandparents) and Samantha. The church was quite quaint, and everyone looked so beautifully dressed. Maria had always gone to church with her family on Christmas but was happy to be going with Samantha's family. Samantha and Maria were getting along very well and were becoming very good friends. They both were 18 years of age, excellent students and had just graduated from high school. They were very similar and getting so close that they seemed like sisters.

Samantha's Grandfather, Ted, has a heart condition, and her Grandmother, Alice, was overwhelmed with his meds and treatments. Samantha had been taking over the care of her Grandpa Ted for the last few months. Samantha discussed with Maria that she is planning to stay and take care of her Grandparents too. Samantha had just graduated from high school and couldn't decide what career path she wanted to follow either. Maria was so thrilled to hear this. Both girls could support each other and continue their friendship.

The girls went to the dinner for the homeless after Church. They stood in line and served mashed potatoes, gravy, and sweet potatoes. They also handed out the tins of cookies. Everyone was so appreciative of the cookies. The homeless had the biggest smiles on their faces, when handed the tin of cookies. The girls realized how lucky they were to have the lives they were living.

After finishing the homeless dinner, Maria went back home to find her Grandpa Joe on the phone with her mother and sisters. Maria talked with her parents and sisters, and they all wished each other a "Merry Christmas.""I hear you decorated the house like a showplace. I hear you also baked cookies and took them to the homeless. Maria, we can't tell you how proud we are of you and how much we love you," Ethel exclaims.

"I know Mom, I love you too so much. I want to tell you something. I was just with Samantha, who is the neighbor next door's granddaughter. She is 18 years of age and from out of state too. She is going to stay and take care of her grandfather, who has a heart condition. We are very similar, and I am so excited to have someone my age close by. I hope you have a wonderful Christmas and I miss you very much."

"Maria, I am very happy to hear you have a friend next door. Kisses from all of us, and give Grandpa and Grandma a kiss from us."

"Love you and talk to you soon, Mom."

Grandpa had prepared a hearty dinner of roast beef, rice, potatoes, creamed corn, and peas. As the family gathered around the table, the room buzzed with comforting chatter. Grandma seemed particularly lively that day, contributing more to the conversation than usual. When dinner wound down, Maria presented each of her grandparents with a tin of the cookies she had baked. Their faces lit up with delight.

"Thank you so much, Maria, I am going to keep my tin of cookies by my bed," Grandma stated, her voice soft but filled with warmth.

"And I'm keeping mine right here in front of me," Grandpa chimed in, his eyes twinkling with mirth. They then surprised Maria with two movie tickets and a dinner voucher for a downtown restaurant. "Thank you both, that was so sweet. Samantha and I can plan a Friday night out," Maria replied, her heart swelling with gratitude.

"This has been a wonderful Christmas, but I am tired," Maria confessed after a pause, feeling the weight of the day's activities. She helped Grandma get ready for bed, and she drifted off to sleep almost immediately, a peaceful expression on her face. Maria then joined Grandpa in the kitchen to help with the cleanup. As they worked side by side, the warmth of the holiday spirit enveloped them, making the fatigue bearable.

In the quiet moments afterward, as Maria reflected on the day, she realized it had truly been a magical Christmas. Christmas 1974 would be remembered fondly, but amidst the joy, her thoughts drifted to Alberto. She wondered what he was doing for Christmas and couldn't help but dream about what might have been if circumstances had been different.

Maria always cherished the two weeks after Christmas because, typically, she would have been on school vacation. Now, as she reflected in the comfort of her grandparents' home, she realized she was on what felt like an unending holiday. She felt incredibly fortunate to be free from school obligations, allowing her to devote herself fully to caring for her grandparents.

On December 31, 1974, the atmosphere at Maria's home was filled with festive anticipation. Maria and Samantha had planned to stay up until midnight to watch the New Year's Eve festivities on television. Samantha arrived at Maria's around 8:30 pm, and soon they were absorbed in the lively beats of Dance Party, dancing together in the living room. Grandma was already tucked into bed, sleeping soundly, but Grandpa Joe couldn't resist joining in. He entered the room and showed off some of his dance moves, drawing laughs and applause from the girls. Samantha always found Grandpa Joe to be a delightful character; his humor and spirited nature made every visit memorable.

Grandpa Joe had prepared a feast of pigs in the blanket, meatballs, chicken wings, popcorn, and brownies, filling the room with the aromas of home-cooked comfort food. The girls were amazed at the spread and eagerly complimented him on the delicious assortment.

"You need to come and sit down and enjoy the food with us. You need to stay awake till midnight to do the countdown," Maria urged her grandpa, her voice playful yet sincere.

"I will try to stay awake," Grandpa Joe responded with a chuckle, his eyes twinkling with merriment as he pulled up a chair to join them. His presence added a special warmth to the evening, making the celebration even more joyous as they all prepared to welcome the new year together.

The girls and Grandpa Joe had a fabulous evening. The girls danced to their favorite songs, and Grandpa joined in at times which made the girls giggle. At 11:50 pm, Grandpa brought out some sparkling apple cider. He poured the three of them glasses into the champagne flutes. At midnight, they toasted, "Happy New Year and Happy 1975". The night turned out to be such an endearing evening and the best New Year's Eve. Grandpa Joe walked Samantha home next door. When Grandpa returned, Maria said, "Grandpa, we had a blast. Thank you for staying up with us and for all the delicious food. You are the best. I love you so much, Grandpa. Happy 1975."

"Love you too, honey. We are so lucky to have you here. Sleep well."

CHAPTER 4-

Alberto drove to the beach the next foggy July morning, Ginger bounding eagerly beside him. The chill in the air did little to dampen Ginger's enthusiasm as she chased after the frisbee Alberto threw, her barks of joy mingling with the sound of the crashing waves. As he watched his dog play, Alberto's mind wandered to Maria — her gorgeous eyes and her beautiful long hair that seemed to dance with the wind. He remembered her sweet demeanor, which, to him, defined the epitome of perfection. Each thought of her sent his heart racing, a mixture of longing and admiration flooding him. Despite spending nearly two hours on the beach, hope dwindling with each passing minute, Maria was nowhere to be seen. With a heavy heart, Alberto decided it was time to leave, promising himself to return the next day.

When he arrived home, his mother, Dorothy, was settled into her home office, papers strewn about as she took a brief pause from her duties. Dorothy, a diligent attorney who split her time between the office and home, noticed her son's somber expression as he entered. Her keen eyes missed little, and the subtle shadows of disappointment on his face were clear to her.

"Alberto, you seem like you have something on your mind," she commented, her voice laced with concern as she peered over her glasses at him. "Is everything alright?"

Alberto sighed, the weight of his unspoken thoughts making him hesitate. He sank into a chair across from her, his eyes meeting hers. "It's Maria," he confessed, the name feeling both sweet and painful in his mouth. "I can't stop thinking about her. She's just... she's amazing, Mom."

Dorothy set aside her papers, giving her son her full attention, a gentle smile softening her features. "Tell me about her," she urged, inviting him to share his feelings, hoping to offer both an ear and her wisdom.

"Oh, Mom, I met this girl on the beach two days ago. Her name was Maria. We really hit it off. We were going to meet the next day at the same spot, but I don't know why she didn't show up. I can't get her off my mind." Alberto's expressions got even sadder; his broken heart could be seen from his expressions.

"I have never seen you so in awe of a girl. Why don't you just call her," asked his Mom.

"She is from out of state, and I don't have her phone number," replied Alberto regretfully.

"Oh Alberto, I am sorry to hear that. I wish there was something I could do to help you," said his Mom trying to ease the pain her son was going through.

"I am planning to go to the beach every morning for the rest of the summer in hopes that Maria will be there," said Alberto hopefully.

"I am going to pray that this all works out for you," said his Mom.

"Thank you, Mom, you are the best," replied Alberto forcing a smile on his face.

Alberto and Ginger went to the beach every morning for the rest of July and all of August. He would throw the frisbee to Ginger and they both would run up and down the beach. However, Maria never showed up. Regardless, Alberto dreamt that one day, they would run into each other again. He felt in his heart that one day, just as spontaneously they had met the first time, they would meet again in a similar fashion. Dorothy could sense how much Maria meant to Alberto. All she wanted was for her son to be happy. Dorothy was glad that he was able to confide in her but wished there was something she could do about the situation.

It was now the beginning of September, and Alberto was going to start working with his Dad, Tony, after Labor Day. Dorothy was an attorney whose focus was estate planning and probate. Her husband was a contractor who basically looked after project management. He used to take on large construction projects and find the most suitable companies to do the necessary jobs. Dorothy occasionally had a probate case where the clients inherited property and then needed to do some renovation work. She used to tell her clients that her husband catered to project management for renovation projects if they were interested. She also used to tell them that her husband tend to save his clients a significant amount of money in comparison to a regular contractor. He finds the appropriate company to do the job at a reasonable price, and then he charges just a nominal fee for his service. He has many vendors that he has been using for many years. He had several projects going on and wanted Alberto to handle the newest project.

Alberto was smart, talented, financially savvy, and a very fast learner. Tony thought that Alberto could try the project management and see if he liked it, and if he did, that would be awesome. They could work together, and one day, Alberto would inherit his company. If he doesn't like this type of work, Tony knows his son will further his education and go on to graduate school.

It was the Tuesday after Labor Day, and Tony introduced the project to Alberto. It was a commercial building on a main street in a small city in California, close to where they lived. The floors were sinking. Tony explained to Alberto that, basically, they were going to demolish most of the building and only leave up the two side walls and the wall in the back of the building. He showed him the plans that the owner had drawn up for the renovation.

"Oh wow, this is going to be a stunning building when it is completed. Do you think I can be the project manager of such a big project, Dad?" Alberto exclaimed.

"You are very smart, and you will need to do a significant amount of research and ask questions, but yes, you will be fine. I will be checking in with you every morning and afternoon so you are not on your own."

Dorothy was very happy that Alberto and his Dad were working together. Alberto was their only child and the father and son have always gotten along very well together. Dorothy also thought that the project would take Alberto's mind off Maria.

Alberto shared with his dad that the first order of business was to address the sinking floors of the building. Tony, lacking immediate contacts for such a specialized problem, listened intently as Alberto laid out his plan. "I've found a structural engineer who has dealt with similar issues before,

Dad. He comes highly recommended and has a lot of experience," Alberto explained, his voice mixed with determination and a hint of excitement at navigating this new challenge.

Tony nodded, visibly impressed with his son's initiative. "Excellent work, Alberto. Let's bring them in for a complete evaluation and get to the bottom of this issue." They hired the company right away, and the structural report soon revealed that the instability was due to groundwater accumulated under the building, tracing back to an old creek. The engineer set to work on a plan to stabilize the structure, filling Alberto with a deep sense of responsibility and eagerness to tackle the problem.

As he immersed himself in the project, Alberto found the work both fascinating and demanding. "Dad, I'm really learning a lot here," he confessed one evening as they reviewed the demolition proposals. "Every day brings something new, and I feel like I'm genuinely contributing."

Tony clapped him on the back, proud and encouraging. "You're doing great, son. Keep at it, and you'll master this in no time."

While working on-site, Alberto often found himself the center of attention from passersby. His tall, handsome figure and piercing blue eyes didn't go unnoticed by the women walking by during their lunch hour. They often threw admiring glances his way, smiling and greeting him warmly. Alberto would return their smiles with a polite "Hello," but his heart wasn't in it to pursue anything further. Despite the attention, his thoughts remained fixed on Maria. The fleeting connection they had shared left a profound imprint on his heart, and he found himself disinterested in exploring new romantic possibilities. In the evenings, he would join his friends for dinner and a movie, enjoying their company but steering clear of discussions about dating.

This reflective state often followed him back to the project site, where he would stand on the sidewalk, overlooking the ongoing work, his mind wandering back to Maria and what could have been. His dedication to the project and his personal resolve not to let his emotional state interfere with his work highlighted the complexity of his feelings and the depth of his character.

The month of September flew by, and the weather was still very warm and pleasant. They started the demolition in the last week of September, which took several days. It was amazing how many trucks it took to get all the debris out of the building. Alberto was standing in the middle of the building, thinking about what I had gotten myself involved in. The plan from the engineer came back and involved a tremendous amount of digging and soil removal, and then concrete was placed to stabilize the building. They were also going to do an earthquake retrofit since this is an earthquake country.

Tony had a company that he had worked with many times for the roofing project. The plan was to finish the roof before the rainy season started. The weather forecast for the rest of 1974 was for a milder and warmer than usual fall, with no rain forecasted till December. They started the roofing project right after the demolition was completed. Alberto was at the building every morning by seven. He was learning so much and was so busy.

The roofing project took till the middle of November to complete. The roof turned out amazing. Alberto knew that digging out of all the soil and laying a new foundation was going to be a huge project. Tony decided since the roof was completed that, they would have some free time till Thanksgiving. Alberto had been working very hard, at least ten hours a day, five to six days a week, for two and a half months. They were ahead on the project, and now they both needed some rest and relaxation.

Alberto was an only child, but the Bertolucci's were a large family. Tony has four brothers and four sisters; they all lived nearby and were coming with their families to Thanksgiving. Tony and Alberto were going to do the shopping and cooking. Dorothy had two cases that were going to court the week after Thanksgiving. She had so much work to prepare and felt bad that she wouldn't be of much help in preparing for the celebration. There was going to be a total of twenty-six people at the dinner. Dorothy was planning to set the table early on Thanksgiving morning.

Tony loved to cook, especially for the holidays. He made the grocery list and planned on going to four stores to get all the ingredients that he needed. It was the Sunday before Thanksgiving; Tony and Alberto set out for the shopping spree early in the morning.

All the stores were crowded, but mainly with women. They went down every aisle of each store. Alberto hadn't gone grocery shopping with his Dad since he was a teen. He remembered how his dad compared prices and got an item for the best price without compromising quality. Alberto has learned a tremendous amount about finances from his Dad, and seeing him shop is a reminder of his financial wisdom.

Around one in the afternoon, they still had one more store to explore but decided to go to lunch. They went to an Italian restaurant, and both decided to have a calzone and a salad. Alberto decided to tell his Dad about Maria. "Dad, I want to tell you something."

"What is it, Alberto?"

"Dad, this summer, I went to the beach every day with Ginger. In July, I met this smart, beautiful girl, Maria, who was eighteen years old and from out of state. We hit it off like we had known each other our whole lives. In my heart, I feel like she is the one. We planned to meet on the beach the next day, but she did not show up. She was with her family on a trip to see her Grandparents. I don't know why she didn't show up, if her parents wouldn't let her come, or what happened. I just can't get over her. I didn't get her phone number because we were meeting the next day. In my heart, I feel that someday we will meet again. Does this sound crazy to you, Dad?"

"No, Alberto, this sounds like you fell hard for this girl in a short period of time. Sometimes, we can never understand the forces of attraction and things like this do happen, but I am so sorry that you don't have a way to contact her. Did she give you any information that could provide a clue, or did you discuss what city she is from or where her grandparents live?"

"No, but she told me she was from a small town in Iowa and that she had just graduated from Lincoln High School. She also said she was going to visit her Grandparents in Northern California."

"The only thing I can think of is to check out Lincoln High School in Iowa and see how many schools are named that in the state. You may be able to get some trail that way. Maybe you can call the Board of Education in Iowa and ask them that question. I hope that you are going to be able to contact her again."

"Thanks, Dad, for the support. You are the best. I feel much better after talking with you."

"I am so glad, and I hope this really works out for you."

After their final store visit, Alberto and Tony packed the car to the brim with groceries, the backseat and trunk bulging with bags as if they were provisioning for an army. By the time they returned home and stowed all the supplies, the afternoon shadows were stretching long; it was nearly four o'clock, and both men were feeling the weight of the day's efforts. Deciding that the cooking marathon could wait until morning, they agreed to an early night. That evening, under the soft glow of the kitchen lights, Alberto's parents found themselves deep in conversation about Maria. They shared a sense of wonder at how deeply their son had been affected by this brief encounter, wishing there was some way he could reconnect with her to explore the potential of what could be.

The next morning broke with the sound of clattering pans and the rich aroma of brewing coffee as Tony started on the Thanksgiving feast. He began with his specialties: homemade ravioli stuffed with a savory blend of meat and spinach and layers of cannelloni filled with creamy ricotta. The kitchen was a whirl of activity, with Tony at the helm, orchestrating the creation of each dish. Pies—pumpkin, apple, and lemon meringue—were lined up like soldiers on the counter next to a towering four-layer chocolate cake that promised to be as decadent as it looked.

Alberto, ever the eager apprentice, assisted wherever he could, marveling at his father's culinary prowess. Despite never having formal training, Tony's skills were a testament to the teachings of his Italian mother and grandmother, whose recipes and techniques had been passed down through generations.

As the days led up to Thanksgiving, the house was filled with the delicious scents of simmering sauces and baking desserts. The menu Tony planned was a lavish spread: the meal would start with a delicate shrimp and crab salad, followed by the rich ravioli. For the main course, guests would help themselves from a buffet groaning under the weight of the traditional turkey and an array of sides like creamy mashed potatoes, sweet potatoes enveloped in a light, sweet glaze, savory stuffing, golden cornbread, creamed spinach, buttery creamed corn, tender green beans tossed with mushrooms, crisp asparagus, and freshly baked rolls.

Dessert was a showcase of Tony's best: in addition to the cannelloni and trifle, guests could indulge in slices of the various pies and the sinfully rich chocolate cake. As he watched his father work, Alberto couldn't help but feel the anticipation building for the holiday feast.

Dorothy, Tony, and Alberto all got up very early on Thanksgiving. Tony was cooking two turkeys, so he was planning that they would be cooked by five thirty. Alberto helped his Mom move the tables, and they set two tables end to end; one would sit fourteen people, and the other would sit twelve. They could all see each other with the tables set this way. Then, they set up the buffet table near the back wall. The dining room was huge, so there was enough space for everything. Dorothy set the tables with Alberto's help. They had fresh flowers throughout the house. The house looked stunning, and the smell of the delicious cooking was beyond words.

It was now around one in the afternoon, and all three of them were taking showers and getting ready for their company. Everyone started arriving around three in the afternoon. Alberto was thrilled to see his aunts, uncles, and cousins. He caught up with his family on their lives and told them about working with his Dad and that he loved the challenge. He also told two of his aunts about Maria. Everyone raved about the amazing dinner. Alberto loved family gatherings, and this Thanksgiving turned out to be such a special day. Alberto was thinking how lucky he was to have such a loving family. The last of the family left just before midnight. Dorothy, Tony, and Alberto put the last of the food away and headed straight to bed.

The next day, all three of them worked on cleaning up, which took most of the day to complete. When they were finished, Tony asked Dorothy and Alberto, "I have something I want to ask you two. I wanted to see if you both would like to go to Puerto Vallarta for Christmas and New Year's."

"Oh, for sure, honey, that sounds so relaxing. I love Puerto Vallarta at Christmas and New Year's," Dorothy responded.

"Sounds good to me, too," Alberto responded after giving it some thought.

"Great, I will make the reservations," Tony replies.

"Thank you so much. You two are the best parents. Sometimes, I wonder how I could have been so lucky. I love you both so much."

"No, we are the lucky ones; you are the kind of child that all parents dream of having, and you are ours. Love you so, so much, Alberto."

All three were so tired that they said good night and went to bed early.

Alberto and his Dad were back at work the first week of December. They were getting bids for digging the dirt and laying the foundation. They settled on the perfect company, which would start the project after New Year's. They were also looking into the retrofit, which would be done after the foundation was completed. Alberto researched about the retrofit. Tony paid Alberto weekly, and he had been saving most of his paychecks and putting them in his savings account. He also saved some of the money in a retirement account for his future.

The women still came by during their lunch hour, and Alberto talked to them every day. No one caught his eye. There were two who were legal secretaries, and two of them were attorneys, and they all worked at the courthouse up the street. Alberto found them all to be very attractive and great conversationalists. He knew that one of the attorneys wanted him to ask her out, but he just didn't feel like dating. Alberto was worried that he would never feel like dating again.

The Bertolucci family left for Puerta Vallarta on the twenty-second of December. They had a smooth flight and arrived at the hotel around nine in the evening. Alberto's Dad made reservations at a very exclusive, upscale hotel on the beach. The three of them decided that the Christmas gift would be the vacation, so they wouldn't be exchanging gifts this year. They went to midnight Mass on Christmas, and it was so enchanting. The Mexican people had children and animals in the entrance procession. The children sang Christmas carols throughout the service. The hotel had shuttled those interested in the Mass and then shuttled them back to the hotel. All three of them were happy that they attended. On Christmas day, the hotel had a lovely Christmas dinner, which was seven courses. They had a huge dining room, so the hotel invited all the families participating in the midnight mass to come to the Christmas dinner at the hotel. The families were so thrilled and appreciative, and the children were just in seventh heaven with all the food. Tony spoke Spanish, so he was able to speak with some of the Spanish-speaking guests, and they praised the owner of this hotel as a very generous man who never forgets his people. Dorothy, Tony, and Alberto had the most amazing Christmas ever.

There were many American families staying at this hotel. Alberto's parents were very talkative and friendly, so they met many people but mainly associated with one couple, who had a daughter who was twenty years old. They were from Texas, and their daughter Marissa was shy and soft-spoken.

Alberto and Marissa would go to the beach during the day as they both loved the sun. Alberto looked at Marissa like a younger sister and would give her advice about college and boys. Both sets of parents could see that their children were developing a friendship, but more like brother and sister. The two families spent much of the week between Christmas and New Year's together. They went on tours to the beach and had dinner together almost every night.

It was New Year's Eve, and the hotel reservation included an exclusive New Year's Eve party at the hotel. The six of them were all going. They all got dressed up and went downstairs to the party, which started at seven. First, there were several tables with oh d'oeuvres, and then dinner started at 8 pm. Dinner was six courses and so delicious. After dinner, starting at 10 pm, there were three rooms with three different genres of music. The first room was Mexican music; the second room was music from the 40s and 50s, and the third room was music from the 60s and disco. Alberto and Marissa both liked to dance, so they danced to 60's music till nearly midnight when they joined their parents for a midnight toast. They all toasted, "Happy New Year and Happy 1975." Their parents were going to continue to do some swing dancing, and Alberto and Marissa went back to the disco. The six of them stayed till around 1:30 in the morning. Alberto was having a wonderful time on New

Year's but also wondered what Maria would be doing then. Alberto realized how fortunate he was as he traveled throughout Europe, Asia, and many other places. He thought about Maria never being out of Iowa and how he desired to show her the world.

It was finally the time to bid farewell. The two families shared contact information and told each other that they would come to visit soon. Marissa was sweet and shy and liked all the advice Alberto had given. She would open up to him like nobody else. She went to an all-girls high school, so in college, she wasn't sure what to expect in a coed college. She learned so much about men from him. She never wanted to talk to her parents about certain issues, and Alberto proved himself to be a great listener; she had found her best friend in him. Alberto also loved talking with Marissa and found a great friend in her, too. Alberto and Marissa planned to keep in contact with each other as friends. Alberto told Marissa, "I will call you when I get home." Both families flew back home on the second of January.

CHAPTER 5-

It was January 1975, a new year with a new beginning. Maria was an excellent caregiver and had the care of her Grandmother down to a precise science. Maria often wondered how long it would take for everything to continue to go so smoothly. Maria and her Grandpa would stay up in the evenings after Elizabeth was asleep, talk for hours, and sometimes watch television. Grandpa and Maria became very close.

Maria's nineteenth birthday was going to be on February 14th – Valentine's Day. Grandpa Joe was so appreciative of everything she was doing he wanted to buy her a car for her birthday. His neighbor who lives down the street has a beautiful red nineteen sixty-eight Chevrolet Camaro for sale at a great price. Grandpa Joe went over to the neighbors three times to look at the car. He also looked through the newspaper want-adds for about six weeks and looked at a few cars, but none of them impressed him. Grandpa Joe took the red Camaro over to his mechanic and had the car checked out. His mechanic's evaluation of the car was that it was in pristine condition, inside and out. He told Grandpa Joe that he felt that it was an amazing find. That's all that Grandpa needed to hear, and he decided to purchase the car. He was so excited about the purchase and knew that Maria was going to be ecstatic.

On February 14th, Maria received many phone calls from her parents, sisters, and friends back home wishing her a happy birthday. At 6 pm, Grandpa Joe, Grandma Elizabeth, and Maria left for dinner. The restaurant was a fancy Italian restaurant in the downtown. They had salad and three types of pastas for dinner. Maria felt so spoiled that her Grandparents would do this for her birthday. The waiter approached with a broad smile, singing "Happy Birthday" as he set a small chocolate cake in front of Maria. As she began to cut into the cake, her knife clinked against something hard. Puzzled, Maria extracted a shiny car key from the frosting.

"Why is there a key in the cake?" she asked, her eyebrows arching in surprise.

"It's a surprise for you," Grandpa replied, his eyes twinkling with mischief.

"What?" Maria's voice quivered with anticipation, her heart starting to race.

"You'll find out very soon," Grandpa promised, a secretive grin spreading across his face.

The excitement was palpable as they quickly finished their cake. Maria, overwhelmed by the moment and the cozy ambiance of the restaurant, expressed her gratitude. "Thank you both so much for this wonderful dinner. It's been so generous of you. I love you both so much."

They stepped out of the restaurant into the crisp evening air. Parked next to their old sedan was a bright red Camaro, gleaming under the streetlights. Maria gasped, her hands flying to her mouth.

"That Camaro is such a beautiful car," she murmured, more to herself than to anyone else.

"That's because it's yours, Maria," Grandpa said, handing her the keys with a proud flourish.

"I don't understand," Maria stammered, her mind racing as she tried to process the reality before her.

"The car is a birthday gift to you. Do you like it?" Grandpa's voice was soft, laden with emotion.

Tears welled up in Maria's eyes as she took in the sleek lines of the Camaro. "Grandpa, Grandma, I absolutely love the car. It's the most beautiful car I have ever seen. Thank you, thank you, thank you. You both are so amazing. I'm just in shock at your generosity and kindness," she managed to say, her voice choked with tears. The gratitude she felt was immense, stirring a mix of joy and disbelief that warmed her entire being.

With a shaky laugh, Maria slid into the driver's seat of her new Camaro, the leather cool against her skin. She drove the few blocks back to her grandparents' house, the engine purring smoothly under her careful touch. She couldn't stop thanking her grandparents, her voice filled with excitement and awe.

Later that evening, around 9:30 pm, still buzzing from the day's events, Maria called her parents. Her mom, Ethel, answered after just one ring.

"Hi, Mom," Maria greeted, her voice still brimming with excitement.

"Is everything okay?" Ethel's tone was laced with concern, sensing the unusual energy in her daughter's voice.

Maria's response tumbled out in a joyful rush, "Mom, you won't believe what happened tonight. Grandpa and Grandma took me out to dinner for my birthday. We had such a nice time. The waiter came and sang happy birthday to me and brought a chocolate cake. While I was cutting the cake, my knife touched something metal, and when I took it out, it was a key. A CAR KEY! Grandpa and Grandma bought a red 1968 Camaro for my birthday. I am so excited and over the moon. It is the most beautiful car that I have ever seen," Maria exclaimed in excitement.

Ethel continued, "Grandpa kept the secret from me, too. I had no idea that they were doing such a beautiful thing. I am glad you are so happy, and you deserve it. You are the best daughter and granddaughter anyone parent or grandparent could ask for. Enjoy the car, and happy birthday again. We all love you so much, Maria. Can I speak with Dad?"

Ethel and Grandpa talked on the phone for a very long time. When Grandpa was off the phone, Maria went over to him and kissed him. "Grandpa, I can't thank you enough. You surprised me beyond words. I am still in shock and can't believe the generosity of you and Grandma. You both are amazing, and I love you both so much." Maria was so excited she couldn't even sleep that night.

The next day, Maria did her usual morning care for Grandma and then helped Grandpa around the house. They needed some groceries, so Maria set out in her new car to the store. When she came back, Maria called many of her friends back home to let them know about her new car. She was in seventh Heaven and so, so excited. Both Grandpa and Grandma were so thrilled to see Maria so happy.

It was continuing to snow lightly in February. Maria and Samantha would take a ride in her new car daily. Maria kept thinking what to do for her Grandparents birthdays, both in March. Grandpa is turning 80 years old on March 25th and Grandma is also turning 80 on March 28th. They were high school sweethearts born three days apart. Maria was talking to Samantha about wanting to have a surprise party. Samantha's Grandparents had a large backyard gazebo, which was perfect for parties. Maria and Samantha went to talk to Samantha's Grandparents. Ted and Agnes told Maria that it was fine and that she could use their gazebo for the party. Maria was so appreciative that she could keep the party a surprise.

Throughout the rest of February Maria and Samantha planned the party. Maria sent out invitations to all her Grandparents' closest friends. She found the addresses in her Grandma's address book. The replies were sent back to Samantha. After all the responses were received, there were going to be 30 people at the party.

The party was scheduled from 2 to 5 p.m. on March 24th. Maria enlisted the help of Samantha and her grandmother Agnes, who was renowned for her baking skills and volunteered to supply the cake and other desserts. The menu included an assortment of hors d'oeuvres, finger sandwiches, and non-alcoholic drinks. Maria had arranged for two local teenagers, both fifteen, to serve the food and drinks, offering them payment for their assistance. The event was to be alcohol-free, with background music provided by a stereo set up in the gazebo. Maria had rented tables and chairs from a party supply store downtown and purchased a variety of decorations to adorn the venue.

Agnes made a phone call to Joe, conveying a casual invitation: "We're having some neighbors over for a gathering on March 24th at 2:30 pm. We would love for you and Elizabeth to join us."

Grandpa Joe's response was warm and anticipatory. "Elizabeth and I will be there. Thank you. We're looking forward to it," he assured her, his voice conveying both gratitude and excitement for the upcoming social event.

Maria and Samantha went grocery shopping the day before the party for all the food and drinks. When they finished shopping, Maria went home for dinner and to help Grandma Elizabeth with her evening care and to get ready for bed. After Elizabeth fell asleep, Maria declared, "I am going to Samantha's house to watch television. Is that ok with you, Grandpa?"

"That's fine and have fun Maria."

Maria and Samantha decorated the gazebo beautifully. They set up the tables and put out the chairs, dishes, glasses, napkins, and silverware. They set up the trays of hors d'oeuvres, made finger sandwiches, and put them all in the refrigerator. They finished around midnight, and Maria planned to come the next day at 1 pm so they could do the last of the preparation.

The two girls who were to serve arrived at Samantha's grandparents' house at the same time as Maria. Maria instructed the girls that she wanted them to walk around with the food trays, but first, make sure every guest had something to drink. Maria had punch, iced tea, coffee, hot tea, lemonade, and raspberry lemonade to drink. It was getting close to 2 pm and they started heating the hors d'oeuvres and other food. Guests started arriving, and the gazebo was filled with chatter. The servers circulated around the guests and got the drinks for everyone. It was now nearly 2:30 pm, and Maria asked everyone, "Please be quiet; my Grandparents will arrive shortly." As Joe and Elizabeth walked through the door, a chorus of voices erupted in a loud "Surprise!" Grandpa Joe's mouth dropped open in astonishment, while Grandma Elizabeth's expression shifted to one of complete bewilderment. Their eyes widened as they spotted the "Happy 80th Birthday Joe and Elizabeth" sign strung across the gazebo. The realization dawned on them that the gathering was in their honor.

"Is this all for us?" Grandpa Joe stammered, his voice choked with emotion.

Grandma Elizabeth, still taking in the scene, murmured softly, "Oh my, what a surprise!"

The party buzzed with energy as everyone mingled and chatted. Even Elizabeth, typically reserved, engaged in brief conversations with old friends, her face lighting up with each familiar greeting. The food was met with enthusiastic approval, with guests complimenting the variety and taste. "Maria and Samantha have outdone themselves," one guest commented, admiring the spread.

Agnes's cake was a centerpiece, drawing admiring glances and praises for its exquisite decoration and flavor. "This cake is just divine, Agnes!" exclaimed a guest, reaching for another slice.

As the party wound down and the last guests departed around 6 pm, Grandpa Joe and Grandma Elizabeth made a point to express their heartfelt gratitude. They approached Maria, Samantha, Agnes, and Ted, their faces beaming with joy.

"Thank you all so much for this wonderful surprise. We've never felt so loved and appreciated," Grandpa Joe said, his voice thick with gratitude.

Grandma Elizabeth, visibly moved, added, "It's been a truly delightful day. Thank you for all the love and effort you've put into this."

Maria hugged her grandparents, feeling a swell of pride and happiness. "You deserve every bit of this joy, Grandpa and Grandma."

As the couple left for home, Maria stayed behind to tackle the cleanup. She hummed to herself, satisfied with the joy the day had brought to her beloved grandparents.

"You are my best friend. Nobody could ask for a better friend than you. I really appreciate all your help and ideas. Thank you so much for everything, Samantha."

"I really enjoyed helping you. It was such a fun time. I really appreciate our friendship and hope that we stay lifelong friends."

"We are attached at the hip; you have me for life."

Maria thanked Samantha's Grandparents and told them "We are so lucky to have such special neighbors as you. Thank you for everything. I can't express my deepest gratitude for all your help."

"You are welcome, Maria. We love you and your Grandparents and were so happy to do it." Maria left and went home. Grandpa was waiting for her. Grandma had fallen asleep when they had arrived back home.

"I don't even know how to thank you, Maria. The party was so amazing and to think at your age you were able to do something like that. There are many adults who could never do anything close to what you did. You are the sweetest, smartest, and most lovely girl. We love you so much. You are the light of our lives. Thank you so much, Maria."

"You're welcome, Grandpa. It was such a pleasure for me to do this for you two. I love you so much, Grandpa. I am going to bed now as I am very tired. Goodnight, Grandpa."

"Goodnight Maria."

It was a spring day in April in California. The rolling hills that surrounded the town were lush, green, and picturesque. The birds were out chirping, and the flowers were blooming. The sun was shining down with its warmth and brightness, reminding Maria of the day she met Alberto. It had been nine months since that day, and it was so fresh in her mind as if it were yesterday. *Alberto, how will anyone compare to you?* Maria thought.

Elizabeth was becoming more confused, less responsive, and more agitated. Maria seemed to have a way with her, but poor Grandpa Joe was beside himself, especially when she acted out. She was starting to have more problems with having accidents. Unfortunately, at times she wasn't aware of when she needed to use the bathroom. Maria didn't want to bother Grandpa when she needed help with Elizabeth, but Samantha would gladly come over to help. Maria knew she was entering a more severe stage of the illness. Maria went to the drugstore and bought all the necessary supplies to care for her grandma.

Maria and Samantha would drive in Maria's car and talk most afternoons when their Grandparents napped. They would talk about their Grandparents' care, boys, family, and especially their hope for their futures, such as what they wanted in a husband and how many children they each wanted. They were each other's backbone and support through some difficult times.

By the end of May 1975, as summer approached, Elizabeth's condition had remained unchanged. Maria had mastered the routine, but Elizabeth was becoming increasingly non-verbal. She would say a few words, but she struggled more with communication and especially with finding the right words. Maria was still able to understand her, but Grandpa was finding it increasingly difficult to communicate with her.

One day, at the beginning of June's early morning the phone rang and Maria answered it and said, "Hi"

"Hi Maria, how are the three of you doing?" Ethel exclaimed.

"We are doing well, Mom. Grandma is having a harder time communicating, and there are a few other things, but I have it under control, and she is happy and comfortable."

"Maria, you are amazing. I want you to know that the whole family really appreciates your selflessness, the wonderful care you are giving Grandma and the unending support and encouragement you give Grandpa. This means more to me and all the rest of the family than you will ever know. Thank you for everything you are doing."

"You're welcome, Mom. I am happy to do it."

"I wanted to let you know the Smiths (Ethel's employer) are going away on vacation for six weeks starting July first. They are paying me vacation pay for the whole time and have paid for airline tickets for Emily, Edith and I to come to California. They are the most amazing employer. I feel like God has blessed me with them."

"I am so happy to hear this, Mom. I am excited to see the three of you. I can't wait till you come. Grandma and Grandpa will be elated. Dad can't come?"

"No, he can't ask for any more time off."

"We will miss him, but this is awesome news. I love you, Mom. I can't wait to see you. Do you want to talk to Grandpa?"

"Yes, love you, Maria. Take care."

Ethel and her Dad talked for a long time. When Grandpa was off the phone, Maria exclaimed, "That is exciting news!"

"It sure is Maria. I am so glad that your Mom and sisters are coming for a visit. Too bad your Dad can't come too. Grandma will be happy to hear this."

Maria went into her grandmother's room and told her of the upcoming visit. She had a large smile and seemed very happy. The month of June seemed to pass slowly as Maria was anticipating the upcoming visit. June is a very hot, dry month with the temperature many days over 115 F. Maria and Samantha frequently in the afternoon would go to the high school pool to cool off.

Ethel, Emily, and Edith were scheduled to arrive at 2 pm on the fourth of July. The airport was located about 40 miles from the house. Maria and Grandpa were set to pick them up, while Samantha stayed home with Elizabeth. Circling the arrival terminal at 2:20 pm, Maria spotted her two sisters emerging from the door and waved to them. The sisters saw the car and waved back. Maria and Grandpa got out of the car, and they all exchanged hugs and kisses. They loaded the suitcases into the trunk, but their reunion was briefly interrupted by a traffic cop urging them to move the car. Quickly, they all jumped into the car, and Maria drove off.

"This car is so beautiful, Dad. That was so incredibly sweet of you two," Ethel stated.

"Maria deserves this and more. She is so compassionate and caring, and she is such a lovely girl. She is taking such good care of Grandma that I can never thank her enough. How are things back in Iowa?"

"Everything in Iowa is good. I have the best employer in the world. The girls are doing well in school, and everyone is happy and healthy."

"Girls, what is new with you?"

"I am going to be in the eighth grade. I love cheerleading and swimming," Emily responded.

"Oh, that's great to hear."

"I am going to be in sixth grade and in the same school as Emily. I am excited to be in a new school." Edith exclaims.

The conversations flowed as everyone tried to update each other on what was new in their lives. The traffic was light since it was the Fourth of July. They arrived home, unloaded the suitcases from the trunk, and went into the house. Maria introduced her mom and sisters to Samantha.

"I have heard that you two are getting along really well. I am so happy that you both are here for each other. It is so nice to meet you, Samantha. Thank you for staying with Elizabeth this afternoon," Ethel states.

"You're welcome. It is a pleasure to meet you, Ethel. I'd better go back to my house and check on my Grandparents now. Bye"

"Goodbye, Samantha, and thank you," Maria, Ethel, and Grandpa exclaim.

Ethel and the girls went into the room to see Elizabeth. They all kissed Grandma, who smiled and seemed happy. Ethel was talking to her Mom, but she had a blank stare and was nonverbal. They left the room and told Elizabeth that they would be back later. They went back to the living room, where Grandpa and Maria were sitting on the couch.

"Does Grandma talk much or is she just tired?" Ethel exclaimed.

"Mom, sometimes Grandma will say a few words, and then other times she has a blank stare. When you talk to her, she seems to understand what you are saying and does follow some commands. She is having difficulty finding the correct words, so I think, at times, she would rather express herself through non-verbal methods. She is doing fine, as she is still eating well and seems happy. She takes her medications, and all her vital signs are stable"

"Maria you are awesome, such an understanding of the situation and you are a such a compassionate caregiver. You should become a registered nurse. You have the calling to help your fellow man and are so caring."

"Mom, I am going to think about that idea. Maybe I should."

Grandpa planned a barbecue for the fourth of July. He fixed hamburgers, hot dogs, potato salad, and chips. They ate outside and enjoyed the warm California evening weather. The sun was going down, and the fireworks were to start in less than an hour. Everyone was outside talking and having a great time. Samantha came over to watch the fireworks as her Grandparents had gone to sleep. The fireworks were starting, and the backyard was the perfect viewing venue. Emily and Edith were very excited. Maria went into the house to make sure Grandma was still asleep. She was sound asleep which was amazing since the fireworks were so loud. After the fireworks were finished, they all went back inside the house. Emily and Edith were tired and so they went right to bed. Grandpa, Edith, Maria, and Samantha stayed up and talked for hours. Edith and Grandpa were so impressed with both Maria and Samantha. They felt that they both were so mature, wise beyond their years and so compassionate. It was way after midnight, and so Samantha decided she better go home.

"My Mom thinks I should become a RN," Maria said.

"You would be a great RN. You love people and are so caring. I have thought of becoming an RN at times, too. That would be great if we both decided on this career and could go to nursing school together."

"That would be awesome. We have a lot to think about. Goodnight Samantha. See you tomorrow."

"Goodnight Maria."

The next morning, everyone was awake by 8 am. The girls were watching television and Grandpa was cooking breakfast. Ethel wanted to see what a typical day taking care of her Mom entailed. She planned to shadow Maria all day. Grandma was awake and cheerful, and the bed was soiled. Maria gave her a rundown of the morning activities.

"The first thing I do is take Grandma to the shower. You can't leave her alone as she is unsteady. I stand by the shower till she is done. You can see she is wearing depends. I then have her put on her robe. I walk her to the sink so she can brush her teeth. I then help her get dressed, but she is no longer able to decide what to wear. Her closet is so frustrating to her so I pick an outfit the night before and ask her if she would like to wear it tomorrow. After Grandma is dressed, she sits in the chair by the bed. I change the bed linens, and on many days, I also need to change all the blankets. I do the laundry almost daily as I don't want Grandpa to be aware that this is going on. Grandpa has enough difficulty trying to communicate with her, and he is not aware yet that she is having frequent accidents. After the bed is made, occasionally, your Mom wants to go back to bed, but usually, she will come and sit in the dining room for breakfast. I always give her a choice and let her make the decision. I believe that letting her have as much control as possible is important. Mom, that is a summary of the morning routine."

Maria I am really impressed how organized and in control of the situation you are. The other thing is you have so much patience and understanding. You are awesome."

"Thanks, Mom." Maria and her Mom finished Elizabeth's morning care.

"Grandma, do you want to go to the dining room for breakfast?"

"Sure." Maria and Ethel walked Elizabeth into the dining room. She was quite unsteady, and Ethel wondered how Maria handled her by herself. Everyone came to the table and enjoyed the beautiful breakfast feast. After breakfast, Grandma wanted to stay up and watch some television with Emily and Edith. They walked Elizabeth to the lounge chair in the living room. She was smiling and watching television.

"Mom, I ask Grandma every two hours if she needs to go to the bathroom. That really helps to prevent accidents during the day. If she happens to stay in bed for a prolonged period, then I turn her from side to side. I encourage Grandma to walk a few times a day to prevent her from losing their range of motion and the ability to walk. I encourage her to drink fluids. I bring her a glass of water, iced tea, or iced coffee every 2 hours to keep her hydrated, especially in this heat. There are times when Grandma will use her utensils and eat by herself and other times when she just plays with her food; I will feed her. I give her protein milkshakes once to twice a day because protein is so important in keeping her muscles strong. Grandpa buys them at the grocery store, and Grandma loves them. She usually takes a nap, about two hours in the afternoon. Samantha's Grandparents nap around 2 pm, so we usually hang out together at that time. Here is the schedule I made for her care and medications."

"The schedule is so impressive; you have it all covered, for sure. Thank you so much for taking such good care of my mom. You cannot imagine how much we appreciate you."

'You are welcome, Mom." As the mother and daughter talked, they suddenly heard yelling and banging in the living room. Grandma was banging her fists and screaming.

"Grandma, what is wrong?" Maria asked concernedly.

"You want to go back to bed. We will take you now." Ethel and Maria walked her to the bathroom and put her back in bed. Then, they went outside to talk in the backyard.

"How much money are you spending on supplies for Grandma a month? "Ethel asked.

"About $50 a month"

"I am going to give you $200 now and then put $75 in your account monthly for the supplies."

"Mom, I appreciate it, but I know you can't afford it."

"But Maria, it is not right. You can't pay for this. I received a very significant raise at my job, so I am able to do it."

"Thank you, Mom."

"No, thank you, Maria," Ethel insisted. Maria was relieved about the financial support; she had been worrying about how she would continue to afford the supplies. She hesitated to ask Grandpa for help, knowing that if he discovered her financial strain, it would upset him deeply. After dinner, Maria and Ethel prepared Elizabeth for bed, and she quickly fell asleep. Having shadowed Maria throughout the day, Ethel came to realize just how much her mother's condition had deteriorated over the past year and how it was demanding an increasing amount of Maria's time and energy.

Maria was so happy to have her mom and sisters visiting. Maria and her mom talked for hours every day. Maria and Ethel went out to lunch several times during their stay. She also showed her mom around the town. She took her sisters to a nearby amusement park, where they played miniature golf and frequently swam at the high school pool. Maria had much more free time since her mom was able to care for her Grandma. Grandpa, Ethel, Emily, and Edith went to lunch at least once a week during their visit, too.

The six weeks seemed to fly by for everyone. They had done so many activities, but most importantly, they had spent quality time with each other. Ethel had a much greater appreciation for the care that her mom required. "Do you want to stay, or is this becoming too much for you, Maria?" her Mom asked.

"Oh no, Mom, I have to stay. Grandpa can't handle the situation. Don't tell him I said that, but it is true. I am fine, and I can't leave now. I really appreciate that you are worried about me, but everything will work out. I am not sure what the future holds, but I am here for the ride. Grandma and Grandpa both need me. I hate to see the three of you leave. I will miss all of you dearly, but in my heart, I know we are doing the right thing."

"Maria, you are so mature and grown up. When you need support or just need to talk, please call me anytime, day or night. I know this situation is difficult, and you are handling it with grace. I don't want you to feel that when we leave, you must bear all this weight on your shoulders only. I know that you have Samantha as a support, which is wonderful, but this is a heavy load that both of you are undertaking. I so admire both of you. Remember, I am always a phone call away."

"Thank you, Mom, you are the best. I have Samantha and Grandpa, but I promise I will call you if I need to talk."

The following day, August 12th, dawned with a bittersweet air as Ethel, Emily, and Edith prepared for their early afternoon flight back to Iowa. Maria and Grandpa drove them to the airport, their hearts heavy with the impending farewell. At the departure gate, they embraced warmly, and tears flowed freely. "I don't know when I'll see you all again," Maria murmured, her voice thick with emotion, "but I'm so grateful we had this wonderful time together."

The drive back was quiet, reflective. Maria and Grandpa returned home to find Elizabeth visibly agitated and Samantha exhausted from the efforts of caregiving. Together, Maria and Samantha gently helped Elizabeth back to bed for her afternoon nap, where she soon relaxed into a calmer state.

"Thank you so much, Samantha, for taking such good care of Elizabeth," Grandpa and Maria said in unison, their gratitude sincere.

Samantha smiled wearily but warmly. "Of course, anytime. I'm glad I could help," she replied, gathering her things. "Goodbye, see you later."

As Samantha left, Maria turned to Grandpa, her eyes still moist from the airport goodbye. "It's hard seeing them go," she confessed, seeking comfort in her grandfather's familiar presence.

Grandpa nodded, placing a comforting arm around her shoulders. "They'll be back before we know it. And we had a great visit, didn't we?" His encouraging voice tried to lift her spirits.

Maria managed a small smile, the weight of the day settling in her heart. "Yes, we did. It was wonderful."

The next few days, the house seemed so quiet with Ethel and the girls gone. Grandma was more confused, but Maria attributed this to trying to get back into their usual routine. Grandpa continued to have difficulty understanding his wife but became more accepting of the situation. On the other hand, Samantha also needed Maria's help more with her grandfather. The months of August, September, and October passed quickly. Maria and Samantha coordinated the care of their Grandparents so they could work together. Elizabeth appeared more distant and less cooperative, so it was taking the two of them to do her care.

It was a sunny, cool day in November, and Elizabeth was more agitated than usual. Maria was unable to calm her down all day. She ate very little for dinner and threw her silverware away during the meal. All this upset Maria and she left the room. To help, Grandpa asked Elizabeth if he could help her with something, but Grandma stood up and threw a chair at him. The chair landed on Grandpa's foot; that hurt, but he claimed that he was fine. He couldn't believe that this had happened. As Maria walked back in the room and saw the incident. She immediately put Grandma back to bed. "Grandma you can't do things like that. Please be good." Maria received just a blank stare back with no response.

"Grandpa, are you alright? I am not sure why Grandma is acting like this today. We need to call her doctor in the morning. What do you think?"

"I am fine, Maria. How was she able to pick up that chair if she could hardly move? You are right. We need to call her doctor in the morning and let her know." The three of them had quite a day, so they all went to sleep early that night.

During the night, around 2 a.m., a loud crash echoed through the dark, silent house. Startled, Maria bolted from her bed and dashed into the living room. There, she found

Elizabeth, her grandmother, wandering aimlessly towards the front door, her expression confused and vacant.

"Grandma, where are you going?" Maria asked, her voice thick with concern as she gently grasped Elizabeth's arm.

"I don't know where I am," Elizabeth murmured, her voice lost and frail. Gently guiding her back to her room, Maria tucked her into bed, soothing her with soft words. Despite her efforts, Elizabeth rose from her bed twice more, each time seeming more disoriented. Maria, with patience worn thin but still compassionate, led her grandmother back each time, reassuring her with a calm, steady voice.

Exhausted and worried, Maria finally decided to sleep on the couch in the living room to keep a closer watch. As she lay down, the quiet of the house was a stark contrast to the turmoil in her heart, her mind racing with concern for her grandmother's wellbeing.

Maria and Grandpa both woke up at about seven in the morning. Maria told her Grandpa that Elizabeth came into the living room three times last night and that is why I am sleeping on the couch. They called her doctor and informed her of the latest incidents. The doctor's office made an appointment for her to be seen the next day.

The three of them went to an appointment the next morning. Grandpa and Maria had difficulty getting her to the office. She was barely able to walk since she would not move her feet and was agitated. After about 45 minutes they got from the car to the office, which was no more than 100 feet. They were late for the appointment, but the office staff understood and were cooperative. Three of them were put in a room right away. The staff took Grandma's vital signs, and by that time, she was totally cooperative. Maria and Grandpa explained to the doctor the latest incidents that have occurred.

The doctor listened to them carefully and then explained, "This kind of behavior can be expected. I will prescribe her medication for agitation. This medication is only to be given when she is displaying moderate to severe agitation. I am prescribing her a low dose. You can give it to her 1-2 times a day only if necessary. Another thing I am going to do is order home-care. I will send a nurse out to help you with her medications and further instruct you on her care. I am also going to send a physical therapist, an occupational therapist, and a social worker. I think this will really help both of you with her care. This is such a difficult situation, and I can see that you both are doing an amazing job. Please let me know if I can be of any further help. I will see her back in the office in two months. "

"Thank you so much. We really appreciate your understanding and compassion and for getting us in for an appointment so quickly," Maria gratefully replied to the doctor. Maria and Grandpa left the office feeling relieved and looking forward to the home-care services.

The next day, the home-care agency called and spoke with Maria. They set up all the evaluation appointments. The first to visit was the Registered Nurse, Beth. She took a comprehensive assessment of the situation and then went over her medications, diabetic care, diet, and activity level. She also told them that they were going to supply a hospital bed, trapeze, commode, and other equipment that would help with the care. Beth was very impressed with Maria since she was nineteen years of age. Maria showed the nurse her vital sign chart, blood sugar readings, medication chart, and schedule. The Nurse demonstrated an easier way of getting her grandma out of the chair. Maria was a sponge and learned all she could from the Nurse. Beth said she would be back in a week. Maria now had a better understanding of the new medication for agitation and felt more comfortable using it as necessary.

Later that day, the Physical therapist came for a visit. She showed Maria an easier way to transfer her Grandma in and out of bed, some range of motion and strengthening exercises, and an exercise program for her Grandma to follow. She also let them know that the equipment would be delivered next Tuesday morning and that she would come in the afternoon to demonstrate how to properly use all of it.

The next morning, the Occupational Therapist arrived and provided utensils with larger grips, which made it easier for Elizabeth to eat. She also demonstrated some upper body exercises to Maria, instructing her on how to assist Elizabeth with these movements to maintain her mobility. Later in the afternoon, the Social Worker visited, bringing a wealth of outside resources that Grandpa Joe and Maria could tap into if necessary.

They had arranged for the nurse to come once a week for the next four weeks. The Physical Therapist was scheduled to visit twice a week for a month. Both the Occupational Therapist and the Social Worker were set to make three visits each, ensuring a comprehensive support system was in place for Elizabeth's care. This network of healthcare professionals provided Maria and her grandfather with much-needed support and guidance as they navigated the complexities of Elizabeth's condition.

The month of November flew by with all the home care that was being provided. The hospital bed and other equipment made a huge difference in Grandma's comfort level. Maria learned so much during this time. When the registered nurse would visit, Maria and Samantha would ask numerous questions. They both were beginning to think more about becoming an RN. Maria and Grandpa were so appreciative of all the skilled care and instructions that they provided. Maria would call her Mom frequently and update her about Elizabeth's care and all that she was learning. Ethel was happy that Maria had this support.

Thanksgiving rolled around, and since Elizabeth was keeping them all busy, they decided not to have any guests. Grandpa cooked a delicious turkey dinner with all the fixings. Elizabeth was more cooperative on the holiday, and she sat at the dining room table. The three of them thoroughly enjoyed Grandpa's feast. After dinner, Grandma went to bed, Maria did the dishes, and Grandpa watched television.

It was the first week of December, and Maria and Samantha were discussing Christmas. They decided to volunteer to serve Christmas dinner at the homeless shelter again this year. Elizabeth had been discharged from home care, and Maria was busy trying to implement all that she had been taught especially the exercise program. She had to feed her Grandma at times, so it would take much longer to do it. Elizabeth only had a few bites at a time, so it took more than an hour and a half to feed her. She was less agitated, and the medication that was prescribed appeared to be helping. Maria decided she would decorate the house the way she had done last year. She did all the decorations in the afternoon when Elizabeth slept. Maria decided not to bake cookies that year but rather bought presents for everyone. Maria did an outstanding job with the decorations and Christmas tree. Her Grandparents were thrilled with how it all came out. Grandpa was in the Christmas spirit and would play Christmas carols frequently throughout the day.

Maria and Samantha would go Christmas shopping in the afternoon when their Grandparents napped. Maria bought her grandma a beautiful pink nightgown with a robe, and for her grandpa, she bought him a small television set for his bedroom. She also purchased gifts for Samantha, her Grandparents, and something for her parents and sisters. She wrapped the presents and put the ones for her Grandparents under the tree and then went to the post office to mail the presents to her parents and sisters. Maria loved the holiday season. The two girls would go out in the evenings after their Grandparents were asleep. Elizabeth, after starting the new medication, was in a quiet phase and did a lot of sleeping. Grandpa felt like he could handle her then, so he encouraged Maria and Samantha to go out for some Christmas fun and magic. The houses in the neighborhood were so beautifully decorated. They would drive down different streets to see all the decorations. They went Christmas caroling with some of the neighbors on the weekend nights and then went over to one of the neighbor's houses for hot chocolate and cookies. They also went to the town's Christmas party held downtown, and they met some teenagers their own age. They really got along well with the girls they met and were happy to have some new friends. The first three weeks of December turned out to be quite an entertaining and fun time for both Maria and Samantha.

Maria woke up on Christmas morning and looked out her bedroom window and saw snow everywhere. It was a glorious winter wonderland outside, and it reminded her of a Christmas morning in Iowa. She wishes both her Grandparents a "Merry Christmas." Maria helped her Grandma with all her care and then got dressed for Church. Maria went to Church with Samantha and her Grandparents again this year. The Church service was beautiful with all the gorgeous flowers around the pulpit, Christmas carols sang during Mass and everyone dressed up in their best clothes. After Church, Maria, Samantha, and her Grandparents exchanged gifts. Maria received a beautiful necklace from the three of them. They all loved Maria's gifts too. Maria bought Samantha a beautiful watch and her Grandparents a lovely vase for their coffee table. After opening the gifts, Maria and Samantha headed to the homeless shelter to serve Christmas dinner. They both wore Santa hats this year to be more festive. They both recognize some of the same people from last year. Both girls realized how fortunate they were to be living the life they had and felt they should never complain, especially when they saw how the homeless lived. They both wished they could volunteer more at the homeless shelter but are so busy with what they are already doing. Samantha and Maria both have such big hearts.

After returning from serving at the homeless shelter, Maria helped her grandpa put the finishing touches on their Christmas dinner. As the meal was ready, she gently wheeled her grandma to the dining room table. They gathered around, immersing themselves in nearly three hours of lively conversation and delightful eating. Grandpa Joe, known for his culinary skills, especially during the holidays, had outdone himself once again, filling the air with the savory aromas of the season.

As they shared stories and laughter, Maria's expression turned thoughtful. "I've been thinking a lot lately," she began, capturing the attention of her grandparents, "I want to become a registered nurse."

Grandpa Joe's face lit up with pride. "That would be the perfect profession for you, Maria. You are so smart and have the patience, understanding, and compassion that nursing demands. You would make an awesome nurse."

"Thank you, Grandpa," Maria replied, her heart warmed by his encouragement. She excused herself for a moment and walked over to the Christmas tree, returning with presents in her hands. "Grandma, this is for you, and Grandpa, this is for you," she announced, handing them their gifts.

"How kind of you, Maria," Grandpa Joe exclaimed, visibly moved. Maria assisted her grandmother in unwrapping her gift—a gorgeous nightgown and robe. Tears welled up in her grandmother's eyes as she touched the soft fabric.

"Thank you," her grandmother whispered, deeply touched.

"You are so welcome, Grandma. I hope you like it!" Maria beamed, pleased with her grandmother's reaction.

"Beautiful," her grandmother managed to say, her voice choked with emotion.

Then it was Grandpa Joe's turn. His eyes sparkled with anticipation as he opened his present and found a small television. "Oh, thank you, Maria. I've always wanted a small television for my room. How did you know?"

"A little birdie told me," Maria winked, sharing a secret smile with him.

"Thank you, thank you, Maria, for everything. These gifts are just perfect. I can't wait for Grandma to wear her beautiful nightgown and robe and for me to watch television in my room." He was overjoyed.

Maria then received a gift from her grandparents—a gold necklace with a gorgeous diamond, earrings, and a diamond bracelet. She gasped as she opened the box. "Oh, my goodness, these are stunning. I've never dreamt that I would have something this elegant to wear. Thank you, thank you. I love the set, and there are no words to describe how surprised and thrilled I am. You two are too kind. Thank you both so much." She stood up and embraced her grandparents, overwhelmed by their generosity.

As she tried on the jewelry, her grandfather chuckled, "You look like a princess, Maria. With those on, you look like a movie star. We better watch out for all those boys out there."

"Oh, Grandpa, don't worry. Remember all I can think about is Alberto. Thank you so much. You two are the greatest grandparents in the world."

"You're welcome, Maria. We love your gifts, and you are such a precious granddaughter with a beautiful heart. Thank you, Maria," her grandfather replied, his voice thick with emotion.

"Your welcome, Grandpa. Is it okay if I call my mom now to tell her about my gift?" Maria asked, eager to share her joy with her mother.

"Of course, Maria," her grandfather smiled warmly, passing her the phone.

"Sure, Maria. Let me talk to your mom when you're finished." Maria called home and spoke to her parents and sisters. They all loved the gifts that Maria had sent them. Maria also thanked them for the Christmas gifts and money they had sent her.

"Mom, Grandma, and Grandpa bought me a beautiful diamond necklace, earrings, and bracelet set for Christmas. They are stunning and look so beautiful. I am so excited and can't wait for you to see them."

"Maria that was so nice of them, but you deserve all the best. You are making a sacrifice, and my parents really appreciate you. You don't realize you are a very special young lady and I hope you know how proud everyone is of you. When I was there last summer, I realized how you had taken control of a difficult situation and handled it with grace with never a complaint, and always with a smile. You are also helping Grandpa feel assured that his wife is receiving the best care possible and all three of you are so happy. Maria, you are amazing, and truthfully, I am in awe of you. Merry Christmas, Maria."

"Oh Mom, I appreciate all your kind words. I miss all of you so much and hope that you have a very Merry Christmas. Grandpa wants to talk to you now." Grandpa talked to Ethel for at least 2 hours. Maria had put Elizabeth to bed and finished all the dishes when Grandpa was finished with the call.

"Oh Maria, I see that the kitchen is spotless. I will empty the dishwasher and you go sit down, watch some television and relax. I really appreciate you doing the dishes."

"Thank you, Grandpa." Grandpa and Maria sat around and watched A Christmas Carol, which finished well after midnight.

"I am going to sleep, Grandpa. I can't thank you and Grandma enough for the beautiful jewelry. I love them."

"You're welcome, Maria. Thank you. Grandma and I love our gifts, too. Have a good night's sleep, sweet dreams."

Same to you Grandpa. Love you."

'Love you too very much."

The next day, Maria and Samantha went for a drive in the afternoon. Samantha loved Maria's jewelry, and they talked about all the gifts that they both received. Samantha was telling Maria that the two girls that they met at the town's Christmas party were having a New Year's Eve party at their house. They were sisters ages eighteen and nineteen. They had invited both Maria and Samantha to come to the party.

They live down the street just a couple of blocks away. Maria wanted to go to the party but felt terrible leaving her grandpa alone on New Year's Eve. Maria told Samantha she would ask her Grandparents and get back to her. Maria was back in her house around 4 pm.

"Grandpa, do you mind if I go to a New Year's Eve party with Samantha? Lisa and Leslie are sisters who live down the street, and we met them at the downtown Christmas party. They have invited us to their New Year's Eve party."

"How old are Lisa and Leslie?"

"They are 18 and 19 years old and very much like all my friends."

"That is fine Maria. I am glad that you have more friends your age. What time will you be home?"

'I would think about 1 am Grandpa."

"That's great Maria. I hope that both of you enjoy the party."

"Thank you." Maria and Samantha really looked forward to the party. They anticipated meeting new people and possibly making some more new friends.

On New Year's Eve, Maria woke up early. She was so excited about the party that night. She did all her usual nighttime care for Elizabeth and then took a long bath, did a facial, and got ready for the party. Her make-up was done perfectly, and her hair was curled. She wore a beautiful blue dress that matched her eye color. She had on the jewelry that her Grandparents had given her for Christmas. Maria came out of her room.

"Oh, my goodness. You look stunning. Maria. Let me get some pictures of you. We can send them to your mom."

"Thank you, Grandpa."

"Be careful, but have fun."

"I will Grandpa. You have a nice New Year's Eve, too."

"I will see you around 1 am. Bye"

"Bye."

Maria went over to Samantha's house and her Grandparents were in the living room. Maria and Samantha both looked so beautiful.

"You two look like you came out of Vogue magazine."

"Thank you. Happy New Year."

"Happy New Year to both of you." Maria and Samantha drove the two blocks to Lisa and Leslie's house. They could hear the music when they approached the house. There were so many cars parked in front of their house and down the street. They were able to find a spot right in front. They went up to the front door, knocked and Lisa answered.

"Come on in. I am glad both of you were able to make it. Let me introduce you to all my friends." They were introduced to everyone at the party. Everyone looked like they were between eighteen years old and twenty- five. Maria and Samantha could feel all the guys checking them out. There seemed to be about 30 people at the party so far. They had food everywhere. They had punch, and they also had alcoholic drinks. Maria and Samantha started talking to two brothers. They both went to college in a nearby town; one was a junior and the other a senior, and both were studying business. Maria and Samantha told them that they were both from out of state, taking care of their Grandparents, who lived next door to each other. Stan and Harry were so impressed with both Maria and Samantha. They talked, then danced, and then talked some more. They all seemed to hit it off very well. Maria liked Harry, but all she could think about was Alberto and contemplating what he might be doing tonight. At midnight, they had a champagne toast and wished each other "Happy 1976," and both couples kissed. Samantha liked the older brother Stan, and Maria liked the younger brother Harry. Maria wasn't sure if she would want to continue this friendship. It was getting close to 1 am.

"I will need to leave soon. I told my Grandpa I would be home around 1 am." Maria exclaims.

"Me too." Samantha says.

"Would you both like to go out to dinner on Friday night, say about 7 p.m.?" Maria and Samantha look at each other.

"Sure, that sounds wonderful." They both replied.

"We will pick you up at your house, and we can double date." The four of them thanked Lisa and Leslie for such a wonderful party. They walked them both to Maria's car, kissed, and said goodnight.

Maria and Samantha drove off. Samantha was so excited, but Maria was less than thrilled. Maria just kept talking about Alberto. Samantha told her that Alberto was not here, and somehow, you are going to have to get on with your life. Maria knew that Samantha was right, but it was hard to accept. They got home and said goodnight to each other.

"Hi, Grandpa. We had a really great time. We met two brothers who are very nice and want to take Samantha and I to dinner this Friday night. Is that ok with you? Happy New Year. Happy 1976, Grandpa."

"Happy New Year to you Maria. What do these boys do? Are they in school, or do they work?"

"They are both in college, majoring in business. I am not sure I want to go because of Alberto, but Samantha is so excited. I am going to go because Samantha likes Stan, and she says that I need to move on. Harry will come to the house to pick me up, so you will be able to meet him."

"That is fine Maria. I am glad that I will be able to meet him.

"I am going to bed. Happy New Year. Love you, Maria."

"Love you too Grandpa very much. Goodnight."

In the first week of January 1976, Maria and Samantha were filled with anticipation for their date on Friday night. Elizabeth had become more active and agitated, often failing to recognize either Maria or her grandpa. Maria was concerned about whether she could leave her grandpa alone with Elizabeth that night, but she decided to wait and see how Friday unfolded.

By Friday, Elizabeth had been calm throughout the day, which eased Maria's worries somewhat. She felt reassured that her grandpa could manage Elizabeth that evening. Right on schedule, Harry arrived at the door at 7 pm. Maria introduced him to her grandpa, and the two men immediately connected over their shared interests in baseball, football, their business studies, and a mutual love for cooking. They engaged in conversation at the front door, discussing their favorite teams and recipes for a good fifteen minutes.

"We better get going," Harry said with a friendly smile. "Samantha and Stan must be wondering what's happened to us. It was great meeting you, Joe. I'm looking forward to continuing our chat soon."

"Have a wonderful time tonight, you two," Grandpa Joe responded, shaking Harry's hand warmly. "Nice to meet you, Harry."

After Harry and Maria left, Grandpa Joe went to check on his wife in the bedroom. He tried to engage her in conversation, hoping to reassure her. "Elizabeth, Maria's date is a wonderful young man. Is there anything you need?"

"Who are you? Get out of here," Elizabeth responded, clearly confused and distressed.

"I'm your husband, Joe. Remember?" he tried to remind her gently.

"I don't have a husband. I'm not sure where my mother and father went, but I've seen you before," she said, her voice tinged with uncertainty.

"If you need anything, just let me know. Goodnight," he said, trying to keep his tone soothing.

"Okay, but please find my mother and father," she insisted, still lost in her memories.

"Okay, I will," Joe promised, though he knew he couldn't fulfill this request. He returned to the living room, his heart heavy, and distracted himself with a football game on TV.

Meanwhile, Maria and Harry stepped out the front door to find Samantha and Stan waiting in a Jaguar convertible parked sleekly by the curb. Maria couldn't help but think about their affluent background, given neither of them worked yet they sported such an expensive car and attended college.

"Nice car," Maria commented as she approached, impressed and a bit curious about their lifestyle.

"Yeah, it's a family thing. We love this old machine," Stan replied with a grin, patting the car's dashboard affectionately.

Harry chuckled, "Let's make tonight memorable," as they all settled into the comfortable leather seats, ready to embark on their evening adventure.

"Your Grandpa is so nice. You are lucky to have Grandparents."

"You are right. I am happy that I am not going to school now, so I am able to care for my Grandma."

"Are you planning on going to college?"

"Yes, I want to be a registered nurse."

"That is such a noble profession." They finally get to the car.

"Sorry, it took us so long. Maria's Grandfather is so cool, and we were having a great conversation."

"Do you two like Italian food? Stan asked.

"We both love it." Samantha and Maria respond.

"Good Italian it will be". They end up taking them to the Italian restaurant that Maria went for her birthday.

"I love this restaurant. It has great food." Maria exclaimed.

"We both love this restaurant too."

They got a cozy table by the window. Stan and Harry told them that both their parents were physicians and that they were fortunate to have a wonderful life. Maria and Samantha saw in these men the same appreciation that they both have for their lives. Stan and Harry both seemed caring, sympathetic, smart, and sweet besides, both were handsome and had great personalities. The brothers find Samantha and Maria to be beautiful, intelligent, caring, very sweet, and sexy. They seemed to have met their match.

The conversation flowed effortlessly during dinner. Maria shared her story of coming from Iowa to take care of her grandmother, who was battling dementia. Similarly, Samantha explained that she hailed from Carson City, Nevada, and was in the area to look after her grandfather, who suffered from severe heart disease. They had both been in their caregiving roles for about a year and a half. Although they hadn't known each other before, their shared responsibilities had made them best friends.

They enjoyed a delicious meal consisting of soup, salad, three types of pasta, and tiramisu for dessert. After leaving the restaurant, they walked back to their car, still chatting amiably.

"Thank you both so much for such a delicious dinner," Maria and Samantha said in unison, their smiles reflecting their gratitude.

"Would you like to go to a drive-in movie now?" Stan suggested, his eyes bright with the idea.

"That sounds like a great plan, thanks," Maria responded, and Samantha nodded in agreement.

"How about 'Jaws'?" Stan proposed, a playful grin on his face.

"Absolutely, let's do it!" they agreed enthusiastically.

They drove to the movie theater, the cool night air swirling around them as Stan lowered the convertible's top. Once parked, Stan dashed off to grab popcorn and drinks for everyone. As the movie began, a hush fell over the group, the suspenseful scenes capturing their full attention. The movie, a classic tale of man versus nature, had them all on the edge of their seats.

During one particularly tense scene, Maria, gripped by fear, involuntarily squeezed Harry's thigh tightly. Realizing her hand was moving higher, she quickly retracted, wondering if she had inadvertently sent the wrong signal. However, the moment passed without awkwardness, and soon they were holding hands, their fingers intertwined.

As the tension on the screen escalated, so did their closeness. Stan wrapped his arm around Samantha, and not long after, Harry did the same with Maria. The screams during the scary parts of the film were mixed with laughter and light-hearted shrieks from Samantha and Maria.

By the end of the movie, as the credits rolled and the resolution washed over the audience, Maria and Harry shared passionate kisses, lost in the moment. Maria found herself deeply attracted to Harry, yet she couldn't stop her thoughts from straying to Alberto occasionally. The evening ended with lingering kisses between the couples, marking a memorable night under the stars.

Elizabeth was quiet during the evening. Grandpa went back to check on her, and she was awake.

"Did you find my Mother and Father?" asked Elizabeth.

"No have you been sleeping?" asked Joe.

"No, I am just here," replied Elizabeth.

"Do you want something to drink?" asked Joe.

"No. Maybe it is poison," Elizabeth replied with concern.

"Just take a few sips. It is good for you," said Joe.

" You are trying to kill me," shouted Elizabeth.

"No, but just go to sleep," Joe replied giving up.

Grandpa got used to Grandma's behavior and didn't take it personally anymore. He realized how difficult it was to take care of his wife and how well Maria was handling the situation. She never complained and always smiled. After taking care of his wife for one night by himself, he felt like pulling his hair out. He looked at Maria like an angel with a very special gift.

The couples continue to passionately kiss. The movie theater had emptied out and they realize their car is the only car left. "Our Grandparents will be wondering when we will be home. This has been such an enjoyable evening and we both want to thank you two so much. We can't wait to see you again." Maria and Samantha exclaimed.

"It had been our pleasure. We can't wait to see you two again." They drive Maria and Samantha home. Stan walked Samantha to her door, and Harry walked Maria to her door. Grandpa opened the front door and asked Harry to come into the house.

Grandpa and Harry talk like they have known each other forever. Maria is happy that Grandpa likes Harry. He says that he will need to leave soon as he has a seminar at school this Saturday.

"Can I come see you tomorrow after the seminar?"

"Sure, I would like that."

"Can't wait." Harry replied and then left.

"I can see you had an awesome date."

"I did Grandpa."

"He seems like such a nice young man."

"I am happy that you have friends here, Maria."

"Thanks. Goodnight, Grandpa."

"Goodnight Maria." Maria got very tired and slept very well that night.

The following day, Maria was anxious and excited about talking to Samantha. They both went for a drive in Maria's car at about 2 pm. Samantha is head over heels for Stan. Maria really likes Harry but is still talking about Alberto.

Maria was back home around 3.30 pm. Elizabeth was anxious and trying to get out of the bed. Maria put her in the wheelchair and let her watch television in the living room. But she started throwing objects and screaming. Maria gave her Grandma one of the relaxant pills. She continued to be agitated so Maria decided to keep her up. They ate dinner around 5:30 pm. Elizabeth wouldn't eat by herself, so Maria tried to feed her. She just spit the food out. The doorbell rang, and it was 7 pm. Harry was at the door.

"Come on in."

"Nice to see you today." Maria introduced Harry to her Grandma.

"Nice to meet you, Elizabeth."

"Same."Grandpa sat with Grandma, who was still in the wheelchair. Maria and Harry went outside to the backyard and talked. Then they kissed, and Maria's heart was beating so fast that she had chills. This had never happened to Maria before, and she knew she was falling for Harry but felt guilty.

"We need to go back inside for a minute. I need to put my Grandma back to bed."

"I will help you."

"Are you sure?"

"Of course."

"Ok, I really appreciate the help." Maria loved Harry helping her put her grandma back to bed. It was so much easier with his help. She found him so endearing that he would help her with this task. Maria and Harry were very similar in personalities, and both had huge hearts. Maria was falling fast for Harry, but in a different way than she did for Alberto. Harry and Maria went back into the living room with Grandpa. Harry and Grandpa talked about so many subjects. It was about midnight.

"I need to leave; it is so late."

"Thanks for coming over. I can't wait to see you again.

"I can come over tomorrow if you want. I can see you need to stay close to the house due to your grandma. You can tell me if I am being presumptuous. I would love to see you."

"Oh, absolutely not. I love having you around here, and so do my Grandparents."

"I will bring dinner for all of us, and I will be here at 6 pm."

"Oh, I will tell my Grandpa, that is so sweet of you."

"See you tomorrow. I can't wait." Harry kissed Maria with such passion that Maria's body was tingled, and her heart fluttered. Maria felt confused; she had fallen for two guys. She thought about how this was possible. She would daydream about Alberto and then about Harry.

At exactly 6 pm, there is a knock on the front door. Harry is there with bags of food. "Hi Harry, come on in."

"Dinner has arrived." Harry brought over Italian food, pasta, salad, and dessert. For Elizabeth, he brought mashed potatoes, sweet potatoes, turkey, and peas. Maria had told him that she likes soft food and is no longer eating Italian or Mexican food. Maria had Elizabeth up in the wheelchair for dinner. Grandpa Joe and Harry started immediately talking about sports.

"We should start eating before the food gets cold," Maria exclaims. They all sat around the dinner table. "This was sure nice of you Harry. Thank you so much." Grandpa Joe enthusiastically says. The food was delicious, and everyone enjoyed their dinner. Maria ate her dinner, and when she was finished, she fed her Grandma. Feeding Elizabeth required a lot of patience. She would take a bite and then not chew her food. Maria worried about her daily caloric intake. Maria decided she would track her daily calorie intake. When Elizabeth was done eating, Harry helped Maria get her Grandma back in bed. Then Maria finished her evening care and medications. Maria then came out into the living room. Grandpa and Harry were deep in conversation.

"Can I borrow this guy for a little while?"

"Sure." Maria and Harry went out to the backyard.

"Thank you so much for bringing dinner over for us. You are so sweet and good-looking. I have never met anyone like you before."

"Oh Maria, you are welcome. I love being around you and your Grandparents. Joe asked me over for dinner tomorrow night. He would be fixing Mexican. I told him, "I will be here. I hope that is ok with you."

"Of course, it is. I am so happy when you are here. I want to tell you something. I really miss you when you aren't here."

"I want to take you out, just the two of us, but I can see it is very difficult for you to leave your Grandpa by himself with your Grandma."

"I appreciate that you are so understanding."

"I can't wait to get you alone, but I do understand."

"I have learned so much taking care of my Grandmother over the last 18 months. First, I have learned patience, to just agree, to distract, to reassure, to reminisce, to encourage, to reinforce, and always ask and never demand. These are the key principles to taking care of someone with dementia or memory loss."

"Maria, you are amazing and will be the best-registered nurse ever. I am going to encourage you to go to nursing school and make sure you do. Also, when you go to school you will be the prettiest girl in your class for sure. Your long flowing hair and beautiful eyes make you a knockout, and you stand out in any crowd. You are so beautiful on the outside but just as beautiful on the inside. You are one of those rare finds that come around once in a lifetime."

"Oh, my goodness, Harry, you make me blush. Such kind words, but look at you. You are tall, extremely good-looking, sweet, compassionate, and so understanding. You are the prize, and I can't believe you would want to be with me."

"Maria, I don't want to scare you since I am older than you, but I can tell you without a doubt I never want to let you go. I want you forever. I know this is a new relationship, but you know when you know. I promise I will take it slow. I don't want to overwhelm you, but you are who I have been looking for my whole life. I want you to go to school and establish your career. I just want you to know I am real and will always be there for you."

"Harry, it makes me happy to hear this. I do want to take it slow. Now, all I can focus on is my grandmother, but you make me feel so special, and I love you for that." They kissed very tenderly in the backyard for a long time. Maria was very confused as she fell deeply for Harry and thought about the day they would get married, but on the other hand, she still dreamt of Alberto.

Elizabeth seemed to be getting worse. She was more confused and brought up relatives from her childhood more often. She believed Maria was her sister and Grandpa was her brother. She could barely move anymore and needed to stay in bed most of the time. She was eating very poorly, but Maria was still able to get her to drink three milkshakes throughout the day. Maria offered her the milkshake every hour that she was awake. Harry came over often and helped Maria with her Grandma. Samantha helped her during the day, and Harry helped her in the evening. Grandpa and Harry became the best of friends.

It was soon going to be Maria's birthday and Valentine's Day. Samantha and Stan had planned to come over and take care of Elizabeth that evening, giving Maria some time to celebrate. Stan and Samantha's relationship had progressed much faster than Maria and Harry's, but both Maria and Harry were genuinely happy for their friends. Stan was supportive of Samantha's ambitions, encouraging her to pursue her education and establish her career before they considered marriage.

The afternoon before Maria's birthday, Samantha and Maria drove to the mall, deep in conversation about their futures.

"I know I am in love with Harry, but I am constantly thinking about Alberto. I am one mixed-up girl."

"Maria, I am sorry about that. I know it must be very hard to sort out your feelings."

"I guess one day it will all become clear."

It was Valentine's Day and Maria's 20th birthday. Her Mom called her early in the morning and wished her a happy birthday. Ethel was happy about her relationship with Harry and heard such wonderful things about him from Grandpa. Ethel couldn't wait to meet him. Her father, sisters, and many friends back home called to wish Maria a Happy Birthday. Her family sent her a gift certificate so she could go shopping for some new clothes. Grandpa and Grandma gave her some money for her birthday. Maria was excited and couldn't wait to go shopping.

It was 7 pm in the evening, and there was a knock on the front door. Samantha and Stan were at the door, and behind them was Harry with a dozen red roses for Maria. Maria looked beautiful and was dressed in a gorgeous red dress. They all talked for a little while, and then Maria and Harry left for an exciting evening out in town. "I am taking you to the city," said Harry excitedly.

"Oh, that sounds great. I am excited as the only time I have been out of town since I have been here is to go to the airport twice." They drive 35 miles and then drive up to the hotel and have the car valet parked. Harry opens Maria's car door, and they walk into the hotel through the swinging front doors. This was a large hotel with multiple red hearts hanging from the ceiling for Valentine's Day. They took an inside glass elevator to the top floor. There was a small fancy restaurant on this floor that rotated 360 degrees. Harry had a special table set aside for them. They sat down, and the waiter handed them the special Valentine's menu. They decided to have salad, steak, lobster, baked potato, and vegetables for two.

"This is so nice of you, Harry. This is such a beautiful hotel. I have never seen a restaurant in the round with a view that is 360 degrees. The view up here is so amazing. It is so festive, and there are so many people here tonight. I have never had a birthday like this before. I love being with you, Harry. I don't think even in my dreams I could imagine such a perfect evening."

"I am so glad you like it here." They both enjoyed the delicious dinner. After dinner, all the waiters came and sang Happy Birthday to Maria. The whole restaurant also participated. They had a chocolate cake with Happy Birthday written on it and 20 candles. Maria blew out all the candles. She cut the cake, and then the waiter brought a large chocolate sundae for them to share.

"Maria, you amaze me every day. You are so sweet, compassionate, caring, and the most beautiful woman I have ever met. I have something for you. Happy Birthday, Maria. I hope you like it," said Harry. Maria opened the box, and there was a gorgeous ring inside. It was an amethyst ring with many diamonds surrounding it. This was Maria's birthstone.

"Harry, the ring is absolutely gorgeous. I love it, and it is stunning. Thank you so much for the beautiful ring and the fantastic dinner. You are too kind. All I can say is I am one lucky woman. I really don't know what I did to deserve someone like you. All I know is that I love you, Harry."

"Maria, I want you to look at this ring and remember I am always with you. I love you too, honey." They left the restaurant and the hotel, deciding to walk to the boardwalk. The boardwalk had a closed-in Ferris wheel, and Maria and Harry decided to ride on it. They got to the top, and it stopped. Harry saw that Maria was getting concerned about how long they would be stuck up there. He cuddled up to her, put his arm around her, and kissed her. Maria forgot that they were stuck and at least there was glass, so they weren't cold. Maria loved kissing Harry, and her heart was beating fast, and she was so happy. It was so romantic being stuck on a Ferris wheel with the man you love. Maria's mind wandered, and she thought, "I can't wait to marry Harry and spend every moment with him." They were stuck on the Ferris wheel for more than an hour and a half. They finally got back down and off it. They walked to the car and then did some more kissing. Then they drove back to Maria's Grandparents' house.

"Thank you, Harry, for the best birthday ever. You made my birthday so special. I can't express to you how much I love the ring. I will never forget this day."

"You're welcome, sweetie. I will call you tomorrow. Let me know if you need any help with Elizabeth. "

"Now I have you with me always. Drive home safely. Bye"

"Bye," Maria walks into the house, and Grandpa is sound asleep on the couch. She debated whether she should wake him up. He had a blanket on and was laying down and looked so comfortable. She didn't t have the heart to wake him up. She left him a note saying that she was home. Grandpa Joe ended up sleeping on the couch all night and said he had the best sleep ever. He also thanked Maria for her note.

Maria woke up early the next morning and called her Mom.

'Hi, Mom"

"Hi Maria. How was your birthday?"

"Mom, Harry took me into the city for a beautiful dinner and bought me an amethyst ring with diamonds around it. He is the best."

"I am happy for you, honey. You deserve all the best." Maria talked to her Mom for a long time and told her all the latest about Elizabeth.

The months of March, April, and May passed by quickly, and Maria found that her Grandma was slipping. She had become harder to arise, and when she was awake, she babbled and made no sense. It was much harder for her to follow directions. Maria had tried to protect her grandpa from some of these realities. Maria was now turning her grandma in bed every 2 hours with the help of Samantha or Harry. She also tried to feed her every 2 hours as she ate only a very little at a time. Maria was doing an excellent job with her skincare as she didn't have any skin breakdown anywhere throughout her body. Both Samantha and Harry have also been great supporters to Maria through these trying times.

Samantha would come over every morning and afternoon to help Maria with Elizabeth's care. Maria felt bad as she was no longer able to leave her Grandma to help Samantha in return. Stan and one of his best friends were helping Samantha with her Grandfather as he was becoming weaker and harder to handle. Maria and Samantha would discuss frequently how lucky they both were to have such wonderful boyfriends.

Maria and Samantha went out to dinner Memorial Day weekend with Harry, Stan and their parents. They finally were going to meet their parents. Their father hired a caregiver for both Maria's Grandmother and one for Samantha's Grandfather so the six of them could go out without any worry. Stan and Harry's parents were both physicians and the sweetest people ever. Maria and Samantha both loved their parents and felt completely comfortable around them. Harry and Stan's parents were so impressed with the two of them and found them both to be intelligent, beautiful, caring and so mature. Maria and Samantha could now see where both Harry and Stan got their compassion, sincerity, and overall great qualities. Their parents told Maria and Samantha that they could call them anytime, day or night if they had any questions about their Grandparents' care. This was such a big relief to them now that they have two physicians available if necessary. Maria and Samantha really appreciated their parents providing the caregivers, volunteering their services and taking them all out for such an extravagant dinner. They both raved about Harry and Stan's parents. Stan and Harry found that after the dinner, their parents were constantly talking about Maria and Samantha and hoped that they would become their future daughter-in-laws. Both Harry and Stan felt the evening couldn't have gone any better. It was important to them both for their parents' approval, and they couldn't have asked for anything more.

Maria talked to her Mom twice a day to keep her updated regarding Elizabeth's condition. During her latest conversation they decided that Maria should call her physician and give her an updated status. Maria was afraid that Elizabeth was not getting enough fluids or calories. The next morning, the first thing Maria did was call her Grandma's physician, who decided that she would send out the home health nurse for a re-evaluation. Maria was very happy to hear that and felt relieved. In the afternoon, the phone rang, and it was the home health nurse, Beth. She made an appointment to see Elizabeth first thing the next morning.

The next day, at 8 am, Beth was knocking on the door. She asked Elizabeth some questions but soon realized she was incoherent. She spoke with Maria and received a thorough update. Beth educated Maria about end-stage dementia. "They lose the gag reflex and are unable to swallow. We can insert a J tube and feed your grandma through her stomach. We might have to restrain her so she doesn't pull the tube out. Maria, it is important now to let your Grandma drink at her pace and only eat pureed foods if she is able."

"I will talk to both my grandpa and my mom regarding this issue."

"I know Maria, this is a difficult situation, and you are doing an amazing job. You told me you were offering your grandma fluids every 2 hours. That is a great idea, so just keep doing that. Near the end, she will stop wanting to eat and just take a few sips of fluids. You are also doing an excellent job with her skin care. We can put in a Foley catheter, which is a tube into her bladder to drain her urine, and that will eliminate her accidents. "

"I am going to discuss all these issues with my Grandpa and Mom. Grandpa Joe was having such a hard time dealing with and accepting all that was going on with his wife, which was why Maria tried to handle as much as possible. She thought he should make the decision on how he wanted Grandma's care to proceed in the future.

"I will be back in two days. Keep up the great work, Maria. If you need the Social worker, let me know, and she can come out and talk to you and your Grandfather at any time. I know these are hard decisions for families, and if there is anything that we can help you with, please don't hesitate to call."

"Thank you so much, Beth. Hopefully, I will have some answers the next time I see you."

"Don't worry, Maria. There is no rush. Please discuss this with your family, and when they have decided, you can let me know." Beth notified Elizabeth's physician, and they were just waiting to hear back from the family about their decision. Maria had a long conversation with her mom about the J-tube and other issues. Ethel called and spoke to the homecare nurse, Beth. Beth and Ethel had a long discussion.

Maria had explained the situation perfectly. Beth praised Maria highly for the care she was providing for her grandma. Then Ethel called her Dad and talked with him for hours. Grandpa Joe decided that he didn't want his wife to have a feeding tube. He was fine with the Foley catheter but thought Maria should make that decision since she is doing the day-to-day care. The nurse came back in two days, and both Maria and Grandpa Joe told her what the family wished.

Harry continued to come over most evenings during the summer to help Maria. Also, on two Fridays a month during the summer, he would hire a caregiver so he could take Maria out on a date. Maria was in love with Harry, and Harry was so in love with Maria. Maria would still think of Alberto at times. Harry never knew his Grandparents and was so fond of Grandpa Joe. Harry became part of the family. The stress of the situation was hard for Maria at times, but Harry was her rock, and without him, she felt she might not survive. Maria was going to see this through to the end, but at times, she felt like saying we need to hire a professional caregiver. Situations would come up for Maria that were difficult, but Maria would just tell herself she was doing her best. Maria, at times, felt like crying but wanted to hold it all together for her Mom and Grandpa.

At the end of August, Elizabeth was hardly drinking any fluids, and her blood pressure was lower than it had ever been. Maria decided to call her Mom and tell her "Mom, I think you should come see Grandma now. I am not sure of anything, but I see Grandma slipping away. The doctor can't predict, but it is a feeling I have after taking care of her for almost 2 years."

"Oh Maria, I really appreciate you calling me. I am going to talk to my employer and then book a flight as soon as possible. Maria, I can't thank you enough. How are you doing?"

'Mom it is really hard to see Grandpa so sad. I think if you come now, you can be a great support for your Dad. I am with Grandma all day now lately and I haven't been able to be there for Grandpa like I would like to. Grandpa loves Harry and he comes early in the morning and stays till late at night. Harry will be going back to school and won't be able to spend so much time with Grandpa. Harry is an angel, Mom, and he comes early in the morning and stays. I love him."

"I know he is Maria. Grandpa talks about him constantly. You two seem like you were meant for each other. I will be there in a couple of days. I will let you know when my flight arrives. Goodnight Maria. Love you."

"Good night, Mom. I love you too." Maria talked to her Mom the next afternoon, and Ethel arrived at 2 p.m. the next day. The next day, Maria drove to the airport to pick her up while Elizabeth was napping. They arrived back at the house around 3:30 p.m. Maria introduced Harry to her Mom.

"Hi Harry. It is so nice to finally meet you. I have heard such wonderful things about you from Maria and my Dad. Thank you so much for always helping with the care for my Mom. Our family really appreciates all your kindness and especially for watching out for my Dad. I am glad that we will have some time to get to know each other."

"Ethel, I am glad that I could be of help. I am so happy to have met you and heard such wonderful things about you, too. I wish this was under better circumstances. Your daughter is so special and means everything to me. "

Ethel went into her mom's room and saw that Elizabeth was awake. She greeted her mom, but Elizabeth had no idea who was at her bedside. She had a blank stare and appeared to be a million miles away. Ethel could see the dramatic changes in her mom since her last visit, which was the previous summer. Ethel and Maria repositioned her and told her they would be back in a little while.

The four of them went into the living room to talk. Ethel was impressed with Harry and had been in awe of Maria since she began taking care of her mom. Ethel believed that her daughter had done a much better job taking care of her mom than she would have been able to do, showing immense compassion and grace without any complaints. It was 7:30 pm when Maria said, "I am going to order dinner." She ordered two pizzas for delivery. Maria and Ethel went into Elizabeth's room to feed her before the pizza arrived. Elizabeth didn't appear hungry or thirsty. She took a few sips and then shut her mouth tightly. Ethel saw how difficult it was for her mom to get the necessary calories. They turned her from side to side. The last time the nurse visited, she had inserted a Foley catheter, which made things easier for both Elizabeth and Maria. Elizabeth seemed happy and comfortable. They both said "Goodnight."

The doorbell rang and the pizza arrived. Harry and Ethel had a great conversation for hours. Poor Grandpa Joe was very quiet and visibly sad. Ethel and Maria wished there was something they could do to cheer him up. He and Elizabeth had been childhood sweethearts, so one could imagine how difficult this situation was on him. Harry had come over to the house almost every day during the summer and had been there from early morning to late in the evening. His senior year in college was starting in two weeks. Grandpa and Maria would miss having him around.

Harry started school in early September and then came over to the house one or two evenings a week and spent all day Saturday there. Maria was so busy with her grandma and trying to comfort Grandpa Joe that she missed Harry when he wasn't there, but she also thought about Alberto at times. She kept asking herself what was wrong with her.

By the middle of October 1976, Elizabeth was barely drinking any fluids. She might have a few bites of either custard, jello, or pudding at each meal. Maria noticed her urine output was decreasing, and her blood pressure was much lower. She was still arousable and said a few garbled words. Grandpa went in and visited his wife several times a day, talking to her and frequently kissing her cheek.

The next morning, Ethel went into her mom's room and couldn't wake her up. She called Maria, who took her blood pressure and found it lower than it had ever been. Maria called the home care nurse, who came to the house that afternoon. The nurse told everyone that at the end, the patient might not be able to be awakened. She noted that Elizabeth looked comfortable and didn't seem to be in any pain. The nurse let them know that Elizabeth could wake back up but that nobody really knew what would happen. As the nurse was leaving, she said, "Call me if there is anything you need."

Maria, Grandpa Joe, Ethel, and Harry stayed in her room for the rest of the day. Elizabeth never woke up, and they decided they would all stay awake and see what happened that night. Harry didn't want to leave, and Grandpa asked him if he could stay. They alternated, with one at a time in her room—either Maria, Ethel, or Grandpa. At 5 in the morning, her respirations became rapid, followed by periods of no breathing. Maria had read in her book that this could happen near the end and was called Cheyne-Stokes breathing. Maria called in the rest of her family into the room, and Elizabeth took her last breath in her husband's arms. Poor Grandpa had never thought it would be this soon. He broke down, as did Ethel and Maria. Maria called the home care nurse, who, in turn, called her doctor. Maria was so appreciative of Harry's support and grateful that he had stayed.

Ethel called her husband and made the arrangements for him, Edith and Emily to fly out in the next couple days. Maria helped Ethel and Grandpa to make the arrangements for her services. Grandma Elizabeth service was going to be in five days. Raymond, Emily and Edith arrived the next day. Harry was happy to meet the rest of Maria's family but wished it was under better circumstances.

The Church was full for Elizabeth's service. They had so many friends in town and nearby. They all loved Maria's Grandparents. Many relatives came from out of town and out of state for the service. Ethel gave the eulogy for her Mom. They had a get-together at the house after the service. Maria loved that her Grandpa had so much support but started to think about what would happen when everyone went home.

Raymond, Emily, and Edith stayed for two days after the service, and then they flew back home to Iowa. The house seemed so quiet now. There was Grandpa Joe, Ethel, and Maria, and everyone was depressed. Harry was back in school, and he would come by the house as much as possible.

Ethel would talk to her dad and tell him he couldn't stay in the house by himself. Maria would also tell her grandpa that he shouldn't stay here by himself.

"Grandpa, you need to be around family, and I won't let you stay in this house by yourself. You need to come to Iowa and help me figure out what college I am going to attend. Grandpa, we have become so close over the last 2 years, and I can't bear to think of you being alone. I need you with me, and so do Mom and the rest of the family. It will take a little adjustment, but you will be happy in Iowa." Maria was so torn as she didn't want to leave Harry and Samantha, but she knew she needed to go back to Iowa.

Maria needed to figure out what colleges and schools to apply to for their nursing program. Maria and Samantha decided that they would apply to the same schools. Hopefully, they will both get accepted to the same college so they can be roommates. Maria was very sad thinking that she was leaving Harry. She had seen him almost every day for the last 10 months. They were best of friends, and she was so in love with him. Harry told Maria how much he was going to miss her. He was planning several vacations when he was out of school so they could see each other. Harry was also planning on going to graduate school and hoped to go to school near Maria's college. Grandpa Joe decided he would give Iowa a try and see if he liked it. Grandpa Joe was going to rent out his house with all the furnishings. Ethel, Grandpa, and Maria packed all his personal belongings and rented a small trailer hitch to attach to Maria's car. Grandpa was going to have his car shipped to Iowa.

The day came when the three of them were going to set out in Maria's car for Iowa. Harry, Stan, and Samantha were helping load the trailer hitch with Maria's and Grandpa's belongings.

"Samantha, I can never thank you enough for all the help and support you have given me over these last 2 years. You are my sister and my very best friend and always will be such. I pray and hope that we get accepted to the same nursing school so we can be roommates. I will miss you more than you will ever know. Good luck with your grandfather."

"Maria, I am really going to miss you. It will never be the same here without you. Keep in touch. We are sisters forever."

"Of course, Samantha, we will talk all the time."

"Stan, please take good care of Samantha and continue to treat her as a princess as you have been doing. She is really special and deserves all the best."

"I will, Maria. We are all going to miss you so much."

"Harry, you have been my rock. Without you, I wouldn't have been able to survive. I will miss you terribly. I can't wait till you come to Iowa in 2 months. I will be counting down the days. I love you."

"Maria, I am going to miss you fiercely. I love you too very much. Drive safely, and please call me when you get to Iowa."

"Grandpa Joe, I am going to miss you too, but I am so happy that you are going back to Iowa. You need to be around your family and just think of all that we will have to talk about after two months." Ethel and Grandpa said their goodbyes. Maria and Samantha started crying, and Harry kissed Maria goodbye. Maria got into the driver's seat and drove down the driveway. Maria, Grandpa Joe, and Ethel were on their way to Iowa.

CHAPTER 6-

It was the first week of January 1975. Alberto and his parents were back from Mexico. It was very difficult to get back in the swing of things after such an enjoyable, relaxing, and fun vacation. Alberto would daydream about Maria and how she touched deep into his soul. He would also think about Marissa and how lovely she was. He had promised Marissa that he would call her when he got back home. He decided that he would call her in a week, right before she went back to college.

Alberto reflected on his conversation with his dad about Maria. She had told him that she graduated from Lincoln High School. He called the operator and asked for the phone number for the Board of Education in Iowa. He called the number and spoke with a friendly lady who answered the phone. He explained his situation: that he was trying to find a girl he had met this summer in California who graduated from Lincoln High School and stole his heart.

"Is there any way I can find out how many high schools are called Lincoln High in your state?"

"Well, I am not supposed to give out this information, but you sound like a nice young man. Hold on, I will see what I can find.

"Sure, thank you."

"Well, there are twelve high schools throughout our state with that name."

"Would you mind giving me the name of the cities where these schools are located?" She went on to name all twelve cities.

"Thank you so much for this information. I hope you have a great day."

"You're welcome. Best of luck in your search. Have a great day, too."

"Thank you."

Alberto had gathered the names of twelve cities in Iowa, each hosting a high school named Lincoln. Over several calls, he obtained phone numbers for each school. One by one, he dialed them, hoping for a breakthrough. Each call followed the same script, "Did you have a student named Maria Hernandez as your Valedictorian last year?" he would inquire, sharing his poignant story with whomever answered. Anticipation filled his voice with each call, but alas, six of the schools outright denied having a student by that name. The remaining six, citing privacy concerns, refused to disclose any information. A sense of defeat began to shadow Alberto's initial hope. He had narrowed down the possibilities to six schools, but the mystery only deepened. Puzzled and growing increasingly desperate, he made another series of calls to the operator, this time searching for any listings for Raymond or Ethel Hernandez in the remaining cities. No leads surfaced, further fueling his frustration. At dinner that evening, Alberto expressed his exasperation, planning to seek advice from his parents on what steps to take next. The sense of a looming, unresolved quest weighed heavily on his heart as he recounted his fruitless efforts.

During dinner that evening, Alberto shared the day's discoveries with his parents. His mother suggested a new angle: "Why don't you call the Iowa operator again and check if there's a listing for Maria's parents in the other six cities?" Motivated by this idea, Alberto immediately contacted the Iowa operator after dinner and inquired about listings for either Raymond or Ethel Hernandez. Unfortunately, this search also yielded no results. Not a single city among the twelve had a listing for Maria's parents.

Frustrated, Alberto reflected aloud, "They could be living in a different city from where the school is located, or maybe they have an unlisted number." His parents listened intently as he mulled over his next steps. "I've hit a real bump in the road. Perhaps I could fly out there and visit each city. I'm sure I'd bump into her sooner or later." But even as he said it, he chuckled at the improbability, dismissing it as a delusional wild goose chase.

"I can't get her out of my head or my heart," he confessed, his voice tinged with a mix of longing and resignation. "She's touched me more deeply than anyone ever has. But maybe... maybe it's time to move on."

His father placed a comforting hand on his shoulder and nodded, "You've done all you can, son. Sometimes, the things we can't change end up changing us the most. Maybe this is one of those times."

The following week, Alberto called Marissa, who was so happy to hear from him. They had a long conversation and a lot of laughing. Alberto wished Marissa good luck in her new semester of college. Alberto liked Marissa and thought she was very sweet, caring, and cute. He thought that maybe someday this relationship may develop into something more. He figured he would just wait and see what happened. Maria was never far from his thoughts.

It was the third week of January, Tony and Alberto were starting back at work. He went back to the building and found there were birds in the attic. They must have gotten in there when the roof was being replaced. He would hear the birds flying around but had no idea how to get them out. He stood in the middle of the building, thinking that this was such a large project, and he contemplated how long it would take to complete it. The engineer had completed the plan for stabilizing the building. The foreman for the excavation project and concrete project dropped by the building. He looked over the engineering plans and discussed with Alberto that the plan would be to start this portion of the work in the second week of February.

It was the second week of February, and the excavation of the soil began. They first had to jackhammer all the concrete and then dig up all the dirt. When the contractor started with the jackhammer, all the birds flew out of the building as fast as possible. Well, Alberto thought there was one problem solved. There were huge piles of dirt. They dug four feet deep and found numerous seashells that had been there for more than one hundred years. According to history books, this area was a wharf a century ago. Alberto found it hard to believe that so much dirt could come out of this area. He needed to hire a dump truck to take all the dirt. The dump truck took at least ten trips to get all the dirt out of the building. This portion of the project took about 2 weeks.

Alberto would be at the building early by seven in the morning and would not leave until after six in the evening. At lunch time, the same women walked by the project every day and would stop and talk to Alberto. One day, when there was no work being done at the building, Alberto went to lunch with these four women. They went to the sandwich shop down the street. Alberto bought them all lunch. They had a delightful conversation, and Alberto found them all to be very interesting, educated, and savvy. They were there for more than an hour, and all the women needed to get back to work. They had really enjoyed spending time with Alberto and hoped that they could have lunch again. "Thank you, Alberto, for the lunch. We will see you tomorrow" all four women exclaimed.

"You're welcome. I had a great time with all of you. See you tomorrow."

In the afternoon, they started laying the concrete, which was a mixture of gravel, pebbles, and sand. They sectioned the building into 40 sections. The plan was to work on one section at a time. This portion of the project was going to take several weeks to complete. They were reinforcing each section with steel rebar. They needed to place the earthquake retrofit, which was the steel beams in the front of the building before the concrete could be finished. They worked on the back half of the building first and then waited for steel beams to be placed before starting at the front of the building.

The middle of April 1975 was set for the retrofit. They had to close the street down and hire a crane operator to place the steel beams in the front of the building. The crane operator lowered the beams to each side of the front of the building. The steel beams were about 24 feet tall, red, and looked just like the Golden Gate Bridge. Alberto was amazed and couldn't believe how the crane operator was able to lower those huge beams into place and how far down they went into the ground. This portion of the retrofit was completed. After the concrete is finished then, the retrofit contractor will come back and finish, which will be to tie and bolt the building.

The laying of the concrete continued through May. There were so many steps involved in the process, and the last step was leveling the concrete so the floor was even. Alberto was learning so many new things every day. He really liked doing this project but was beginning to see that he couldn't do it for a lifetime.

The framing contractor came in and placed the beams throughout the building. After the framing and the concrete project were done, the retrofit contractor came back and tied the building with bolts to the beams near the ceiling. The new concrete, framing, and retrofit were completed by the middle of summer.

Alberto has been speaking with Marissa at least once a week since Mexico. They were getting closer, and Marissa valued Alberto's opinions. Marissa was slowly falling for Alberto. Alberto was starting to have feelings for Marissa, too. He would also think about Maria frequently. Alberto's friends would tell him you are going to have to get over Maria and move on with your life. He knew his friends were right, but it wasn't easy to do. Maria left a hole in his heart.

Alberto's and Marissa's Moms would talk almost every day since Mexico. They have become the best of friends. They planned a family vacation for August so both families could spend two weeks in Hawaii together. One week was planned for Kaanapali, Maui, and the second week would be in Honolulu, Waikiki. They planned it so that Marissa's family would fly to California and meet Alberto's family and then they could all fly to Hawaii together. Marissa and Alberto were both looking forward to the vacation and seeing each other. They both had been to Hawaii several times before and loved it there. Alberto had been working ten or eleven hours a day, five or six days a week, for the last seven months and he was more than ready for a vacation. Marissa had the most challenging semester so far and was ready for some relaxation, too.

The second week of August rolled around, and the Bertolucci family was on their way to the San Francisco International Airport. They met Marissa and her parents at the airport. Alberto gave Marissa a kiss when they first saw each other, and Marissa's heart was pounding. The six of them boarded their flight and had a very enjoyable flight to Maui.

Alberto found Marissa to be much more talkative, engaging, and mature. She appears to have grown up a lot since Mexico. He looked at her and thought maybe this relationship would develop into something special.

They arrived at the hotel in Maui and it was only two in the afternoon Hawaii time. There was enough of the day left for some adventure. They all unpacked their suitcases and were deciding what to do next. Marissa and Alberto decided that they were going to the beach. Marissa had brought five bathing suits with her and was trying to decide which one to wear. She decided to wear her purple bikini. The two of them walked hand in hand to the beach. They bought a sandwich and drink to eat for lunch on the beach. When Marissa took off her cover-up and Alberto saw her purple bikini, his eyes almost popped out. In Mexico, he saw Marissa as a shy, immature girl, and now he is looking at her and sees a more mature twenty-year-old woman. He realized that he had started to have real feelings for her and wanted to pursue her as more than just friends. They were both very hungry, so they ate their lunch right away. Then they lay in the sun, put suntan lotion all over each other's body, and listened to music. They kissed frequently and told each other how happy they were to be together. Marissa knew she was falling for Alberto and was happy to see Alberto return the affection. They stayed at the beach till six and decided they better go back and get ready for dinner.

Their parents had made dinner reservations at a fancy restaurant on the beach. The six of them walked to the restaurant in the warm, beautiful, breezy air, and all of them were so happy to be together. Marissa looked gorgeous in a strapless long dress in teal blue. They had a delicious dinner and great conversations. Then Marissa and Alberto excused themselves, thanked their parents for the wonderful dinner and went walking on the beach. They both took off their shoes and walked barefoot, hand in hand, for quite a distance. Alberto stopped and started kissing Marissa passionately and her body was tingling.

"Marissa, you are such a beautiful, smart, sweet woman, and I am starting to fall in love with you. You are everything I ever wanted."

"Oh, Alberto that makes me so happy to hear this. The first day I saw you in Mexico, I was taken with you. I was afraid I might be too young and inexperienced for someone like you."

"No, Marissa, what I like about you is that you are real, and there is no pretense about you. I want to be in an exclusive relationship with you and see what happens."

"Oh, of course, Alberto, there is nobody but you for me."

"We both are so lucky that we come from such nurturing families and we both have such exceptional parents who love us dearly."

"You are so right Alberto. I have always felt I was so lucky to have such wonderful parents and now I have you. I have definitely won the lottery for sure." They continue kissing on the beach with the wind blowing through their hair. Alberto was so happy about Marissa, but at times, the beach would remind him of him and Maria on the beach. They spent a wonderful week in Maui learning to surf, scuba dive, played beach volleyball and spent a lot of time lying in the sun. They both went to dinner almost every night with both sets of parents and had a most memorable week.

As their flight descended from Maui to Honolulu, the six travelers were captivated by the bustling activity below. Upon arrival in Waikiki, they were swept up in the vibrant energy of the place. After settling into their hotel, they all agreed to unwind at the pool, soaking in the warm Hawaiian sun and the soothing sounds of the waves.

The week in Waikiki was filled with adventure and bonding. Marissa and Alberto, along with their parents, immersed themselves in the rich cultural tapestry of the island. They explored scenic locales, visited Pearl Harbor, enjoyed the immersive experience at the Polynesian Cultural Center, and reveled in the excitement of luaus and boat rides. Throughout the activities, their parents' joy was palpable, thrilled by the deepening bond between their children.

On their final evening, Alberto planned a romantic dinner for just the two of them. After a delightful meal, they strolled along the beach, the sunset casting a warm glow around them. The moment felt right, and Alberto, his heart pounding with anticipation and a touch of nervousness, turned to Marissa.

"Marissa, I've been thinking... How would you feel about celebrating your twenty-first birthday in Las Vegas? We could fly out on December 28th, celebrate your birthday, and ring in the New Year together. What do you think?"

Marissa's eyes lit up with surprise and excitement. "Oh, Alberto, that sounds incredible! There's no one else I'd rather be with to mark such a special occasion. Thank you for thinking of such a thoughtful gift."

"Great, it's a date then," Alberto replied, his voice filled with affection. "I'll start planning our trip. I promise it will be a birthday to remember."

"Alberto, you're too sweet," Marissa responded, her voice thick with emotion. "I can't wait for Vegas. Just knowing I'll be with you makes it all the more special. I'm going to miss you so much until then."

"And I'll miss you too," Alberto said, squeezing her hands gently. "But time will fly by fast with your senior year keeping you busy, and before you know it, it'll be December."

Their conversation continued into the night, their words weaving a tapestry of dreams for the future, as the rhythmic waves provided a serene backdrop to their heartfelt declarations.

The next day, the six of them packed their bags and were on their way to the Honolulu airport. They boarded their flight home. They arrived back in San Francisco, it seemed, in no time at all. Marissa and her parents said their goodbyes to Alberto, Dorothy, and Tony. Marissa was crying saying her goodbye to Alberto. They kissed, and then Marissa and her parents headed to their connecting flight. Alberto and his parents left the airport and drove back home.

It was Labor Day weekend and Alberto was reflecting on what a wonderful vacation they just had. He was falling for Marissa, but still at times couldn't help but think about Maria. He felt he was sure a mixed-up guy.

It was the second week of September, and Alberto was back working at the building. He was getting bids for the electrical work to be done. He had to deal with the natural gas and electrical power provider on how to set up the electrical panel and gas lines. This was very difficult for Alberto to understand since everyone he spoke to at the company had a different answer on how it should be done. Alberto asked his dad to intercede as he was becoming so frustrated with this portion of the project. They both went and sat down at the gas and electric company early in the morning waiting to speak to someone who could help them with this dilemma. Tony could see why Alberto was so frustrated with it. Tony took the helm of this portion of the project. They kept switching the person handling this situation, and nobody had an answer. Unfortunately, this went on for months and this delayed the completion of the project. Alberto learned that not everything would go as planned.

Alberto would talk to Marissa frequently in the evenings. He shared his frustration with the building project with her. She reassured him that he was doing an awesome job and every project had its bumps. She said, "Remember your Dad is very proud of the job you are doing." Alberto always felt better after talking with her. He let her know the plans he had made for her birthday- a New Year's getaway. He made reservations at Caesars Palace for a six-night stay. Marissa was so excited and couldn't wait till finals were over; it was vacation time.

During the months of October, November, and December, the plumber and the electrician worked at the building. The plumber laid drains and vent lines and ran copper supply lines. The electrician wired the electrical and put plugs on the floor and walls. It was the third week of December, and all the contractors working on the building were planning to take the next two weeks off for Christmas and New Year's. This Friday would be Alberto's last day at the building for more than two weeks.

It was Christmas morning, and the Bertolucci family was planning on going to Tony's brother's house for the day. Dorothy, Tony, and Alberto exchanged their gifts before they left. Alberto was thinking about Marissa and the upcoming vacation but also had Maria on his mind. They had a wonderful Christmas with 30 family members at Tony's brother's house.

It was December 28th, and Dorothy drove Alberto to the airport for his flight to Las Vegas. Alberto boarded his flight and was anxious to see Marissa. Her flight landed about an hour before Alberto's. She was waiting at the gate when Alberto deplaned. They kissed and were so happy to see each other.

"There is so much activity at this airport with slot machines and all the people. I am so happy to see you, Alberto."

"I have been looking forward to this vacation. I missed you, Marissa. You look beautiful, and I am so happy that we are having this time together."

"Me too. I have missed you so much, too, Alberto."

They went to the baggage claim and collected their luggage. Then, they made their way to the front of the airport to hail a cab. The cab drove down Las Vegas Boulevard. Marissa was amazed by the dazzling lights and glitter of Las Vegas. Overwhelmed with excitement, she marveled at the city's vibrant energy—it was her first time visiting. As they pulled up to the front of Caesars Palace, her eyes widened in awe at the stunning fountain and the grandeur of the hotel. She felt a rush of exhilaration as the iconic architecture unfolded before her, the hotel's opulence far exceeding her expectations.

They checked in and Alberto had made reservations for a suite on the top floor. They walked into their room, and Marissa was awestruck by the view from the room and the room itself. Marissa was just beside herself, thinking that Alberto had done all this for her birthday. She was falling more in love with him every day. They decided to unpack and then go get some dinner. Marissa changed into a beautiful purple dress, and Alberto put on a pair of nice slacks with a button-down shirt, and they headed out to dinner. Marissa gazed at Alberto across the candlelit table, her eyes reflecting the soft light as she marveled at how handsome he looked. They had dined at the steak restaurant on the first floor of their hotel, savoring each bite of steak, baked potatoes, vegetables, and a decadent baked Alaska for dessert. Each moment felt surreal to Marissa, like a dream she never wanted to wake from. As they finished their meal and strolled around the hotel, the clock struck midnight. Alberto turned to her, his eyes warm with affection, and whispered, "Happy Birthday, darling."

"Oh, thank you, Alberto. Thank you for such a delicious dinner," Marissa responded, her heart swelling with happiness.

"You are twenty-one now. Would you like to try your luck at the slot machines?" Alberto suggested with a playful smile.

"Sure, that sounds fun," Marissa replied, her excitement bubbling over.

Alberto ordered a celebratory drink for each of them, and they found a promising slot machine. Marissa's excitement grew as she started winning, her machine chiming merrily, while Alberto found less luck on his. As the night deepened to 2 am, they decided to retire to their room. Marissa, having won $400, attempted to share her winnings with Alberto, but he graciously declined.

Once they were back in their room, Alberto's kiss deepened with passion. "Marissa, I don't want you to worry, but we will take things at your pace. I would love to take things to the next level. I have been dreaming of that day, but if you aren't ready, it is entirely up to you. I love you and want to be with you. You are my everything," he confessed earnestly.

"Thank you, Alberto. I really appreciate you being so considerate. I can't wait till we take it to the next level, but I am not ready now. I love you and want to spend the rest of my life with you," Marissa replied, her voice filled with love and a hint of anticipation. They prepared for bed, and soon, Marissa emerged in a beautiful purple nightgown. They cuddled close, Alberto's hands gently caressing her back and legs, enveloping her in a sense of security and profound affection. They drifted into sleep wrapped in each other's arms.

The next morning, they awoke late, their lips meeting in a gentle, lingering kiss. "Do you want to stay in and order room service for breakfast?" Alberto asked softly, brushing a lock of hair from her face.

"That sounds wonderful," Marissa murmured, nestling closer to him. They enjoyed a leisurely breakfast in bed, and then Alberto offered, "Marissa, would you like a back rub?"

"Sure," she replied with a relaxed smile.

A knock at the door announced the arrival of a male and female massage therapist. After an hour of soothing massages that melted their stress away, another knock brought in a makeup artist and hairstylist to prepare Marissa for the evening. Alberto excused himself, giving her space to be pampered. When he returned three hours later, Marissa was transformed, her beauty accentuated for their special night. She was stunned by the effort Alberto had put into making her feel cherished on her birthday.

Dressed elegantly for the evening, Marissa in her striking long black dress and Alberto in a sharp gray suit, they turned heads as they walked through the hotel. Alberto had made reservations at the Bacchanal buffet, where they were seated at a secluded table, served by six attentive staff members. The eight-course dinner was unlike anything Marissa had ever experienced.

"Marissa, you are so special. I wanted to do something for your 21st birthday that you will always remember," Alberto said, his eyes gleaming with affection.

"Thank you, Alberto. This dinner is out of this world. I love you so much. I will never forget this day," Marissa responded, her voice thick with emotion.

"I love you, Marissa. I have something for you. I hope you like it." Alberto handed her a beautifully wrapped box. Inside, Marissa found a diamond pendant and matching earrings, sparkling with promise and luxury.

"They are gorgeous, Alberto. I love them. I will treasure them always," she exclaimed, her eyes misty with tears of joy. She donned the jewelry, feeling like a goddess, and prepared for the rest of their magical evening. Marissa was so excited she could barely speak.

"There is more to come," Alberto said, winking at her with a big smile.

They headed out of the restaurant into a waiting limousine. They drove down the strip to a theater in the round, and they saw in the lights "Sony and Cher." They are Marissa's favorite performers. They stepped out of the limousine and were ushered to front-row seats. Marissa was so excited and couldn't believe this was happening. The show was incredible and during the show,

"We have a 21st birthday here tonight. Her name is Marissa. Please stand up, Marissa," Cher said. The whole theater sang Happy Birthday. She was so thrilled and could never imagine anything like that happening to a girl like her. After the Sony and Cher show ended, they took a cab back to Caesars Palace.

"Alberto, I can never thank you enough for how special you made my birthday. I absolutely love the jewelry. The dinner and show were out of this world. I love you with all my heart and soul and want to be with you forever. Thank you so much for everything. You made my 21st birthday a day I will never forget. "

"Your very welcome Marissa. I am glad you are happy. I wanted this day to be special. I love you, Marissa."

Marissa and Alberto were so enjoying their time in Vegas. Marissa was starting to like gambling but only wanted to gamble a little. The next day they went to the spa, did some shopping and really enjoyed each other's company. They had a wonderful time on New Year's Eve. The hotel had a party, which included a six-course dinner and dancing, which was part of the hotel stay. They danced all night and loved the music. At midnight they had a champagne toast, and both said, "Happy New Year, Happy 1976." Marissa had never had such a great vacation. She was so sad to be leaving Alberto.

On January 3rd, they checked out of the hotel and took a cab to the airport.

"Alberto, I can't thank you enough for everything. You made my birthday so special. I am going to miss you terribly. I love you so much, and it is so hard to be away from you. I want to move to San Francisco after I graduate from college. I want to go to graduate school, and hopefully, I can find a school near you."

"Marissa I am coming to your college graduation in May. I am glad that you had a great birthday. I would love it if you moved to San Francisco after graduation. I love you."

"I am happy you are coming to my graduation. I can't wait to see you." They both kissed goodbye and went to their assigned gates for their flights home. They both thought about the awesome vacation they just experienced. They were both so in love.

Marissa returned to her final semester of college and shared the story of her incredible 21st birthday with all her friends. They unanimously agreed that Alberto was a keeper and that she was exceedingly fortunate. Knowing well that Alberto was exceptional, Marissa dreamed of a future with him. She informed her parents of her decision to move to San Francisco after graduation and her plans to apply to graduate schools in California.

Meanwhile, Alberto resumed work on the building project in the second week of January. The work on the electrical and plumbing systems extended through March. Eventually, Tony managed to resolve the complications with the gas and electric company. Though some of the gas meter work had to be redone, they finally had a solution to the ongoing issues.

As spring approached in late March, the days became sunnier, flowers bloomed, and birds sang, heralding the new season. The team began installing the sheetrock, taping, and painting the interior of the building. In April, they installed the HVAC system, fitted all the bathroom fixtures, and completed the tiling in the front part of the building. A potential issue with the building's sewer system arose, but after consulting three different companies, they concluded that only one line needed updating—a relief for the project.

By May 1976, Alberto was in search of a contractor to apply smooth stucco to the exterior of the building. He soon found the perfect team for the job. The work was scheduled to begin within a week and was expected to take two months. During that week, the installation of new windows in both the front and back of the building marked another step forward in the extensive renovation.

The women who worked up the street would still come by the building almost daily. They would tell Alberto how beautiful the building looked and that the architecture was gorgeous. He talked to them almost every day and always appreciated their feedback. He had become very friendly with them, and they were a daily fixture in his routine.

In the middle of May, Alberto flew to Dallas to attend Marissa's college graduation. Alberto and Marissa had been talking on the phone at least once a day since their Vegas trip. He was going there for four days since there was so much going on with the building project. Their reunion was charged with palpable excitement and emotion. As Alberto stepped off the plane and into the bustling Dallas Fort Worth airport, Marissa was waiting with a wide, eager smile. The moment their eyes met, a wave of warmth washed over them, diminishing the distance that had separated them for too long.

"Hi, Alberto. I have missed you so much," Marissa said, her voice thick with emotion as she reached out to pull him into a tight embrace.

"Hi, Marissa. I am so happy to see you," Alberto replied, his tone conveying the depth of his feelings. The joy in his eyes reflected the genuine affection he felt.

"You must be so excited about your graduation," he remarked, holding her hands and studying her face, as if trying to memorize every detail.

"I am, Alberto, but I'm much more excited about seeing you," she confessed, her cheeks flushed with happiness. "Thank you for coming to my graduation. It means everything to me."

"I wouldn't have missed it for anything," Alberto assured her, his voice earnest. Their heartfelt reunion underscored the deep connection they shared, setting the stage for the significant celebrations awaiting them.

The next afternoon was Marissa's commencement ceremony. Her parents, aunt, uncle, and Alberto were in attendance. She went to a very large school with many graduates. She was graduating with a B.A. in business. After the ceremony was finished, Alberto presented her with two dozen long stem red roses. She loved the roses. She was so happy that her family all loved Alberto. After the ceremony, the six of them went to a very fancy restaurant to celebrate. Alberto presented Marissa with her graduation gift. It was a large hand-painted picture of the two of them from their Las Vegas trip with the caption on the bottom reading: "Congratulations on your college graduation, my love. I am so proud of you. I have no doubt our future is going to be great."

Marissa loved the gift, and it was such a special keepsake. She was looking forward to putting it in her new apartment in California. Marissa and Alberto had a wonderful time during his visit to Texas. It was Monday evening, and Alberto was heading back to California. Marissa was planning on moving out to California in August and should be at Alberto's home by the 18th. Marissa wanted to be there by August 20th, which was Alberto's birthday. The plan was that her parents would help her move. The three of them would drive Marissa's car with her belongings from Texas to California. After that, her parents would fly back home. In three months, Marissa and Alberto would both be living in California, and they were excited.

Alberto was back at the building on the third Tuesday in May. The smooth stucco project was going well. The color was a neutral brown and added such a flair to the outside of the building. The foam design on the outside of the building added the final touches. The project was finished the second week of August. It had taken two years, but Alberto saw the project through to completion. Tony was so proud of his son and his accomplishments. People would walk by and say this is one of the best-looking buildings in town. They would also comment on the beautiful architecture. Alberto had learned a tremendous amount about construction, himself, and, more importantly, what he wanted to do for the rest of his life. Alberto told his parents he wanted to become a doctor. He plans on applying to medical school, and hopefully, he could start in the Fall of 1977. His parents were happy that he knew what direction he wanted his life to go. They were also happy for Alberto that Marissa was moving to California. She was planning on going to graduate school starting in the Fall of 1977 too. Marissa and Alberto would have one year till they both go back to school. Alberto was counting the days till Marissa and her parents would arrive, which should be in ten days.

CHAPTER 7-

At the beginning of November 1976. Maria, Edith, and Grandpa pulled up to their house in Iowa in Maria's car. They had been on the road driving from California for the last five days. Maria was so excited to be home as she had been away for two years. She was thrilled to see all her friends again. She was so happy that Grandpa had come to Iowa, too. They had become so close over the past two years. She planned on making sure that Grandpa was happy and thrived in Iowa. Edith and Emily came running out of the house to greet the three of them. They said welcome back to Maria and gave their Mom and Grandpa hugs and kisses.

As everyone entered the house, they immediately began to catch up with each other. Maria eagerly showed Grandpa his new room, complete with an adjacent bathroom. She, along with Emily and Edith, meticulously unloaded all their belongings from the trailer hitch. Maria carefully hung all of Grandpa's clothes in his closet and organized his other items in the drawers. She left some things unpacked, wanting Grandpa to feel involved by deciding where they should go. Her efforts were driven by a deep desire to make Grandpa feel comfortable and settled in this new chapter of his life.

By 6 pm, the day's activities had stirred up quite an appetite among them. Maria decided to order pizza, thinking it would be a simple yet comforting meal for their first evening together in Iowa. The pizza took about 45 minutes to arrive, just as Raymond was walking through the door, returning from work. His face lit up with joy as he greeted his wife, daughter, and father-in-law, relieved and delighted to have his family safely back home. That night, they stayed up until midnight, their conversations weaving through memories and plans for the future. Maria shared her intentions to take Grandpa on a tour of the town the next day, showing him essential spots like the grocery store, library, and senior center, hoping to help him integrate into their community smoothly.

Everyone was awake by 8 am the next day. Emily and Edith were off to school and Raymond was off to work. Ethel fixed her Dad, Maria and herself a delicious breakfast. They all sat around after breakfast and drank coffee. Grandpa was planning on doing the cooking for the evening meal each night. Ethel and Maria were so happy to hear this as this was Grandpa's favorite pastime.

Maria and Grandpa left the house around 11 am. Maria gave her Grandpa the guided tour of the city. He found the city to be much larger than what they had described. She showed him the beautiful Senior Center and thought that he could participate in some of the activities and get to know some of their neighbors. The last stop was the grocery store. Ethel had given them a list of groceries that were needed. Grandpa had made his own list of necessary ingredients needed to prepare dinner for the next few nights. They had five bags of groceries that Maria unloaded from her car. Grandpa fixed a delicious dinner that evening, and everyone sure loved his cooking. They were all thinking and dreaming about the delicious dinners they would be having in the future. They were all so happy that Grandpa had come to live with them.

Maria decided she was going to call Harry tonight.

"Hi Harry,"

"Hi Honey"

"We are home. We had a nice trip. Grandpa seems to be happy here."

"It is great to hear from you. I miss you so much. I am glad that Grandpa is doing well."

"I am home with him during the day, so I can hang out with him. How is school?"

"Finals are in a couple of weeks. I am just studying for them."

"You will do well as you always do. I miss you too. Only seven weeks till I will see one handsome guy. I can't wait till we are together."

"Me either. I love you, Maria."

"I love you, Harry." They talked for almost two hours. Maria went straight to bed after their conversation ended.

The weeks passed, and everyone settled into a routine. Ethel had gone back to work. Maria and Grandpa would be together during the weekdays unless Maria was doing odd jobs, such as babysitting, cleaning houses, or cooking for neighbors' families. She decided not to get a full-time job as she felt she would be away from Grandpa too much. She was afraid he would be lonely being in the house all day by himself. Maria was making good money at the odd jobs and saving it for college. Grandpa would go to the Senior Center in the afternoon when Maria would work. He was meeting and making many nice friends and seemed to be the life of the party. Grandpa missed Elizabeth so much, but he was distracted, and keeping busy was helpful.

It was Thanksgiving, and Grandpa fixed the ultimate feast. Emily and Edith couldn't believe all the food that Grandpa had prepared. They both loved his cooking and loved getting to know him better. Grandpa would watch television in the evenings with Emily and Edith. Occasionally, they would watch a dance party, and Grandpa would get up and show them his moves. Grandpa made the girls giggle all the time. All their friends loved to come over to see Grandpa, too. Maria also introduced Grandpa to all her friends. They all thought he was funny, full of wisdom, encouragement, and inspiration. Grandpa became the talk of the town. Maria was so happy that Grandpa was appearing to thrive in Iowa.

Maria would talk to Samantha on the phone every day. They decided on three colleges to apply to their nursing program. Two colleges in Iowa and one in California. They both had completed their essay and applications and sent transcripts and recommendation letters to each college. They both were applying for financial aid and scholarships. They were supposed to hear back either in March or April of next year. The scholarship process was tedious, but both girls had 4.0 GPAs with numerous awards and extracurricular activities. They both had a good chance of obtaining scholarships. It was difficult waiting, but their future would be determined soon. Would they both go on to be RNs and go to nursing school together? Only time will tell.

It was December 20th, and Harry would be arriving today on an afternoon flight. Maria and Grandpa were going to the airport to pick him up. They arrived at the airport, and Harry was standing on the arrival walkway with his luggage. Maria put her flashers on and got out of her car. Maria and Harry kissed, and the cars behind them started to honk. Harry loaded his suitcases into the trunk, and they both jumped in the car. Grandpa and Harry started to talk right away, and they talked all the way home. Maria could see that her Grandpa was so happy to see Harry. They pulled up to the house and unloaded his suitcases.

Edith and Emily came running up to Harry to greet him. Ethel welcomed Harry and told him,

"We are all so happy that you could spend the holidays with us."

"Thank you. I am so thrilled to be here."

Maria showed Harry where he would be staying. They have an in-law unit in their backyard. It is a small bedroom with a bathroom and a small kitchen. Raymond built this addition several years ago, and it came in handy for guests.

"I love your house, Maria. It is such a cute farmhouse. The house is decorated so beautifully for Christmas."

"Thanks. My parents bought it many years ago, and it was all run down. My Dad remodeled the house on weekends. It took him about four years to finish. I was little at the time, but I was always trying to help him. He worked so hard as a supervisor on his labor job during the week and then would do this project on the weekends."

"Maria I am so happy to see you. I have missed you so much. I love you more than you will ever know."

"Harry, I have missed you terribly. I love you so much, too. I am happy that we have these two weeks together."

Grandpa cooked a delicious dinner, and Harry told everyone, "You are all so lucky to be able to eat Grandpa Joe's cooking. He is the best cook ever."

"Thank you, Harry, for such a nice compliment." Harry and Grandpa continued having long conversations, and at times, Raymond would also participate long into the night.

The next day, Maria took Harry around town to show him her favorite places. She also introduced him to some of her friends. They went to a beautiful park downtown, sat on the grass, and started kissing. Maria is so happy to be in Harry's arms and feels so safe and loved.

"Maria, I love kissing you and holding you in my arms. In my eyes you are an angel."

"Harry, you make me feel so safe and loved."

"Maria, I want to tell you about graduate school. I can't find the graduate program I am looking for in Iowa. I have applied only to graduate school in California. I know that will be two more years that we will be in different states, but you will be in nursing school and will need to study. I think I would be a distraction."

"Harry, I am sad to hear this, but I want you to go to the best graduate school possible. Samantha and I applied to nursing schools, two in Iowa and one in California. You never know how this will turn out."

"We will have a winter break, spring break, and all of the summer we can spend with each other. Two years sounds like a long time, but it will go by fast. Maria, I want you to know even if we are miles apart, you are always on my mind and in my heart. We will get our degrees and go on to have a wonderful life. You are my soulmate and my everything."

"Oh Harry, I can't wait till we can be together every day for the rest of our lives. You are such a generous, loving, and handsome man. I ask myself every day how a girl from Iowa got so lucky. You are my everything, too."

It was December twenty-third, and it was Harry's twenty-second birthday. He received a call from his parents, Stan and Samantha who wished him a happy birthday. Grandpa fixed Harry's favorite meal for lunch. The whole family was home, and they celebrated with a cake and gifts. Harry was just like one of the family, and that made Maria very happy.

Maria took Harry out to dinner in the city, which was about 45 miles away. Maria looked stunning and took him to a very elegant restaurant. She had been working hard at various odd jobs and was happy to spend her money on him. She decided to give him a gold ring with the inscription, "You are mine forever; love you babe." Harry was so happy with his gift.

"Thank you, Maria. I will look down at this ring and think of you every time I look at it." Harry had the best birthday ever.

It was Christmas morning. The Hernandez family and Harry went to church services. They came home, and then Maria and Harry helped Grandpa prepare dinner. Before dinner, they all sat around the Christmas tree and opened gifts. Edith and Emily played Santa and handed out the gifts. Everyone was thrilled with what they received. Maria thought about the homeless shelter and how she had spent the last two Christmases serving food for the needy.

"Harry, I was thinking that the last two Christmases, I served food at the homeless shelter in California. There are so many people who are less fortunate than us. We need to never forget how lucky we are and should always try to help the less fortunate."

"Maria you are so selfless and always thinking about others. That is one of your qualities that I love so much." The family had a beautiful and special Christmas especially with everyone together to celebrate.

The week between Christmas and New Year's had been very special for both Maria and Harry. Maria had taken Harry all around Iowa, introducing him to the state she loved. During that time, they had grown much closer, sharing dreams about their future, discussing how many children they wanted, and opening up about their deepest aspirations. Maria introduced Harry to most of her friends who still lived in Iowa, as well as those who were home for the holidays. Her friends had found Harry to be charming, good-looking, and incredibly sweet. They all remarked that Maria had truly hit the jackpot, hoping to someday meet someone as wonderful as Harry.

Harry had secretly discussed with Ethel his plan to return for Valentine's Day to surprise Maria for her 21st birthday. Ethel agreed to pick him up at the airport at 12 pm on

February 14th. They both decided to keep this a surprise, sharing it with no one else.

It was December thirty-first, New Year's Eve, marking exactly one year since Maria and Harry had met—a year filled with significant moments and deep connections. They attended a New Year's Eve party hosted by Maria's best friend from elementary and high school. Dressed elegantly, they mingled and laughed, with Maria glowing in her outfit and Harry at her side, perfectly complementing her. Harry listened intently as Maria's friends regaled him with tales of Maria's high school escapades, giving him a fuller picture of her life before they met.

As midnight approached, Maria leaned into Harry, her eyes sparkling with excitement and affection. "It's been a wonderful year with you, Harry," she whispered, moments before the clock struck twelve.

Harry, feeling a rush of affection, replied warmly, "And there are many more to come, Maria." As the room erupted in cheers, they kissed, their lips meeting as they whispered in unison, "Happy New Year, Happy 1977." The warmth of their embrace and the promise of future joys filled the air around them, making the moment unforgettable.

"To my partner in life, my best friend, and my love, all the best is yet to come. Love you, Harry."

"Love you, Maria." They left the party around 12:30 am and went back home. Ethel and Grandpa were still up watching all the celebrations on the television. Maria and Harry decided to join them. Harry and Grandpa got into a deep conversation while Maria talked with her Mom. It was now 2:30 am and they all decided to go to sleep.

Harry and Grandpa watched football from early afternoon till late in the evening on New Year's Day. Raymond worked on the holiday. He had a second job as the manager of a hardware store on weekends and holidays. Maria spent the day with her mom and sisters. The whole family had a delightful first day of the year 1977.

Soon came January fourth when Harry would have to fly back home. He thanked everyone for their amazing hospitality. Maria drove Harry to the airport. Maria started to sob when Harry got out of her car.

"I wish we could spend every day together. I love you, Harry. Have a safe flight. Call me when you get home."

"Love you, Maria. Thank you for everything. I will call you."

Maria returned home from the airport. Ethel and Grandpa talked about Harry and said he was a wonderful boyfriend. They told Maria how lucky she was because he was so kind-hearted and generous. "I know, and that is why I am so in love with him."

The month of January passed with several heavy snow and storms. Maria watched several children who were on break from school at her home. Grandpa had the best time with all the children around. It was now the beginning of February, and it would soon be Maria's 21st birthday. Maria talked to Harry at least once a day. They had long conversations every night, but she had no idea he was coming for her birthday.

Then came February 14th, which was also Maria's birthday. Ethel told Maria that the family was taking her out to dinner. Ethel left the house around 11 a.m. and informed Maria that she was going shopping. Ethel drove to the airport to pick up Harry. They returned to the house around 1:30 p.m. Harry went and knocked on the front door. Maria answered the door and was almost going to faint. He presented her with a dozen long-stem pink roses.

"Thank you, Harry, for the beautiful roses. Come on in. How did you get here from the airport? I am so happy to see you, but I had no idea you were surprising me. I am in complete shock."

"Your Mom is the only one who knew."

"You and my Mom are sure sneaky. Well, all I can say is you sure made my day. I can't believe you came all this way for my birthday. "

"I love you, Maria. The twenty-first birthday is a special one. I couldn't miss it. You are my everything."

"I love you, Harry." Grandpa was so surprised to see Harry, too. Grandpa and Harry started talking non-stop. Ethel and Harry had pulled off this surprise with nobody suspecting anything.

The whole family went out to dinner that night at a fancy Polynesian restaurant with hula dancers and waterfalls. They had an exquisite Hawaiian dinner with six coarse meals. Maria, Emily, and Edith all participated in the hula dancing. Everyone in the restaurant sang Happy Birthday to Maria. After dinner, when they were all back home, Harry told

Maria," I want you to pack some clothes. I am taking you away for a couple of days. We will leave in the morning."

"Where are we going?"

"It is a surprise. Pack a couple of nice dresses, your bathing suit and shorts, and you should be fine. Maria, I have something for you." He hands her a gorgeously wrapped small box from Tiffany's. It was a 14k gold collar necklace. Maria was stunned and speechless for a minute.

"Oh Harry, I love the necklace. It is the most beautiful gold necklace I have ever seen. I have always wanted a gold necklace. Thank you so much. I don't know what to say."

"It looks amazing on you. It brings out your beauty even more if that is at all possible. You could win for Miss Universe, for sure. You are the prettiest girl I have ever laid eyes on, and you have the biggest heart, too. I am glad you like it." They kissed for what seemed like hours. Maria was so attracted to Harry and couldn't wait for the next day. Everyone else went to sleep a long time ago. Harry was sleeping on the couch that night and Maria went to her room.

Maria and Harry woke up around 9 a.m. Ethel and Raymond had gone to work, and Emily and Edith had already gone to school. Grandpa fixed breakfast for them. The three of them talked for some time after breakfast. Maria and Harry told Grandpa that they were going away for a couple of days. They told him they would be back on Thursday.

"Does your Mom and Dad know you are going?"

"Yes, they both know."

"Be good, you two, and have fun. See you Thursday."

"Love you, Grandpa."

"Bye Joe."

"Love you two. Drive carefully." They got in Maria's car, and Harry offered to drive. They loaded their suitcases and took off.

"I am so happy to get you alone Maria. I hope you like where we are going. I thought we could get away and celebrate together."

"I am so excited, but I have no idea where we are going."

Harry drove on the Interstate going south. They drove for about four hours. They chatted away about a million subjects. The time flew, and Maria saw that they were in Missouri. Then they reach Branson Missouri. They pulled up to the hotel, and the bellman unloaded their suitcases. They checked in, and Harry had reserved a suite. They go up to their room, and there is a hot tub. Maria couldn't believe what a lovely room it was with a hot tub. They both unpacked their suitcases and changed their clothes. Maria put on a beautiful green dress, and Harry changed into some dress slacks. They went to have dinner at the steakhouse. After dinner, he asked her if she would like to try some gambling. Maria was attracted to the slot machines. However, she had never gambled before since she just turned 21 years old. They were winning on their machines and having so much fun. They gambled for a few hours, and they both continued winning. They took a break and went to the lounge to listen to the music and do some dancing. They both loved to dance and were good dancers. They went back to the same machines and continued to be lucky. It was about 2:30 am, and they decided that they were tired and would go back to their room. Maria went into the bathroom, changed into her bathing suit, and put on the jets in the hot tub. Harry changed into his swim trunks, too. They sat in the hot tub, kissed, and enjoyed each other and the warm water. They sat in there for more than one hour and then decided to get out. Maria changed into a beautiful nightgown, and Harry put on a different pair of shorts. They decided it was time to sleep. Maria was dreaming of what it would be like to take this relationship further. She knew Harry loved her and wondered when the time would be right. She was so attracted to him that, at times, she wanted to go for it. Harry cuddled Maria tightly and they kissed goodnight. Harry was being a gentleman, and Maria appreciated it.

They had slept in until 11 am the next morning, reveling in the luxurious comfort of their room. Harry suggested Maria wear her bathing suit under her clothes for a surprise he had planned. Eager with anticipation, Maria followed his lead down to the spa. Harry had organized a day of pampering for them both. Maria was scheduled for a facial, massage, manicure, and pedicure, while Harry had a massage lined up and planned to spend the rest of the day relaxing in the whirlpool, sauna, and hot tub. After a light breakfast at the spa's restaurant, they separated for their treatments. Between appointments, they reunited in the hot tub, the warm water enveloping them as they shared serene moments.

Maria found the spa day profoundly relaxing and enjoyed every treatment. After their spa experience, they returned to their room to change before heading out for dinner at the buffet restaurant. The evening extended with a bit of gambling, where both Maria and Harry found luck on their side. It was well past 2 am by the time they decided to return to their room, exhausted yet content, and they quickly fell into a deep, restful sleep.

The following morning, they woke up refreshed, packed their belongings, and checked out of the hotel. Over breakfast, Maria couldn't hold back her gratitude, her eyes sparkling with tears of joy. "Harry, I can't thank you enough for this wonderful vacation. You've thought of everything. You never cease to amaze me. I love you so much and can't wait to spend every day with you. I wish we didn't live so far apart."

Harry, taking her hand across the table, reassured her with a tender look, "Maria, we will live in the same state again someday. Until then, we must treasure our moments together and keep them close to our hearts."

Feeling overwhelmed with emotion, Maria added, "I couldn't have imagined a better 21st birthday. Thank you for everything, Harry."

They arrived back at Maria's house around 6 pm, just in time for dinner. Everyone was already seated at the table. "You guys made it back just in time for dinner," Grandpa noted with a smile.

"Thanks, Grandpa. We're starving," Maria replied, her happiness evident in her voice.

Ethel, curious and smiling, asked, "Where did you go?"

Maria's face lit up as she recounted their trip. "We went to Branson, Missouri. Harry thought of everything. We had wonderful dinners, did a bit of gambling, but the best part was spending a whole day at the spa. I had a facial, massage, manicure, and pedicure. It was an amazing time."

Ethel, looking at Harry with a grateful expression, thanked him, "I'm so glad to hear that, Maria. And thank you, Harry, for spoiling my daughter on her 21st birthday. I can see she had the best birthday ever."

"It was my pleasure, Ethel," Harry responded warmly. "Maria deserves the best in life, and that's what I plan to give her forever." His words filled the room with a sense of enduring commitment and love.

Maria, Emily, and Edith cleaned the kitchen after dinner. Grandpa, Raymond, and Harry got deep in conversation about sports. Maria talked with her mom and gave her more details about her trip.

On Saturday afternoon, Harry had a flight back home. Maria drove Harry to the airport. When he got out of her car, she started crying. Maria was upset because she thought she would not see him for a long time. They kissed and waved goodbye as he walked inside the airport. Maria drove off, still crying.

Maria got back home and thought that Samantha's 21st birthday was on June 1st and Harry's college graduation was on June 2nd. She discussed this with her Mom and decided that she would go to California and surprise them both. She called and spoke with Stan and then his parents about the surprise. They figured out all the details and were so delighted that Maria would be there. Stan would pick Maria up at the airport at 12 pm on June 1st.

Throughout March, April, and May, Maria was very busy doing odd jobs, mainly babysitting and house cleaning, to earn money for her trip and for college. She talked to Samantha and Harry every day. She was careful to keep the secret. She spent many days with her grandpa. They were so close, and he seemed happy in Iowa. Grandpa loved helping Maria with her preschool children. She took care of 4 toddlers all of them were 3 years old. She watched them during the day when their parents were at work. Maria was so good with the kids that when their parents picked them up, they didn't want to leave and started crying. Maria dreamt of the day when she would have her own children. She was also excited to find that very soon, both she and Samantha would know if they had been accepted into nursing school. Maria anticipated her trip to California and dreamed about her and Samantha being roommates and going to nursing school.

At the beginning of May, Maria ran out to catch the postman, and he handed her the family's mail. There were two letters addressed to her. They were from the two schools she applied to in Iowa. She was accepted into the nursing program at both schools. She ran into the house to tell her Grandpa and called her Mom at work. She called Samantha, but her mail hadn't arrived by then. She called Harry that evening to let him know about her acceptance letters. It took another week before both girls received responses from all three schools. They both were accepted at two schools. The

University of Iowa was the nursing program in which they both were accepted. They could be roommates after all. They were on cloud nine. This school wasn't too far from home. Maria was happy that she could keep an eye on her Grandpa on weekends. They both received full scholarships and a grant to pay for room and board. Maria and Samantha started talking about how they wanted to decorate their dorm room. They were thrilled beyond words.

It was June 1st, and Ethel drove Maria to the airport early in the morning. When her plane landed Stan and his Mom were there to greet her.

"Hi, Maria. We are so happy to see you. Both Samantha and Harry are going to be so surprised. You look wonderful. How is Iowa?" Stan asked.

"I am happy to be back in California. I couldn't miss Harry's graduation or Samantha's birthday."

"We are going out to dinner: myself, Harry, you, Samantha, our parents, and Samantha's Grandmother. They both will be shocked when you walk into the restaurant." Maria was staying at their parents' house.

They had celebrated Samantha's birthday at a fancy downtown restaurant. Harry, his dad, Samantha, Stan, and Samantha's grandmother were already seated when Harry's mom entered with Maria. Both Samantha's and Harry's jaws dropped in surprise. Harry leaped up and ran over to kiss Maria, while Samantha rose to embrace her tightly. The dinner was filled with lively conversation and laughter. After dinner, their parents drove Samantha's grandmother home, while Maria, Harry, Samantha, and Stan headed out for drinks at a lively spot that featured dancing. They danced until the band stopped playing, making Samantha's birthday truly memorable, especially with the surprise appearance of her best friend.

The following afternoon marked Harry's commencement ceremony. He graduated with a B.A. in business and had been accepted into the school's master's program starting in the fall. Stan, Samantha, both sets of parents, aunts, uncles, and Maria were all present to celebrate. Maria was thrilled to be part of the ceremony. Afterwards, their parents hosted a grand graduation party at their home, attended by about 100 guests. A professional party planning service and caterer had been hired to manage the festivities. Harry spent the evening introducing Maria to many of his friends. They danced, sang, and chatted the night away, with the party continuing until around 1 am. Maria had gifted Harry an engraved briefcase with his initials, a nameplate for his desk, and a stunning watch, which left him deeply touched and grateful for her thoughtfulness.

Maria stayed in California for two more days. During that time, they explored Northern California, visiting various attractions and enjoying a day at an amusement park. Sadly, when it was time for Maria to leave, emotions ran high. Harry drove her to the airport where they shared a tearful goodbye, with Maria crying as she walked into the terminal.

Back in Iowa, the summer unfolded beautifully. Maria and her mom went shopping for dorm room essentials, aiming to make her and Samantha's room the most stylish in the dorm. Maria enjoyed a relaxing summer swimming, playing tennis with her sisters, and boating with friends. As the days to their move-in day on September 4, 1977, ticked down, Maria and Samantha eagerly anticipated the start of their new adventure in nursing school. They were both buzzing with excitement, looking forward to their future as roommates and future nurses.

CHAPTER 8-

On the 18th of August,1976, Marissa and her parents arrived at Alberto's parent's house. It took them four days to drive from Texas. They had a trailer hitched behind Marissa's car with all her belongings. Her parents thought of renting a hotel room nearby, but Dorothy and Tony convinced them all to stay at their house. The Bertolucci's owned a huge house, which was about 8,000 square feet, in Hillsborough, a suburb of San Francisco. Marissa and her parents were to stay in a wing of the house, which was used for guests. They settled in and unpacked their suitcases. Marissa's parents, Anne and Dave, planned to stay and help Marissa find an apartment and stay until she was settled in.

It was August 20th, and it was Alberto's birthday. The six of them went to the country club for dinner to celebrate. Alberto introduced Marissa to his friends. They had an outstanding dinner and then danced afterward. All three couples were out on the dance floor for most of the evening. Marissa loved slow dancing with Alberto. The dancing ended at 11 pm. Their parents were tired and went home. Marissa and Alberto decided to go to a nearby restaurant for after-dinner drinks. Marissa gave Alberto an album with pictures of the two of them from their various trips. Each picture had a meaningful saying underneath it. She also gave him a basket full of his favorite things. Alberto couldn't believe how creative and thoughtful a present Marissa had given him. They so enjoyed this time together by themselves.

"Alberto I am so happy to be in California and near you. We can spend so much time together now."

"Marissa I am so looking forward to having this year together before we both go back to school. We can really get to know each other and spend some quality time together. I love you and want to thank you for the heartwarming gifts."

"You're welcome, Alberto. I love you so much, too." They went back to Alberto's parent's house. Everyone was already asleep. They laid on the couch in the living room in each other arms and kissed passionately. Alberto touched her from her neck to her shoulders and down both arms. His eyes elude love, safety, and respect. Then he moved his hands and touched her legs gently and tenderly. Marissa was so happy to think that they could be in each other's arms all the time. They were so much in love and expressed it very tenderly. Alberto had a special birthday, and he spent it with his love.

Marissa and her parents had planned to look for apartments for rent the following day. Waking up to a beautiful morning, Dorothy prepared a sumptuous breakfast for all six of them. Around the table, they engaged in deep and lively conversations, enjoying each other's company. Later that morning, Alberto, Marissa, and her parents left to hunt for apartments. Marissa was keen on living in San Francisco, anticipating her schooling there or in Berkeley. They discovered a charming two-bedroom apartment on Nob Hill, complete with a swimming pool and an exercise room. Her parents fell in love with the apartment instantly. Marissa felt that this part of the city was perfect for her, and Alberto agreed, noting it as a safe area for her to live. The commute from Alberto's parents' house to the apartment would take about 30-45 minutes. Upon returning to Alberto's parents' house, they all agreed that the Nob Hill apartment was ideal for Marissa.

Marissa was thrilled to be in California and decided to sign a year's lease for the apartment, which would be available to move into in a week. Over the next few days, Alberto, Dorothy, and Tony took Marissa and her parents around the San Francisco Bay area, showcasing its beauty. "This is such a stunning place, isn't it?" Marissa remarked, her eyes sparkling with excitement. Her parents nodded, visibly pleased, knowing Marissa would be in good hands.

Moving day arrived quickly. Marissa had rented some elegant furniture, which was due to arrive that afternoon. Alberto helped unload the trailer hitch of all her belongings. Marissa's mom decided to stay a few days to help her organize and decorate. They spent the next two days arranging the furniture and personalizing the space. "I think it needs a little more color over here," her mother suggested, pointing towards the living room. They made several trips to the store, picking up additional necessities to make Marissa's new home comfortable and inviting. By the end of their efforts, Marissa looked around her newly decorated apartment and felt a deep sense of satisfaction. "It's perfect, mom. It really feels like home," she said, her voice full of emotion. Her mother hugged her, sharing the joy. They were both pleased with the outcome, feeling a profound connection to the new space that Marissa would call home.

Marissa and her Mom went back to Alberto's parents' house. Her parents were planning on flying home in two days. Her parents spent the last two days with Marissa and

Alberto. Dorothy and Tony had both gone back to work this week. Marissa's parents asked Alberto to take good care of their only daughter. Alberto assured her parents that she would be in good hands and that he would always be there for anything she needed. He told them that he was so in love with their daughter and that he would always watch out and protect her. The six of them went to the airport to see her parents off. Marissa started crying when saying goodbye to them. This was the first time Marissa had been away from Texas.

The four of them drove back to Alberto's parents' house. He told them that he was going with Marissa to her apartment and was planning on staying for a few days. He wanted to help her get acclimated to her new surroundings. Also, they both needed to finish applying to school. Alberto was going to help her with her applications to graduate school, and Alberto also needed to work on his personal statement for medical school applications.

Alberto and Marissa arrived at her Nob Hill apartment.

"You and your Mom did an amazing job decorating. This place is very cozy, cheerful and charming. You should be very happy here."

"I will be now that I am near you. We have so many things to do. Where do we start? Go hang your clothes in my closet so they don't get wrinkled."

"That's a good place to start."

"Are you hungry Alberto?"

"A little. Maybe we should order pizza?"

"Sounds good to me." Marissa and Alberto were excited to spend their first night in her apartment. After dinner, they watched some television and decided to go to bed.

"Can I ask you something, Alberto?"

"Anything, of course."

Do you ever think about taking our relationship to the next level?"

"All the time, but I don't want to pressure you. I want you to be comfortable and for it to be when you are ready. I want it to be a very special moment in our lives."

"Now that we are both in this apartment, I think I am ready. You don't have to worry I just started taking the pill."

"I am going to plan a very special evening very soon. Let me surprise you. I am so happy to hear this but remember if you change your mind and don't feel ready just let me know."

"Of course, babe. I love you so much."

"I love you too."

The next few days, they drove all over the city, and he showed her many places of interest, such as Coit Tower, Golden Gate Bridge, Lombard Street, Chinatown, Cable cars, Golden Gate Park, and Alcatraz. They also found the local grocery store, cleaners, library, and shopping mall. They both wanted to find employment for the next year till they started school. They applied at restaurants, amusement parks, grocery stores, and hospitals. It turned out that they both found employment at the same restaurant. It was a very exclusive restaurant on the Wharf. Marissa was going to be the evening hostess. Alberto's position was for an evening shift waiter. The salary was excellent for restaurant work. Many high-profile clients were regulars at this restaurant. They were both starting as of September 15th. Marissa was so happy that they were working together in San Francisco.

In the two weeks before starting work, they both wanted to complete the process of applying to graduate school and medical school. Marissa applied to two schools in San Francisco and one in Berkeley. She had her applications completed, undergraduate transcripts, GMAT score, three letters of recommendation, and entrance essay. She mailed these off, and all she could do was wait.

Alberto went to Stanford for his undergraduate studies and is hoping to go there for medical school. He applied to two additional medical schools. He has already sent in his applications and MCAT scores. Alberto worked at Stanford University Hospital during his undergraduate studies. He worked in several departments, such as admitting, as an OR tech, and as an ER tech. He submitted his personal statement, which included a description of why you are interested in this school, what skills would make you a good doctor, and what you can add to the school. Also, the statement informed the school of what field of medicine one planned to pursue. He sent out all the additional information necessary to complete his application process. Alberto stayed at Marissa's apartment but did go home to see his parents for a few days.

Alberto planned their special night. He wanted to do it before they start their jobs. He had a catered dinner with salad, steak, lobster, potato au gratin, broccoli soufflé, and chocolate cheesecake for dessert. They had champagne and wine to drink. Marissa came back to her apartment, and it was all decorated with roses and candles throughout. He was such a romantic at heart.

"I can't believe how you were able to transform my apartment. "

"I want this night to be special and one you will never forget."

"Everything looks amazing. You have outdone yourself." They ate dinner by candlelight. The food was out of this world. They sat around and drank champagne for at least two hours after dinner. They started kissing then Alberto carried Marissa into her bedroom. There were rose petals all over the bed. They were up most of the night and made love four times. He was gentle and slow, and they had a night they will never forget. Marissa was so happy to have made love with the most amazing man. She wanted Alberto to stay at her apartment every night. His parents weren't happy that he was spending so many nights there. Marissa didn't want her parents to know that Alberto had been staying at her apartment either.

They both started their job at the restaurant on the same day. They went through orientation together. Neither one of them had ever worked at a restaurant. They both liked their job. The tips at times were amazing. Marissa made a perfect hostess, but all the men who came in by themselves would try to flirt with her. She had a sense of being somewhat shy. At times, men would hand her their business cards and expect preferential seating. Other men would try to slip her some money, but she was all business, and that didn't work in Marissa's eyes. They both met famous people at times, so the job turned out to be quite interesting. They both worked 4 evenings a week, but not always the same evenings. Alberto would stay at Marissa's apartment the nights that he worked. They both would get off work between 11pm and 1 am. They became so close and inseparable. They thought that it would be a long time before they could get married. Alberto needed to finish medical school and an internship, and maybe they would wait till after his residency. Marissa had the perfect life with the perfect man. What more could she want.

On Thanksgiving, Alberto, Marissa, and his parents went to Tony's sister's house for the day. There were 28 family members at the dinner. They were happy to meet Marissa. She fit in so well with his family and they all loved her. Marissa missed her parents on Thanksgiving, but she was happy they were coming for Christmas.

On December 23rd, Marissa's parents arrived at the airport. Marissa and Alberto went to pick them up. They stayed at Marissa's apartment. On Christmas, they went to Alberto's parents' house, and they planned on a joyful, relaxing day. They had Christmas carols playing in the background, the house was beautifully decorated with a tree, which was 20 feet high, and the table was elegantly set. The house glistened as bright as the stars, and the aroma of the food was breathtaking. Tony had fixed a magnificent dinner. They had several courses and took time between each course. The six of them had a stimulating conversation through dinner. The parents were the best of friends, and their children were dating. Is there anything better in life?

They had decided that the six of them would go to Lake Tahoe for the New Year's weekend. Marissa's birthday fell on December 29th, and both sets of parents took her out to lunch that day, showering her with love and good wishes. Later, Alberto whisked her away for a romantic dinner, where they shared laughter and dreams for the future.

The following morning, bright and early at 8 am, Dorothy, Tony, and Alberto arrived to pick up Marissa and her parents. Despite the snowfall that made the roads slick, requiring chains on tires, their drive up to the mountains was filled with excitement and anticipation. It was Marissa's parents' first visit to Tahoe, and they were instantly enchanted by the panoramic views, the serene lake, and the cozy, inviting atmosphere. "Could you imagine having a cozy cabin here?" Marissa's father mused aloud, capturing everyone's imagination with the idea.

New Year's Eve was a gala affair at their hotel, which hosted a party included in their stay. Dressed in their finest, the group enjoyed a festive evening of dinner and dancing that lasted until 1 am. The music spanned genres from disco and swing to soft rock, smooth jazz, and soul, setting the stage for a night of joyous celebration. Marissa and Alberto watched their parents dance with a mix of admiration and joy, inspired by their grace and vitality. As midnight approached, they all joined in a chorus, "Happy New Year, Happy 1977! To the most amazing year ahead!" The night was filled with laughter and memorable moments, making it truly unforgettable.

On January 2nd, they drove back from Tahoe. Marissa's parents were staying for two more days, giving them a little more time to savor the family's company. They spent January 3rd resting and later gathered at the Bertolucci's house for what would be a farewell dinner. Over the meal, Marissa's parents expressed their deep gratitude to Tony, Dorothy, and Alberto for their incredible hospitality. "You've made us feel so welcomed; it's been like a home away from home," Marissa's mother said, her voice thick with emotion. "Thank you for making these holidays so special," her father added, his tone sincere.

As they reflected on the past two holiday seasons spent together, they pondered what the next year might bring. "Here's to future holidays, perhaps even more joyful and family-filled than the last," Alberto toasted, raising his glass, everyone echoing his sentiment with warm smiles and clinking glasses. The night was a beautiful end to their visit, filled with promises of more joyous gatherings in the years to come.

Marissa missed her parents when they left, but she started back at work which kept her busy. The owner offered Marissa the bookkeeper position since she had a degree in business. They offered Alberto the shift manager position. They both were thrilled that the owner wanted to promote them. There would be a significant salary increase with both positions. Marissa was thinking she might be able to keep her job while going to graduate school, but Alberto knew he wouldn't be able to keep his job during medical school. Marissa accepted her job offer, but Alberto declined his opportunity.

Marissa was in training in February and March. She loved learning new skills. She assumed the new position in April. This job had flexibility, as she could work in the restaurant office or from home. Marissa thrived in her new position and loved it. Alberto remained in his position as a waiter. He would stay at her apartment the nights he worked. She would feel lonely the nights she was at her apartment by herself. She loved San Francisco and thought that when they both started school, they would not be able to see each other as much as they have been able to lately. She was sad to think of this but tried to distract her mind from this thought.

Alberto had an interview with the Stanford medical program. He and Marissa were very excited. The interview went very well, and Alberto made a great impression. They both anxiously waited to see what they would be doing in the Fall.

In May of 1977, Marissa was accepted into a graduate business program in San Francisco, which started in the fall of 1977. Everything seemed to be working out for her as she could go to school, keep her apartment, and keep her job, too. Alberto was accepted to medical school at Stanford in the fall of 1977. He was so thrilled but knew he had a lot of work and a long road ahead of himself. He thought of Marissa and what she would need to give up while he was in school. They wouldn't be able to see each other as often as they would like, and studying would now need to be their priority. They both knew in the end it would pay off, but they both needed to shift their priorities. They would have to make the most of the little time they'd have together. Life was good and falling into place.

During the summer, Marissa took a two-week vacation and went back to Texas to see her parents. She and Alberto spent as much time together as possible. Alberto started medical school in late August, and Marissa started graduate school in the first week of September. Alberto quit his job the first week of August. They both relaxed and waited for school to start.

CHAPTER 9-

It came the third week of August 1977; Stan and Harry drove Samantha to school in Iowa. Samantha's parents wanted to drive her, but they had to pick up Samantha's Grandparents and move them into their house in Carson City, Nevada. They planned to hire a caregiver to take care of them. Samantha's parents appreciated all the outstanding care Samantha had given her Grandparents, but they were so happy that she was going to nursing school with Maria.

The three of them arrived at the Hernandez house after driving for 12 hours a day for four days. The family was so happy to see the three of them. Maria was super excited to see them, and they had seven days till it was move-in day. Stan and Harry would stay in the in-law unit in the back, and Samantha would stay in Maria's room. Maria and Harry gave Samantha and Stan a guided tour of Iowa. They drove all over and had a wonderful time. Grandpa fixed incredible meals for everyone. Maria and Harry were so happy to be able to spend this time together before they both started school.

The September 4th, 1977, was the move-in day for Maria and Samantha. They packed three 'v8cars with their belongings. Maria, Samantha, and Ethel drove to the campus. Grandpa also joined them as he wanted to see the college and the dorm. Maria was very happy that Grandpa was part of the day. They drove up to the campus in Iowa City, and it was beautiful, so lush and green. The campus looked much bigger than they had anticipated. They walked around campus and found their dorm. They went downstairs to register. Their dorm room was on the third floor and was the last room from the elevators. Maria and Samantha liked their room and were happy with its location. They all helped unpack the three cars. They decided that they would all go to dinner after they finished unloading the cars. Stan and Harry had a flight back home the same day at 9 pm. Harry had to start school in two days on Tuesday, Sept 6th.

Grandpa and Ethel liked Maria's school and the dorm and were very happy with everyone they met that day. They went to a restaurant that was close to the school. After dinner, Ethel and Grandpa said goodbye and drove back home. Maria and Samantha drove Stan and Harry to the airport. Samantha was very upset as she had seen Stan every day for almost two years. Stan and Harry got out of the car at the unloading level of the airport and kissed their girlfriends, goodbye. Samantha started crying, and then Maria started too. The men gather their suitcases, and they both give them a final kiss goodbye. They walked through the airport entrance, waved, and sent a kiss to them. Maria drove off, and they were both still crying.

They arrived back at their dorms around 8:30 pm and decided to unpack the rest of their belongings and arrange their room, which turned out quite cute. As they reviewed the welcome week activities for freshmen, they experienced a mix of emotions. Although saddened by their goodbyes to their boyfriends, they were also excited and thrilled for what lay ahead. Both were exhausted from the day's events and decided to call it a night early.

The following morning, they woke up around 10 am. The communal bathroom, located down the hallway near the elevators, was huge and meant to accommodate the entire floor. They gathered their essentials and headed down the corridor. The bathroom quickly became a place of conversation and a way to meet their dorm-mates, many of whom were also freshman nursing students. They appreciated their dorm's location, especially loving the view from their window which spanned the entire campus. Positioned across from the commons, which housed the dining facility, it was conveniently located for their daily needs.

Feeling hungry, Maria and Samantha headed for a late breakfast, though by the time it was 11:30 am, lunch was being served. They presented their dining cards and were greeted with a vast array of food choices. The cafeteria-style setup allowed them to choose freely, with hot items served directly by staff. They collected their meals and found a relatively empty table where they sat down to a leisurely lunch, discussing the practicality of stocking some food in their room, especially since Samantha had brought a mini-refrigerator.

They also expressed concerns about the shared amenities—there was only one phone for the entire floor and a single television room, which made them worry about availability when needed. Despite these adjustments, the thrill of dorm life outweighed any inconveniences.

Returning to their floor, Maria and Samantha met more dorm-mates, all of whom were exceptionally friendly and pointed out how fortunate they were to room with their best friend. Feeling grateful, Maria decided to seize the moment and call her grandpa, delighted to find the communal phone available. The warmth and support of their new friends deepened their appreciation for each other and their shared journey in nursing school.

"Hi Grandpa"

"Hi Maria. How are you?"

"We are doing well. I just wanted to check on you and see how you are doing."

"I am good, but the house seems quiet without you."

"Grandpa you should go to the senior center this afternoon."

"Great idea, Maria. I will go there and see what is happening."

"I want to give you our floor's phone number. Please give it to Mom, too."

"Ok"

"Let me know if you and Samantha want to come for dinner anytime. I will cook anything that you two would like."

"Thank you, Grandpa. I am going to go, but I will talk to you soon. Love you."

"Love you too. Say hi to Samantha"

"Will do, bye Grandpa." Then Samantha called her parents and gave them the floor's phone number, too. They looked at the list of freshman activities and saw that there was a welcome dinner that night at 6 pm. They decided to attend it.

The dinner had been set in one of the large halls. As Maria and Samantha walked in, they observed appetizers being passed around and everyone mingling. They chatted with several out-of-state students, enjoying the warm and lively atmosphere. Then the host called everyone to their seats. During dinner, several speakers introduced the freshmen to college life, outlining the available activities and sports. Despite the interesting presentations, Maria and Samantha noticed some male students were more focused on them than the speakers, drawn perhaps by their striking appearances and vibrant personalities. They met many friendly students that evening and were glad they had attended the event.

The next morning, they eagerly checked the list of classes for the first semester. Maria and Samantha found they shared classes in Anatomy and Physiology, Microbiology, and the corresponding labs. They were also enrolled in Psychology and Philosophy, although their schedules for these did not coincide. Together, they headed to the bookstore to purchase their textbooks, which were surprisingly heavy—a stark reminder of the challenging curriculum ahead.

They relished the welcome week activities, especially looking forward to the welcome breakfast for freshman nursing students. With 105 in their cohort—102 women and 3 men—the speaker introduced them to what they could expect in the nursing program, further fueled by an encouraging speech from the Dean of the Nursing department. The air buzzed with excitement and anticipation.

At dinner on Friday night in the commons, Maria and Samantha settled at their usual table. Soon, two male students approached and asked if they could join them. The girls welcomed them warmly. The newcomers were freshmen on football scholarships: one, a tall, dark-haired quarterback, and the other, a blonde punter, both studying business. As they conversed, time flew, and before they knew it, the commons were about to close.

"Hey, just so you know, we both have boyfriends back in California," Samantha mentioned gently, setting expectations.

"And they're brothers, actually," Maria added, smiling. "But we're happy to make new friends!"

The boys agreed, respecting their boundaries. As they left the dining hall, Maria whispered to Samantha, "Imagine, the two most eligible freshmen wanting to sit with us!"

The adjustment to college life during the first week was more challenging than Maria and Samantha had anticipated. They struggled to balance their schedules, ensuring they had enough time for breakfast before rushing to their early classes. The academic load was intense, with copious amounts of reading and study required from the outset.

"You realize we're not the big fish in the pond anymore," Maria said one evening as they sat surrounded by textbooks.

Samantha sighed, replying, "I know, it's humbling but exciting too. We're just going to have to support each other and work harder."

Their close friendship became a point of envy among other students, highlighting how fortunate they were to have a pre-established relationship unlike many who were still navigating the complexities of new roommate dynamics.

Phone calls with Harry and Stan were bittersweet and too brief, often cut short by the line of students waiting to use the communal phone.

"We'll catch up properly soon," Maria promised Harry during one hurried conversation, feeling the pang of missing him more sharply in that moment.

As they hung up, both women felt a mixture of loneliness and motivation. They were determined to make the most of their opportunities despite the sacrifices required by their demanding schedules.

They both learned so much, and it was all so interesting. They would visit their first anatomy lab on Saturday. The lab was a two-hour class taught by medical students. Cadavers were used so the students could learn about the organs, bones, muscles, tendons, and such. They had a female one semester and a male the next. This was used not for dissection but to identify different parts of the body. These were donations and gifts from people who chose to give their bodies to science. They dedicated themselves to promoting and further educating the next generation of students. The experience was surreal, and the students were grateful for this opportunity to learn. Some of the students were very uneasy about the thought of that, but it was best not to let fear or imagination get the best of you. The lab was the place where all that they had learned in class, came together.

Maria and Samantha handled the anatomy lab well, but both felt totally exhausted after class. They decided to go back to their room and take a nap. They also decided that Friday night would be their one and only night without studying. That semester, the courses were difficult, and they planned on giving it their all and more. They didn't realize how difficult nursing school would be, but they both loved the challenge.

They informed Grandpa and Ethel during the week that the two of them planned on coming over Sunday afternoon to visit and that they could stay for dinner. Grandpa and Ethel were so excited to see them. The drive from school was just a little over an hour. Maria and Samantha had a great visit, and everyone was excited to hear about the school. They let Maria's family know that they have a tremendous amount of studying to do, and they wouldn't be able to come over as much as they would like. Everyone was happy that the two of them were together and were such great supporters of each other. They wanted to stay longer but told the family that the 6:30 am alarm would be going off soon. They said their goodbyes and were on the road again.

The next morning came fast, and they had thirty minutes to eat breakfast and get to class. The football players came to their table, and they didn't want to be rude but explained that they were in a hurry to get to class. Maria and Samantha couldn't understand why they would want to hang around them since they told them there was no chance of a relationship beyond friendship. Maria and Samantha were so sweet and caring, and it seemed like everybody wanted to be their friend. They both felt that they were shunning their family, boyfriends, and everyone at school who wanted to be their friend. They hoped that they all understood they weren't ignoring them, but that time was so limited. Time was flying by, and it was almost Halloween and midterms.

Maria and Samantha frequently went to dinner at different times, and the football players always seemed to be at dinner at the same time. The four of them have dinner together frequently. The football players asked Maria and Samantha to go to the homecoming dance in two weeks. They both were stunned that they would ask them. There were so many other female students who would die for this opportunity. They both were flattered but didn't want to go because of Harry and Stan. Jim and Jack, the football players told them that they would have a much better time with the two of them than any other classmates. Maria and Samantha reiterated that they can only be friends. Maria, at times, was still thinking about Alberto. She realized that she was still mixed up and needed to just focus on her nursing. They both discussed the homecoming with their parents and decided that they both would turn them down. It turned out that the football players hadn't gone to the dance after all. They only wanted to go with Maria and Samantha and not with anyone else.

On the night of homecoming, many of the nursing students attended the dance. Maria and Samantha could see all the couples going to the dance out their window. They felt good about their decision and decided to study for the midterms that evening.

Maria and Samantha would try and talk to Harry and Stan every other evening. They both missed them so much but were so busy that couldn't call them as often as they wanted. They would study very hard and many times would decline their friend's invitations to many events. Philosophy and Psychology weren't too difficult, but it was the Anatomy and Physiology and Microbiology that they really needed to focus on. Their friends couldn't understand how they could spend so much time studying.

It was Thanksgiving weekend, and they were going to spend the weekend at Maria's house. There were some students who lived too far away from home to go back for a long weekend. Maria invited two students on their floor from Hawaii to accompany them to her house for the weekend. They both were so thrilled about the invite. They were both freshman nursing students, too. Grandpa, Ethel, and Raymond were happy that Maria was coming home with three friends for the long weekend. Grandpa decided to go all out for dinner. When the four arrived at Maria's house they were enthusiastically welcomed. Edith and Emily were so happy to see their sister and her friends. Grandpa was his usual, charming self and had such an endearing personality that everybody loved him. Ethel and Raymond were so happy to see their daughter and her friends. Ethel asked numerous questions about school, and she was happy to see that they were all friends.

Thanksgiving dinner consisted of four courses, and Grandpa had fixed a spread of about twenty dishes for the buffet. The Hawaiian students were used to going to Luau's but had never seen a buffet like this before. The four of them did numerous activities over the long weekend. They went black Friday shopping the next day. Then, on Saturday, they decided to take Edith and Emily to the amusement park. On Sunday they just hung around the house and rested. Maria had great conversations with her Mom, Dad, and Grandpa. After dinner, the four planned to go back to the dorm. The Hawaiian students thanked Maria's family for their amazing hospitality. Grandpa and Ethel told them both that they were welcome anytime. The four drove back to school and arrived at the dorms at 8:30 pm. They all had such a remarkable weekend, and now it is time to get back to the reality of school.

Then came Monday morning, and it was less than three weeks before finals started. They realized how much studying they needed to do before finals. They both went to the lab two or three times a week to review the different muscles and their insertions and origins. They decided to make flash cards so they could quiz each other. They both have two papers due in a couple of weeks and decide to finish those before studying for finals.

It was one week before finals, and they had both turned in their papers. They were ready to make their plan for studying. They decided they would study every night from 7 pm till 3 am. They were planning on drinking a lot of coffee to stay awake. The studying was going well and each night they needed to drink more coffee to stay awake. Once in a while, one of their friends came to their room and studied with them. It was Friday night, and they went out to dinner to give themselves a break. On the weekend, they planned on studying from 9 am to 3 am, an 18-hour study session both days. The flashcards were an excellent idea. On Sunday morning, they decided to review everything just one more time. By then, they were drinking 2-3 pots of coffee each day. They both were tired and very wired. They decided to take a two-hour nap. After they woke up, they decided to go to the Commons for dinner and ran into the football players. The four of them had a very pleasant conversation during dinner. Jim and Jack thought that maybe their relationship would end, and they could rescue them. They were respectful of Maria's and Samantha's relationship with Harry and Stan but still dreamt that one day they both would be their girlfriends.

It was finals week, and Monday morning was their first final. Maria and Samantha arrived at class fifteen minutes early. They both felt as prepared as possible. They finished their test with half an hour to spare. It was difficult to know how you did, but they both felt happy when they left the test. They went back to their room to study for the next final. They both had two more finals in the next two days. In their anatomy and physiology lab final, there were flags numbered one to fifty, and they needed to identify what the organ was or the name of the muscle with its origin and insertion site. After their finals were completed, they both were exhausted. Samantha was flying home in two days. Maria decided she would stay at school till Samantha left. The day after their last final they both slept till three in the afternoon. They packed their clothes to bring home for their six-week vacation. The second semester started the first week of February.

Maria had driven Samantha to the airport for her flight home. At that time, neither of them had figured out what they would do during their vacation, aside from spending Christmas and New Year's with their families and the month of January with their boyfriends. They planned to reunite in February.

When Maria arrived home, she was greeted warmly by her grandpa, parents, and sisters. With Christmas just seven days away, she initially wanted to sleep for days, something that worried her family due to her uncharacteristic quietness and frequent naps. Despite their concerns and suggestions to visit a doctor, Maria reassured them, "I'm just exhausted, really. A few days of rest and I'll be as good as new." True to her word, after a few days, she revived and was eager to start Christmas shopping. The holiday was beautiful, filled with joy as the whole family was together. Maria missed Harry, but she knew the importance of this family time.

On December 30th, Maria picked up Harry from the airport. As they embraced, she couldn't hide her joy, exclaiming, "Harry, I am so thrilled to see you. I've missed you terribly."

Harry, holding her close, replied warmly, "Maria, I've counted every day until I could hold you again. I love you so much."

"I love you too, Harry, so much." Their arrival at home was met with excitement, especially from Grandpa, whose smile was the broadest. Maria and Harry attended a New Year's Eve party hosted by one of Maria's friends, where they had a fantastic time. Harry enjoyed getting to know Maria's friends better, deepening his connections. The three weeks flew by, allowing them both to grow closer and reconnect on a deeper level. Harry expressed his happiness about Maria's passion for nursing school, knowing she would excel as a nurse.

By the first week of February, Maria and Samantha were back at school, refreshed and ready to tackle the challenges ahead. They were continuing with the same classes but switching from psychology to nursing research this semester.

On their first night back, they encountered the football players at dinner. The conversation stretched long as they shared stories of their holiday adventures. Maria and Samantha enjoyed the chat but were mindful of setting boundaries.

Maria laughed softly during dinner, saying, "We really enjoy these chats, but just so we're clear, we're here as friends, nothing more!"

Samantha nodded, adding, "Absolutely, we've got some amazing boyfriends waiting for us back in California."

Despite their clear stance, several cheerleaders eyed the football players with envy. Maria and Samantha were well-liked for their humble, caring natures, which sometimes sparked jealousy over their looks, intelligence, and the attention they received from two of the most eligible bachelors at school. Yet, their kindness made them beloved figures on campus, navigating the complexities of college relationships with grace.

The first week of the second semester started just like the first semester did with significant reading due before the next class in most subjects. At least they both have adjusted to school, so it made it a little easier. They decided to do what they did last semester, which was to study every night but Friday. Maria and Samantha would have to go to the library more that semester due to the nursing research class.

Maria looked out her window Friday night and called Samantha to come over. They see fifteen to twenty male and female students streaking by their windows very fast. They both heard that this might happen, but they would never do anything on this level. The temperature was 10 degrees Fahrenheit, and there was snow everywhere. There were a couple of freshman nursing students in the pack, but they both felt that nursing students would be too mature to do something like that. The student organizers called this activity the welcome back parade. The organizers had hoped that they could get at least 100 to participate. Maria and Samantha decided to leave campus and went to see a movie.

They both couldn't believe how difficult nursing school was, and the second semester seemed harder than the first. They would spend all their time not in class, studying. Jack and Jim told them they should get away from their studying more often. The four of them decided to go to the school's basketball game next Friday. They went to get ice cream after the game. They decided that they would all go together to all home games held on Friday night. Maria and Samantha looked at Jim and Jack as their brother. The school was winning and was going to the final four basketball championships. The whole school was so excited. Jack and Jim asked Maria and Samantha to accompany them to the final four playoffs. The school was hiring buses to take the students, and they would be gone for four days. It sounded like a lot of fun, but they thought that if they went, they would be leading them on. They politely declined and explained that Maria's family, especially her grandpa, was so looking forward to them coming home during Easter Break. Jack and Jim tried to get them to change their minds, but they understood.

Maria, Samantha, and the two Hawaiian students went to Maria's house for a week for Easter break. Maria's family was so happy to see all of them. They had a relaxing week, which included many enjoyable activities. Grandpa was so elated to have the company and was his usual character.

After the week off, they were back at school, and finals would be in six weeks. It was hard to believe that their first year of nursing school was almost finished. Maria and Samantha started realizing that next year, they would start their clinical rotations. They would be wearing their student uniforms with caps and be assigned to different hospitals with each clinical rotation. They were starting to study for finals. They were going to follow the same routine as the previous semester. They both aced their finals this semester and were going to be Sophomores. Summer 1978 was upon them, and they were excited to have some time off.

Samantha went home to her parent's house in Nevada for the summer. They stored her belongings at Maria's house. Maria had a job for the summer at the local hospital to work as a nursing aide on the medical-surgical floor. Samantha was able to find a nurse's aide job at her local hospital on the pediatric floor. The two girls would see each other again in about ten weeks. Stan and Harry had planned a summer vacation with Samantha and Maria to Hawaii for the last two weeks in August. They were renting a house in Maui. Both Maria and Samantha enjoyed their summer jobs as nursing aides. They both loved the patient contact and all the skills they acquired during the summer program.

They both were so excited to spend time with their boyfriends. It was August, and the four of them met at the San Francisco International Airport and flew directly to Maui. The house they rented had three bedrooms right on the beach. They decided to go to the grocery store and get food to fill the refrigerator. They were all so happy to be together. Samantha and Stan had a much more intimate relationship than Harry and Maria. Maria wanted to take things slowly. She missed Harry so much that she often thought about taking their relationship to the next level.

They went snorkeling, scuba diving, boating, and water skiing. They ate breakfast on their patio each morning and went out to dinner in the evenings. Both of their relationships were flourishing. They couldn't be happier but wished they could spend every day together. They knew they would look back on these days as some of the happiest days of their lives. They were all excited about what the future would hold. Maria and Samantha had an amazing vacation and were more in love with their boyfriends with each passing day. They both couldn't wait for them to be their husbands. They both felt so lucky to have met these wonderful men that New Year's Eve in Northern California. So much has happened since that day, and there was so much to look forward to in the future.

It was September; Maria and Samantha were back at school and were now Sophomores. They were both in the same resident hall on the third floor but a couple of rooms away from their last year's room. Harry was starting his last year of graduate school. Maria and Samantha went to the nursing school and saw their list of classes for the semester. Maria's clinical rotation was Medical-Surgical and Samantha was in the Operating Room. They had two classes together and had their clinical rotation on the same days. That night, they went to the Commons for dinner and ran into Jack and Jim, the football players. They stayed there for hours talking about their summer. Jack and Jim still held out hope that Maria and Samantha could be their girlfriends.

The school started in the morning, and it was the first day of the clinical rotation. They were so proud to be dressed in their nursing school uniform. Maria had eight other students in her rotation. She had a patient with Congestive Heart Failure. They learned about giving bed baths, Intravenous hydration, and fluid restrictions. Her homework assignment was to make a nursing care plan for her patient. Samantha was in Operating Room rotation and was assigned to observe a surgery for a hip replacement. Three students were assigned to watch the surgery and one of them fainted. Samantha was happy that she was able to watch the whole surgery with no ill effects. Her assignment was to develop a post-op nursing care plan for this patient. They both worked diligently on their care plans. They both loved the patient contact and helping people in their time of need.

They both looked forward to this semester and all the learning that will occur. This semester seemed a little easier than last year. They felt they were going to have a great year. They both loved their clinical rotations and patient care. They were excited to follow up with their patients and see their progress. Maria learned so much from her patients. She learned how important it is for the patient to feel dignity and respect and be part of the care plan. She loved educating her patients about their illnesses and how to manage their symptoms. Samantha found the Operating Room to be very interesting but knew that she would not want to work in that area after graduation. She liked patient contact more, communication, and teaching. The year passed very quickly, and it was almost near the semester finals.

They both studied very hard for their finals. Samantha and Maria did very well on their final exams as usual. It was fall break and December of 1978. They both were going home to their families for the break. Maria had a wonderful time visiting with all her family and friends during the school break. She caught up on all that was going on in her town. She spent a significant amount of time with her grandpa. She felt so close to him and was sad that during the school year, she couldn't spend more time with him. The two of them went everywhere together. They were both so excited that Harry was coming for the last two weeks of January. Harry arrived on January 15th and has become part of the family. The year of 1979 started out gloriously. Harry and Maria took Grandpa with them everywhere. The rest of the family was either back at work or back in school. Maria and Harry would go out in the evenings by themselves.

"Harry it is getting harder and harder to have these two, week vacations and then not see each other for months. I love you Harry and miss you so much."

"I know Maria, I feel the same way. We have a plan, and we both must get our education first. We will go on to have a wonderful life and will look back fondly on this time. Maria, I love you with my whole heart and soul and can't wait for you to be my wife."

It was the end of January, and Harry was flying home to start his last semester of graduate school. Maria was going back to school in a few days.

It was the first week of February and Maria and Samantha were back at school. Maria had the Operating Room as her clinical rotation and Samantha had Medical- Surgical rotation. Each semester seemed a little easier, but they both studied most of their free time. They were still friendly with the football players, who had started to talk with some of the school's cheerleaders. Samantha and Maria were happy to see them venturing out and starting to date.

The semester flew by swiftly as Maria and Samantha settled into a steady routine. They would speak with Harry and Stan almost every night, sharing the day's events and their plans. Stan had already graduated and was working as a stockbroker in San Francisco, while Maria hoped Harry would secure a job in Ohio after his graduation that spring. Maria had grown to love medical-surgical nursing, particularly cardiovascular care, and envisioned specializing in that field. She cherished the patient interaction, communication, assessment, and especially educating patients about their conditions.

Two years of nursing school had vanished in the blink of an eye. Maria found herself on a plane, heading to attend Harry's graduate school graduation—a weekend filled with countless festivities. She was overjoyed to reunite with Stan and their parents. Maria held a deep affection for Harry's parents and admired the kind of in-laws they would be. She felt incredibly connected to Harry's mom, perhaps even more so than with her own mother. As she contemplated her future, Maria felt fortunate about the prospect of marrying into such a caring, understanding, and loving family.

Maria spent two exhilarating weeks in California, reveling in every moment. During her stay, Harry was applying for jobs in both San Francisco and Iowa, but Maria secretly prayed he would secure employment in Ohio, allowing them to be closer to each other. The constant farewells and tears at airports were wearing on her, and she longed for a time when their goodbyes would be fewer and further between.

Finally, Harry landed a job offer in San Francisco to be a stockbroker at the Pacific Stock Exchange. He called Maria that afternoon in July and told her the good news. She was so happy for him that he landed his dream job but sad for herself that they would still be apart. Maria kept telling herself to be happy for Harry, not to be selfish, and to think about herself. Maria would frequently daydream about Harry and, at times, still thought about Alberto and what could have been.

CHAPTER 10-

It was the last week of August 1977. Alberto was spending the last night at Marissa's apartment for some time. It was Saturday night, and he started his first year of medical school at Stanford coming Monday. Marissa cooked a delicious dinner with his favorite dessert, strawberry shortcake. The two of them had become so close over the last year spending so much time together. They both knew that things were going to change drastically. Free time would then become scarce, and they knew that it would be of the utmost importance to spend their free time wisely. Marissa was sad to see Alberto leave and knew that this was going to be a long journey. She supported her boyfriend and wanted the best for him.

Finally, Monday morning arrived and Alberto began his first day of medical school. He recognized two classmates from his undergraduate studies, which eased his nerves slightly. The initial two years of medical school were known to be the most grueling, filled with a massive influx of information from various science classes including anatomy, biochemistry, microbiology, pathology, and pharmacology. Moreover, he was enrolled in a course designed to teach the basics of interviewing and examining patients. Alberto's schedule comprised four classes with corresponding lab sessions; the lectures lasted an hour each, while the labs extended for at least two hours. Despite the daunting workload ahead, Alberto felt prepared to meet the challenge head-on.

Returning home around five in the evening, Alberto found his parents eagerly awaiting details of his day. He reassured them that everything had gone smoothly and mentioned reconnecting with his former classmates. That evening, Dorothy prepared Alberto's favorite meal, which he gratefully acknowledged.

"I'm heading to my room to review my textbooks and plan out my study schedule," Alberto announced after dinner.

"Oh, Alberto, everything will fall into place. You're incredibly intelligent," Dorothy encouraged.

"Thank you, Mom," he replied, touched by her confidence in him.

Opting to share his day with Marissa, he gave her a call. She was delighted to hear from him.

"Hi honey," he greeted.

"Hi babe, how was school today?" Marissa inquired, her voice warm over the phone.

"It was overwhelming," Alberto admitted. "I was flooded with information. Luckily, I know a couple of people in my class from before."

"That's great! It's always good to have familiar faces around," Marissa responded supportively.

"I've just realized how much we need to learn when I looked at the textbooks," Alberto sighed.

"You are so capable and I have no doubt you'll excel. You always rise to the occasion," Marissa encouraged him.

"Thank you, Marissa. I love you so much," Alberto said, his voice softening.

"I love you too. Now go hit those books, and we'll talk soon. Bye," Marissa replied, giving him the space he needed to focus.

With that, Alberto's first week at medical school flew by. Meanwhile, Marissa, feeling his absence particularly on her days off, had chosen to work from home on her bookkeeping job. The day after Labor Day marked the beginning of her own academic journey in the graduate MBA program at a nearby college. She was thrilled to escape the stifling heat and humidity of Texas for the cool, foggy climate of San Francisco—a city she was growing to love. Excited for this new chapter in her life, she planned her schedule around her classes and work, looking forward to immersing herself in her studies while managing her time effectively. She resolved to call Alberto after her first class to share her experiences, just as he had done with her.

"Hi honey"

"Hi beautiful. How was school today?"

'I love the campus, and all my classes seem interesting."

"I am glad to hear that."

"How are you?"

"I am amazed at how much reading and studying we have to do. I want to see you, but I am already behind on my reading."

"I understand, don't worry. I love you."

"Love you." Marissa tried to sleep and thought about Alberto and the time they had spent together. She thought of his strong arms cuddling her while they slept, all the amazing, kind, thoughtful ways, and how loved and safe she felt with him. She tried to distract her mind and tell herself that they would be together again soon. Getting an education was important to them so they could have a life filled with love, adventure, travel, and all the good things this world has to offer.

The months passed and both Marissa and Alberto were extremely busy. Marissa tried to come to Alberto's house on Saturdays and spend time with him. They loved seeing each other, but wished they had more time to spend together.

Marissa's parents were coming the week of Christmas until January 3, 1978. They stayed at her apartment while they visited. She was so excited to see them. Both Alberto and Marissa finished with finals and were on winter break. Alberto would have three weeks before his next semester began. Marissa would be out of school for six weeks, which included all of January.

On December 23rd, Marissa picked up her parents from the San Francisco airport. Together, they headed to the Bertolucci's for dinner. The reunion was heartfelt as everyone caught up on the recent happenings in their lives. Dorothy and Anne, who talked on the phone nearly every day, were particularly joyful to meet in person again. The camaraderie among all six was palpable, creating a warm and welcoming atmosphere.

By Christmas Eve, the festive spirit was in full swing as they attended midnight Mass at the beautifully adorned Cathedral in San Francisco. The church was a sight to behold, festooned with holiday decorations that sparkled under the soft glow of candlelight. Everyone was dressed in their holiday best, their faces alight with joy. The children's choir added to the enchantment, their voices angelic as they sang Christmas carols. As the Mass concluded, the Bertolucci's warmly said, "We'll see you tomorrow at 3 pm."

"Thank you. We can't wait," Marissa and her parents responded, looking forward to more shared moments.

On Christmas Day, Marissa and her parents arrived at Alberto's house, arms laden with gifts. The Bertolucci home was elegantly decked out for the occasion, the dinner table impeccably set, creating a backdrop of refined holiday elegance. They spent hours in the living room, enjoying champagne and engaging in animated conversations that reflected their deepening bonds.

Gift opening was a delight, with heartfelt expressions of gratitude and joy as each person unveiled thoughtful presents from one another. Tony, renowned for his culinary skills, excelled himself with a sumptuous six-course meal that left everyone thoroughly impressed and deeply satisfied.

As dinner wound down, they returned to the cozy ambiance of the living room, continuing their lively exchanges until the early hours. By 1 am, they had made plans to ring in the New Year together at a party in Union Square.

Expressing immense gratitude for the hospitality and the splendid dinner, Marissa and her parents were effusive in their thanks to Alberto and his parents. The warmth and generosity exchanged were a testament to the close-knit ties between the two families. They looked forward to reuniting on December 29th to celebrate Marissa's birthday, already anticipating another joyful gathering.

The week between Christmas and New Year's Eve, Marissa and Anne did some shopping, and when they finished, they would meet her dad for a late lunch. They also went sightseeing, and she showed her parents around the city that she had come to love. Marissa had a wonderful birthday and so enjoyed this special time with her parents and the Bertolucci's.

It was New Year's Eve, and Marissa and her parents were waiting for the Bertolucci's to arrive. Alberto knocked on the front door and saw Marissa.

"You look stunning sweetie. You always look beautiful, but you look even more gorgeous tonight. You should be a model."

"Thank you, Alberto. You look so handsome that I got chills looking at you." The six of them set out for the hotel. This was the third New Year's Eve that the six of them have spent together since they met in Mexico back in 1974. All six of them looked gorgeous and festive. Marissa and Alberto loved seeing their parents all dressed up, dancing, and enjoying themselves. Their parents were young at heart and did not look their age at all.

"I still have a week off from school when your parents leave. I can't wait to get you all to myself, my love."

"I know I have been thinking about that too, but I am having a wonderful time with my parents. Love you so much."

"Love you too." They all had a fantastic time this evening and New Year's Day 1978 was upon them.

On January 3rd, Marissa and Alberto were driving her parents to the airport. Marissa was sad to see her parents go, but she knew she would see them again soon.

Alberto was staying at Marissa's apartment for the week till school started. They were unable to keep their hands off each other as it had been a long time since they had been in each other's arms. They made love so many times during that week. Marissa never wanted this week to end and would dream what it would be like to be with Alberto every night. The week came to an end, and Alberto needed to go back home and start his spring semester, which started in two days. Marissa still had three weeks off from school but had so much work to catch up on for her job. She felt so lonely when Alberto was gone. She tried to remember all the good times and daydream about their future.

The second semester flew by for both of them. The second semester of medical school seemed more challenging than the first. Marissa had more classes and less time to do her accounting job. They talked on the phone about twice a week. They were unable to see each other very much this semester due to their schedules. They were able to spend some time during Easter break, and when they returned to school, it was almost time for finals. After finals, summer 1978 was upon them.

Alberto had two months off for summer but was taking one class during the summer. Marissa had three months off from school but was still working. They were able to spend more time together during the summer. He would go to Marissa's apartment on the weekends. He still needed to do some studying, but she loved having him there. The summer has ended for Alberto. He was starting his second year of medical school in August. Marissa was taking two weeks off from her job and flying home to Texas. She had a great time in Texas, visiting with her parents and all her friends. Marissa started back to school the day after Labor Day.

In the autumn of 1978, the weather was beautiful and so warm. They saw less of each other this year than last year. Marissa's parents invited Alberto and his parents to come to Dallas for the holidays. The four of them were coming for two weeks. Marissa was so excited to show Alberto where she was from and grew up, and especially to introduce him to all her friends.

Dorothy, Tony, Marissa, and Alberto all flew to Dallas on December 23rd. Anne and Dave were excited to see all four of them. They were all going to stay at their home. They have five bedrooms with plenty of room for everyone. The house was beautifully decorated for Christmas. They all had a wonderful Christmas and were so happy that all six of them could be together for the holidays.

Anne planned a surprise birthday party for Marissa on her birthday, December 29th. Alberto was in on the secret and took her out for the day. They were to be back at the house at seven in the evening. Alberto took her out to lunch that day and went shopping for a birthday gift. Marissa loved shopping with him. He bought her three new outfits, two pairs of shoes, two purses, and some earrings.

"Let's go home and put your presents away, and then we can go back out tonight."

"Sounds good honey."

The moment Marissa entered her home on her birthday, she was met with shouts of "Surprise!" from a crowd of friends she hadn't seen in ages. Overwhelmed by emotion, tears streamed down her face as she took in the sight of the beautifully catered party, complete with a live band playing in the living room. The effort her parents had put into organizing such a magnificent celebration touched her deeply. They had even ensured all her friends could meet Alberto, who quickly won everyone over with his charm and kindness. The party carried on until after 1 am, filled with laughter and heartwarming conversations. Marissa's friends remarked that finding Alberto was like striking gold—they found him good-looking, sweet, compassionate, and funny.

As the night wound down, Marissa expressed her gratitude. She thanked her parents for their incredible generosity, Alberto's parents for making the journey, and Alberto for being her steadfast partner. The two weeks with her parents and the Bertolucci's flew by, and soon they were on a plane back to California, anticipating her upcoming graduation.

The spring semester of 1979 passed swiftly. On May 25th, Marissa graduated with an MBA under the sunny San Francisco sky, the air warm with temperatures in the eighties. Alberto, along with both sets of parents—Anne, Dave, Dorothy, and Tony—proudly attended the outdoor ceremony. Afterwards, they celebrated at the Fairmont Hotel, reveling in Marissa's accomplishment and the promise of her future.

Despite the joy, Marissa felt a pang of longing; she wished she and Alberto could marry immediately rather than waiting until after his graduation. She understood the rigorous demands of his medical studies and knew she must not distract him. Yet, she couldn't help but yearn for the day when they could be together without the separations imposed by their academic commitments. She dreamed of a life where they could share every day and night, wrapped in each other's arms, building a future filled with love and adventure.

CHAPTER 11-

It was the fall semester of 1979, and Maria and Samantha were now junior nursing students. They could hardly believe they had passed the halfway point to becoming registered nurses. They decided to live in the dorms for another year, planning to get an apartment near campus for their senior year. Although they were in the same dorm, they ended up on different floors. Despite this, they loved being roommates and cherished the familiarity they shared, especially as many other students from the past two years had moved off-campus.

"Can you believe we're juniors already?" Maria exclaimed, her eyes wide with disbelief as she unpacked her suitcase.

"I know, it feels like just yesterday we were clueless freshmen," Samantha replied, laughing as she hung up her clothes.

As upperclassmen, they felt a sense of responsibility to help the freshmen acclimate to dorm life. They had considered becoming resident assistants, but decided against it, recognizing the role would demand too much time that they needed to devote to their studies.

They received their class schedules for the semester, discovering they both had classes only on Mondays, Wednesdays, and Fridays. Maria was assigned to her clinical rotation in Obstetrics, while Samantha would be in

Psychiatry. With two days left before classes started, excitement and a bit of anxiety filled the air.

"Obstetrics, huh? You'll be delivering babies!" Samantha teased, nudging Maria playfully.

"Yeah, and you'll be dealing with the mind. We'll make quite the team," Maria responded, smiling.

Despite her excitement, Maria couldn't help but think about Harry. She wished he had landed a job in Iowa. She knew the experience he was gaining at the Pacific Stock Exchange was invaluable, but she missed him tremendously.

"I really wish Harry was here," Maria confided to Samantha one evening as they sat in their dorm room. "It's so hard being apart from him."

"I know, Maria. But think of how amazing it'll be when you finally reunite," Samantha reassured her. "And hey, we've got a lot of work to keep us busy."

Determined to stay occupied, Maria and Samantha both applied for jobs for Tuesdays and Thursdays, their class-free days. Maria landed a job at a nearby pharmacy for 16 hours a week, while Samantha secured a position in the School of Nursing office.

"This pharmacy job will be good for me," Maria said, holding up her new uniform. "It's only 16 hours a week, but it'll keep me busy."

"And I'll be in the nursing office, probably filing papers and answering phones," Samantha added, rolling her eyes. "But hey, it's a job."

Their days soon filled with classes, work, and endless study sessions. The fall semester of 1979 seemed to flow more smoothly as they thrived in their clinical rotations. Maria's thoughts often drifted to Harry, especially during quiet moments at the pharmacy or late at night in her dorm room.

"I think about Harry every day," Maria admitted to Samantha one night. "I can't wait until we can take our relationship to the next level."

Samantha nodded understandingly. "I get it, Maria. But just focus on your studies for now. The time will pass faster than you think."

Maria knew Samantha was right. For now, she poured her heart into her studies and clinical rotations, finding solace in the knowledge that every day brought her closer to reuniting with Harry.

The fall semester of 1979 seemed to be easier for both of them. They were both thriving in their clinical rotations. Maria was doing her Obstetrics rotation and started thinking about having a family with Harry. She thought about him every day and couldn't wait till they took their relationship to the next level. Samantha sometimes told Maria about her and Stan's night of passion relationship, and Maria wanted that too with Harry. Harry had been very respectful of Maria, but Maria wanted to connect with Harry on a much deeper level.

Harry had two weeks, from Christmas Eve till January 6th off from work. He was coming to spend his vacation with Maria. She was ecstatic and couldn't wait to tell him her plan.

Harry arrived on Christmas Eve, and the whole family was so excited to see him. They had a wonderful Christmas, and so many wonderful gifts were exchanged. Maria whispered in Harry's ear,

"I have one more gift for you. Come out to my car." They walked out to her car, got in, and turned on the heat.

"I have been thinking about something for a while, honey. I want to take our relationship to the next level."

"Are you sure you don't want to wait till we are married?"

"No, I am sure. I love you so much."

"Ok, I have an idea. What do you think if we go to Branson, Missouri, on New Year's Eve? I will make it a night you will never forget."

"Sounds perfect. I am so excited to get away with you alone."

"I will make the reservations. You have no idea how excited I am, Maria."

It is New Year's Eve and Harry and Maria were both packed. They said their Goodbye and Happy New Year to Maria's family and headed out the door. There was significant traffic, but they arrived at the hotel around 5 pm. They changed their clothes and set out to the hotel's party. Maria looked stunning and Harry was in awe that she was his girlfriend. Maria also felt so lucky to have Harry, who was sweet, caring, smart, charming, and so good-looking.

They went to the New Year's Eve party. They had a delicious dinner and danced all night to different genres of music. They are having the best of their time. It was about 2 am and they decided to do a little gambling. Both of them were winning, but Harry was thinking about the special night he had planned for them.

It was 2 30 a.m., and they went back to their suite. Maria saw the hot tub filled with water, and she noticed rose petals on the bed and chocolate and champagne on the bedside table.

"Oh, I can't believe how thoughtful you are."

"I want this to be a very special night." Harry started kissing Maria passionately. He started to unbutton her dress. She started to unzip his pants, and he took off his shirt. They slipped into the hot tub and were toasting with champagne.

"Do you know how much I love you, Harry. I can't wait till we spend every night together. You are my person. I know that we are soul mates and God put you here for me."

"Maria, I love you so much. I can't wait to be your husband and spend the rest of our lives together. I am so happy that you want to make love."

The water started to cool, so he carried Maria to the bed. He kissed her passionately over her whole body. Maria felt tingly and had never felt so loved. Their bodies rubbed against each other. Harry was gentle with Maria, and she loved it. They made love three times during the night. The night was perfect, and they both fell asleep in each other's arms.

They both awoke around 10:30 am. Harry ordered room service for breakfast, and they ate in bed. After eating, they made love again. They decided to go back to sleep for a while.

They woke up and decided to shower together. Maria loved soaping Harry's muscular, toned body and Harry did the same for Maria. They decided to stay in the room and have room service bring dinner. They had a delicious dinner and just talked about their future plans and goals. They sat at the table talking for quite a while, and then Harry carried Maria back to bed, and they started making love again.

"This was such a special night and one I will never forget. I love you so much, Harry. I know it is going to be even harder to be away from you now."

"I know my dear, but just think it won't be long till we are back together again. Summer isn't too far away." They drove back to Maria's house, and everyone was happy to see them. Harry had four days till he left. He spent some quality time with Grandpa on his last couple of days. Maria drove Harry to the airport, and she started crying before they even got there.

"Honey why are you crying."

"I am going to miss you so much."

"I know, but time will go by fast, and we will see each other soon."

The spring semester of 1980 in nursing school had started. Maria and Samantha were incredibly busy with school and work. Maria often reflected on the amazing time she had just spent with Harry. One evening, she decided to divulge to Samantha that she and Harry had a night of passion.

"Samantha, I have something to tell you," Maria began, her cheeks flushing slightly.

"What is it?" Samantha asked, curiosity piqued.

"Harry and I... we were intimate," Maria confessed, her eyes sparkling with emotion.

Samantha's face lit up with excitement. "Oh my gosh, Maria! I'm so happy for you two!"

"I can't stop thinking about him and how he makes me feel," Maria admitted, a dreamy look on her face. "We're so lucky to have met these amazing brothers. Our lives have forever changed since that day."

"Absolutely," Samantha agreed, grinning. "Best friends, sisters, and one day, sisters-in-law."

The spring semester soon came to an end, marking the conclusion of their junior year. Both Samantha and Maria were thrilled to be spending the summer in California. Harry and Stan shared an apartment in downtown San Francisco, and Maria and Samantha arrived the first week of June, filled with anticipation.

"Welcome to San Francisco!" Harry greeted them warmly, pulling Maria into a tight hug.

Stan smiled at Samantha. "We've been counting down the days until you got here."

One evening, Stan and Samantha decided to go out to dinner, leaving Harry and Maria alone.

"Enjoy your night out!" Maria called after them as they left.

As soon as the door closed, Harry turned to Maria with a mischievous grin. "I have a surprise for you," he said, starting to unbutton her clothes.

"Lead the way," Maria whispered, her heart racing.

Harry led Maria to his room, where rose petals were scattered everywhere. Maria's eyes widened in awe.

"Harry, you're so romantic. I can't imagine my life without you. You are my soulmate; you complete me and hold the key to my heart," she said, her voice filled with emotion.

"Maria, you are so special and the love I thought I would never find," Harry responded, his eyes reflecting his deep feelings for her.

They made love many times that evening, savoring every moment together.

"Harry, you are absolutely amazing. I never knew I could feel so loved and cherished," Maria murmured, resting her head on his chest as they finally fell asleep in the early morning hours.

During the days, Stan and Harry went to work, while Maria and Samantha cleaned the apartment and prepared dinner for their return.

"This is a glimpse of what married life will be like," Samantha mused one day as they set the table.

"Yeah, I can't wait to be Harry's wife," Maria replied, smiling.

In the afternoons, Maria and Samantha often went shopping, spending quality time together. They also grew closer to Stan and Harry's parents, cherishing the bond they formed over the summer.

"Your parents are wonderful," Samantha remarked to Stan during a family dinner. "I feel like I'm part of the family already."g

"They adore you," Stan replied, squeezing her hand.

As summer came to an end, it was time to return to school. They spent many hours discussing their future plans.

"Samantha, what are your plans after graduation?" Maria asked one evening.

"I plan on coming back to California, finding a job, and living with Stan," Samantha replied confidently.

"I'm hoping to stay in the Midwest to be near my family, especially my grandpa," Maria said. "I want to find a job there, and I'm hoping Harry will be able to find a position so we can move in together."

"We'll make it work, Maria," Samantha reassured her. "No matter where we end up, we'll always be best friends and sisters."

Maria nodded, feeling a sense of comfort. "You're right, Samantha. We'll always be there for each other."

The last year of school was the easiest of all the years. They were excited to start their career as registered nurses. Graduation was upon them. All of Samantha's family and Maria's family attended their pinning ceremony and the commencement. It was so hard to believe that four years had passed. Samantha and Maria were best friends and sisters, and they knew that they would miss each other terribly, but they would keep in contact daily. Stan proposed to Samantha in front of her family, and everyone was so excited for the upcoming wedding. Summer 1981 was upon them with so many exciting things to come in the future.

CHAPTER 12-

In the summer of 1979, Marissa had graduated from her MBA program. Alberto had taken 2 months off from school, planning to return in the middle of August. Marissa had quit her job at the restaurant, opting to search for new employment in the fall. Alberto was thrilled that she was taking a break for the summer. Being prudent with her finances, Marissa had saved a significant amount of money, so quitting her job for the summer posed no financial burden. Deciding to forego any classes during the break, Alberto chose to spend the entire summer with her. He stayed at Marissa's apartment, giving them a taste of what married life could be like. Their intimacy deepened frequently, and Marissa marveled at how fortunate she was to have met Alberto in Mexico. However, Dorothy disapproved of him living there over the summer. She spoke with Anne almost daily, struggling with the guilt of hiding this arrangement from her. One morning, a week into their vacation, Alberto sprung a surprise on Marissa.

"Marissa, I have a surprise."

"I booked a trip for us to Europe for 5 weeks, and we leave in a week."

"Oh, that is so exciting."

"I am going to show you around Europe."

"I can't believe you had time to plan our trip with how busy you have been. What countries are we going to visit?

"Italy, France, Greece, and England. I am so excited and can't wait. I will need to buy some new clothes before we leave."

"I will take you shopping tomorrow."

"There are no words to describe how much I love you. You are too good to be real. You are so considerate, handsome, and an amazing soul. You are my soul mate and my everything."

The following day, they went shopping, and both purchased new clothes for their trip. Marissa adored shopping with Alberto as he was always so complimentary and had impeccable taste in fashion. She eagerly anticipated their marriage, wondering how she would endure the wait until he completed his residency.

They packed their clothes and headed to the San Francisco Airport, brimming with excitement. Having traveled to Europe multiple times before, Alberto was set to be an excellent tour guide. They flew to New York, enduring a three-hour layover before their flight to Rome was called for boarding. Marissa was amazed at the size of the aircraft—a new 747—towering and majestic, ready to whisk them across the ocean.

During their flight, Marissa and Alberto discussed their future plans in depth. She had decided she wanted to pursue a career as an office manager for a large family practice, believing that this experience would prepare her to manage Alberto's practice once he was ready to establish it. Alberto cherished the idea of them working together as a married couple, though he cautioned that the next five years would be hectic and demanding. They talked excitedly, their voices mixing with the hum of the plane as they flew toward new adventures, their future together unfolding before them.

"I will be finishing medical school and then be an intern and a resident."

"Oh Alberto, I don't like to think about those years. I am afraid I will miss you so much and it will make me sad. I just want to focus on this amazing vacation we are embarking on and how awesome you are."

"Sure honey. No, I am the lucky one. You are so sweet, caring, authentic and my soul mate." They had a delicious lunch, which made them both sleepy. They both fell asleep for a couple of hours. They awaken to the pilot saying,

"Put your seat belts on. We will be landing shortly." The plane landed, and the trip of a lifetime began for Marissa and Alberto. They deplaned and went to get their suitcases from the luggage carousel. They walked out and caught a cab.

"We are going to the Hotel Eden."

When they drove up, Marissa was amazed at how beautiful the hotel was, and that they would stay for a week in Rome. Alberto liked the first-class accommodations, and so did Marissa. They both agreed on almost everything, and it seemed to be a match made in heaven.

The bellman brought their suitcases to the room, and Alberto tipped him. The room was stunning and had a large tiled hot tub in the middle of it. Marissa started unpacking and hanging both her and Alberto's clothes up. Alberto started kissing Marissa and took her clothes off and his, too.

They filled the hot tub and got in. The warm water was so relaxing after the long trip. They kissed and made love in the hot tub two times.

"Alberto, you are amazing; where do you get all your energy."

"Looking at you just sparks my flame. I can't get enough of you." He carried her to the bed, and they were intimate one more time. They both felt asleep naked in each other arms.

The next morning, they both woke up around 10 am. They would be in Rome for a week and needed to plan their sightseeing activities. On the first day, they went to the Colosseum and Palatine Hill (an ancient part of the city, one of the seven hills). They went to Monti for an authentic Italian lunch. The food was out of this world. Marissa thought that her clothes wouldn't fit her soon. Everything shut down for two or three hours in the afternoon, around two or three in the afternoon. Marissa and Alberto decided to return to their room and nap.

They napped for two hours and then decided to get up and have dinner. They went to the Via del Corso for some shopping and to buy some souvenirs before dinner. They had dinner and were exhausted from the time change, so they went back to their room. They soaked in the hot tub, and then they had a night of passion. They both seemed like they couldn't keep their hands off each other. Life could not be better.

The next day they set out to the Trevi Fountain and the Spanish steps. Marissa felt she was living a dream as she was in Europe with the man she loved. She kept thinking, how did I get so lucky.

The week went by quickly, but they saw so many tourist sites and some off-the-beaten-path sites that only Italians usually visit. The last day in Rome was Sunday and they went to the Vatican to see the Pope. They were both Catholics so this is a very special day. They stood among all the other tourists and then the Pope started Mass. At the end of Mass, the Pope came out and mingled with his followers. Marissa and Alberto were very close to the Pope and he blessed them both. This was one day that neither one of them would ever forget.

The next day, they were to board the train to Venice, which would take about four hours. The high-speed train had just started running a few months ago. The scenery was so beautiful through the countryside. They passed through Florence, Bologna, and the regions of Lazio, Umbria, and Tuscany. They arrived at the Venice train station around 10:30 am. They decided to walk on the Grand Canal and had some lunch before checking into their hotel. They had pizza for lunch and walked to their hotel, which was the Hotel Danieli, which overlooked the Grand Canal. Marissa couldn't believe what a gorgeous hotel they would be staying in for a week.

They went to their room and unpacked their belongings.

"You just amaze me, Alberto. You have thought of everything."

"I wanted this to be a special trip for us. I have been to Europe several times and wanted to share some of my favorite places with you."

"The hotel is magnificent and right on the Grand Canal."

"I thought we could have this as our home base for the week and venture out to different cities from here."

"Oh, it sounds glorious to me."Marissa started kissing Alberto passionately, and she started to unzip his pants.

"Guess what I am thinking. Oh, I am so turned on by looking at my awesome, sexy, and handsome boyfriend. I don't have any panties on."

"Now you don't have any clothes on." Their night of intimacy was way beyond any night of passion that they had previously experienced.

"I could lay next to you with our naked bodies rubbing against each other for hours. I was shy when we first met, but I feel so loved and treasured and definitely coming out of my shell."

"When we are affectionate, let me know what you like. This is where you are safe and can say anything, honey."

"Oh, I know Alberto. You are amazing, and I can't wait to be your wife. I can't wait till we have a family. You are going to make the best Dad ever."

"Thank you. Marissa, you are going to make the sweetest mother ever."

"Alberto, I just want to lay next to you for a while." Alberto rubbed her thighs and kissed her on the neck. They continued their night of passion, and sometime during the night, they fell asleep.

The next morning, they woke up and realized that they never left the room the night before.

"Alberto, that was the most amazing night ever."

"I never knew how connected and spiritual you can feel when inside the woman that you love so much."

"Do you want to take a shower together? I love soaping your sexy body."

"Of course, honey."

They were both ready for the day. They decided to visit the Rialto Bridge, St Mark's Square, St Mark's Cathedral, and Doge Palace and take a canal ride. They did so much walking that they both had huge appetites. They ate dinner at the hotel and were both exhausted after eating. They went back to their room and fell asleep immediately.

They woke up in the morning, and Marissa said,

"You know sweetheart sometimes I think I am in the middle of a dream. I wake up and see this gorgeous man with his arms around me. I think, how can I be so lucky? You are handsome, considerate, sweet, and the best lover ever. Sometimes, I am afraid I will wake up and find out this is all a dream."

"No, Marissa, this is as real as it gets. I love you so much. I could sing it off rooftops."

"You are so romantic, Alberto. You give me goosebumps. I love you so much, Alberto, and never knew a love so deep is possible."

"Marissa, just talking like this is such a turn-on. We have all day and I want to give you so more loving this morning."

"Oh, Alberto, that sounds amazing. I love you inside of me more than I can ever express." They had an awesome morning filled with so much passion.

"Alberto, you are more than the total package and always want to find ways to please me. I never imagined I could love someone as much as I love you. I have completely fallen for you. You are the first thing I think of in the morning, the last thing I think about at night, and I think about you all day."

"Marissa, I know you would like to get married sooner than later, but I need to finish medical school. You would be a beautiful distraction."

"Oh, Alberto, I completely understand, and sometimes in life, the best things you have to wait for, and that statement can be no truer than in this situation. I just want you to know how much I want to be your wife."

"Well, Marissa, I know, and I can't wait to marry you too."

They left the room and tried to figure out where to go for dinner. They walked around the canal shops and had dinner. They went back to their hotel suite and planned their sightseeing for the next four days. They went to Florence, Pisa, and Tuscany. They had an awesome time in Venice and the surrounding area and are now off to Paris.

They were going by train to Paris from Venice. They would need to make one transfer to France. Marissa and Alberto enjoyed the spectacular view of the French countryside. They ate lunch in the dining car and returned to their seats for a nap. The train approached the Paris metro station. It was time to disembark the train and explore Paris. They hailed a cab, and Alberto said,

"We would like to go to the InterContinental Paris Le Grand Hotel."

"Sure," stated the cab driver.

They arrived at the hotel, a majestic-looking hotel that opened in 1862. Marissa had taken French classes in high school. She was so happy to see all the famous places she had learned about in school. They stayed in Paris for a week. They visited the Eiffel Tower, Louvre Museum, Notre Dame Cathedral, Palace of Versailles, Champs de Elysees, and the Arc de Triomphe. Marissa found Paris to be such a romantic city. They ate fabulous pastries and had the time of their life. One evening, they went and saw the Moulin Rouge. They loved Paris so much they really didn't want to leave, but it was time to head to Athens.

They took a cab to the Charles de Gaulle airport and were on a TWA flight that left in two hours. Marissa knew less about Greece than she did about Italy and France. The plane landed after they had flown for four hours. She had bought a book about Greece at the airport and read it on the flight. They were staying at the Hilton Hotel Athens.

When they arrived at the airport, Marissa noticed that everyone in Greece had dark hair, which made her and Alberto blend seamlessly into the local crowd. They decided to stay in their hotel room that evening and order room service, craving some quiet and affectionate time together. Alberto undressed to his briefs while Marissa opted for her bra and panties. They cuddled up for a two-hour nap, recharging after their journey.

Upon waking, they ordered dinner, dressing again before the food arrived. Alberto had arranged for fresh red roses to be placed on the table, adding a touch of romance to their evening. After they finished eating, Alberto cleared the table and turned to Marissa with a playful grin. "Oh, good looking. What do you have planned?" Marissa asked, her voice tinged with excitement and curiosity. "I am going to take you on an adventure of a lifetime, and hopefully, we will have a night we will never forget," Alberto replied. His words sparked a wave of anticipation in Marissa.

Alberto began by kissing Marissa tenderly on every inch of her body, heightening the intimacy of their connection. He then took some massage oil and began to sensuously massage it all over her body. Marissa, feeling the sensual tension rise, reciprocated by massaging Alberto with the same oil. They continued this passionate affection for over an hour, each moment deepening their bond and affection. The night evolved into one of profound passion; their lovemaking was both gentle and fervent, a perfect reflection of their deep emotional connection. They discovered new depths of their relationship, each touch and whisper adding layers to their love. They finally drifted off to sleep around four in the morning, utterly content and intertwined.

The following morning, refreshed yet still basking in the afterglow of their romantic night, they decided it was time to explore Athens. They visited the Acropolis, wandered through the Acropolis Museum, admired the Parthenon, and explored the temple of Zeus. They even embarked on two boat excursions, visiting two of the Greek Isles, fully immersing themselves in the beauty and history of Greece.

As their time in Athens concluded, they boarded a plane for London. The four-hour flight passed quickly, and soon they were navigating through Heathrow Airport. They checked into the Four Seasons London at Hyde Park, a plush hotel that promised a luxurious stay. Over the next five days, they toured the iconic sights of London—the Tower of London, Buckingham Palace, the Natural History Museum, Tower Bridge, and Big Ben. Each landmark visit filled Marissa with joy, especially Buckingham Palace, as she had always been fascinated by the royal family.

It was their last night in Europe. This had been a trip for the storybooks in Marissa's eyes. She had come to know Alberto even better, and he was even more charming and sweet as time went on. They had a lavish dinner that night and then headed to their room early. They packed and will have to be at the airport by five in the morning for their flight home.

They were at Heathrow Airport three hours before their flight. There were so many people already in line so early in the morning. They boarded their plane for San Francisco, which would be around a twelve-hour flight. The flight was smooth, and they took a couple of naps. Marissa said,

"Alberto, I don't even know how to thank you for the most amazing trip of a lifetime. I can't believe all that we explored in five weeks. Thank you for making me the happiest woman on the planet. I feel so close to you and can't wait to spend the rest of my life with you."

"Believe me, Marissa, you gave it to me in ways I could never have imagined. I love you for all eternity, and our love will continue to grow. I want you to remember when we can't be together how much I love you. I never want you to forget that. I love you more than you will ever know."

They arrived back at the San Francisco International Airport and hailed a cab back to Marissa's apartment. They both called their parents and let them know they were home safe, and told them all about their trip. Alberto had one more week that he could spend at Marissa's, and then he would start school, and Marissa would look for a job. They made more cherished memories that week. It was going to be very difficult when Alberto left, but the time had come, and he was going back to his parent's house in Hillsborough and starting school in the morning.

Marissa sat in her apartment alone, wondering if everything that had happened was just a dream. But no, it was her real life, and this was what she had to look forward to when they were married. She knew she needed to be supportive of Alberto's schooling and find ways to keep herself occupied.

Alberto returned to school for his third year, which, along with the next, would be spent in the hospital on various rotations. He was excited to care for patients and apply the knowledge he had acquired. His rotations included Emergency Medicine, Internal Medicine, Neurology, Pediatrics, Psychiatry, Surgery, and Women's Health, starting with Internal Medicine. Alberto loved being a medical student in the hospital environment; he found it challenging and rewarding, and he felt he was exactly where he needed to be in life. He was also pleased that he had waited until the age of twenty-six to start medical school. He missed Marissa deeply but knew it would be worth it in the end.

Marissa decided that the first thing she needed to do was update her resume. She took it to a certified professional resume writer to have it professionally created. Excited about getting a new job but missing Alberto intensely, she researched all the Internal Medicine offices that had advertised for an office manager. She sent her resume and cover letter to five offices and waited to hear back. Marissa received responses from two offices and went on to interview with both. One of the offices called her back for a second interview. This office was large, with nine Primary Care Physicians and thirty-three staff members. The physicians were impressed with Marissa, and she felt that this would be a great place to work. They offered her the job, and she accepted.

Eager to share her good news, Marissa decided to call Alberto.

"How are you honey?"

"I am good and love my clinical rotation. It is so stimulating, and I love working with the patients."

"I knew you would love your clinical. You are going to make an amazing doctor. I have something to tell you. I got the position of Office Manager for an office with nine Primary Care Physicians in the City. The doctors were all so nice. I think it will be a great fit for me."

"Congratulations, Marissa. I am so happy for you. I love you and miss you so much."

"Thank you, Alberto. I love you and miss you so much, too."

"When do you start?

"I start on Monday."

"I am so excited for you. I am going to have to go. One of the other students is asking for some help with her patient. I will talk to you soon."

"Sure honey, bye."

"Bye"

Marissa called her parents next with the exciting news. They both were so thrilled for her. She went shopping and bought herself several new business outfits for work. Marissa started on Monday and loved her new position. She had a tremendous amount to learn, but she did an amazing job. All the employees seemed very happy that Marissa was their new manager. She conducted frequent staff meetings so she could learn the workings of the office. Sometimes, especially on Fridays, she went out with her coworkers for drinks and dinner. The fall in San Francisco had gorgeous weather, and she loved her life. The only thing missing was Alberto.

It was now December 1979, and Alberto had just a few days off from school until his next semester began. He came to Marissa's apartment on Christmas Eve. They hadn't seen each other for quite a while. They exchanged gifts and had a romantic evening filled with lots of lovemaking. They went to Alberto's parents for Christmas. On New Year's Eve, they decided to stay in and watch the celebration on television. They had a very romantic nine days, and then Alberto returned to school.

The year was 1980, filled with much learning for both of them. Alberto was learning how to do patient assessments and so many other skills. Marissa was learning all the skills necessary to run the office. She absolutely loved her job and loved teaching and directing others. She hired and trained all the new employees. She had definitely found her niche.

As 1981 approached, Alberto was in his final year of medical school. Time seemed to have flown by incredibly fast. Marissa and Alberto had struggled to see each other as often as they would have liked throughout the year. Alberto applied to several programs for his Internship and Residency, causing Marissa great worry that he might have to leave the area. However, relief washed over both of them when he was accepted into the program at Stanford. With the pressure of his medical boards looming, Alberto was buried in his studies, anticipating his graduation in June.

The day of Alberto's graduation from medical school finally arrived. Anne and Dave joined to celebrate his milestone. Marissa swelled with pride over his achievements. Following the commencement, Dorothy and Tony hosted a large celebration at their house. While Marissa had met most of his family previously, she was excited to meet the remaining members. The party, complete with a catered meal and a live band in the backyard, turned into a memorable occasion. Amidst the festivities, Alberto had planned a special moment. In front of both families, he dropped to one knee and proposed to Marissa.

"You taught me the meaning of love. You bring out the best in me. I never knew I could love someone as much as I love you. Please make me the happiest man on this planet. Will you marry me?"

"Yes, yes!" Marissa exclaimed.

Both families erupted in joy, having grown close over the years, and were thrilled about the upcoming union. Tears of joy streamed down Dorothy and Anne's faces. Marissa gazed down at her engagement ring, stunned by its beauty. Alberto had now become an MD and was engaged to the woman of his dreams. Shortly after, he received the fantastic news that he had passed his medical boards. Life couldn't be any sweeter, and there were so many beautiful things to look forward to.

CHAPTER 13-

It was the summer of 1981, and both Samantha and Maria had graduated from nursing school. Samantha was preparing to move to San Francisco to live with Stan. She planned to take the nursing boards in California and then seek a nursing position.

Meanwhile, Harry had been secretly searching for a job in either Des Moines, Iowa, or Chicago. He wanted to surprise Maria with his plans. After a successful job hunt, he secured a position as a supervisor at a firm in Des Moines, complete with a great salary and excellent benefits. The firm was very impressed with Harry's skills. He hoped that Maria could find a nursing position in Des Moines so they could move in together. He was set to start his new role on July 1st.

Deciding it was time to share the exciting news, Harry called Maria.

"Hi Maria," he greeted.

"Hi babe. How are you?" Maria responded with a smile.

"I am beyond good," Harry replied, his voice bubbling with excitement.

"Wow, that sounds wonderful! What has you so excited?" Maria asked, her curiosity piqued.

"I have some great news to tell you. I just landed a supervisory position in Des Moines, starting on July 1st."

"Congratulations, Harry! Oh, my goodness, I can't believe it. This is so exciting, and I am so happy, surprised, and speechless," Maria exclaimed, her voice filled with a mix of joy and astonishment.

"I was thinking, if you can find a nursing position in Des Moines, maybe we could move in together," Harry suggested tentatively.

"Oh, that sounds incredible. I can't wait until we are together every day. Although, if I tell my parents and Grandpa about us moving in together, they won't be happy. They all love you so much, Harry, but they can't condone living together. It might sound strange, but perhaps I could get my own apartment close to yours, and we could still be together. We'll need to discuss this more later," Maria reasoned, her voice tinged with a hint of concern.

"Maria, I do understand, and I don't want you to upset your parents and Grandpa," Harry reassured her.

"When are you planning on coming out here? You can stay at our house until you find an apartment. Des Moines is about forty-five minutes from our house, so it's not that far. The traffic in Iowa is much less than in California. My family would love for you to stay with us," Maria offered warmly.

"Thank you, Maria. My last day at my current job is Friday, June 11th. I'll get a trailer, pack all my things, and probably leave San Francisco around June 14th. Then I'll drive to your house. I'm not sure how many days it will take to get there, but I am so excited," Harry shared, his voice filled with anticipation.

"I can't wait to tell my family. I'm studying for the nursing boards, which I'll be taking on July 15th," Maria added.

"You will do well, Maria. You are so smart," Harry complimented.

"Thank you, Harry. I'm going to start looking for nursing positions in Des Moines."

"Well, I'm going to let you go, honey. We'll talk soon," Harry said, preparing to end the call.

"Love you so much. Bye," Maria said affectionately.

"Bye, babe. Love you," Harry replied, and they both hung up, their hearts full of excitement and plans for the future.

Maria was so excited and happy. She told her family that Harry had landed a job in Des Moines, and they were all so thrilled. She told them that he should arrive June 18th or 19th. Her parents were fine with him staying at their house till he found an apartment. They offered since they have room in their house that he could stay in definitely. Maria thanked her parents for such a generous offer and told them she would ask him. Maria really appreciated her parents' offer, but they were ready to be on their own. She told them that he wouldn't be far away and could come to her house on weekends. They didn't know that Maria was planning on hopefully finding a position in Des Moines and living there, too.

Harry arrived at the Hernandez house with a large trailer attached to his car with all his possessions. The family was so delighted that Harry was staying with them, especially Grandpa. Maria felt awful that she needed to study for her nursing boards, but Harry spent much of the time with Grandpa.

On the weekend Maria and Harry drove to Des Moines so he could find where his job was located. It took them exactly forty-five minutes to get there. Maria and Harry hadn't had any alone time since he arrived. They couldn't wait to be alone together. They told Maria's parents that they would stay overnight and look at apartments on Sunday. After finding where his job was located, then they checked into the Hilton hotel. They put their belongings down and started taking off their clothes. Maria remembered that wonderful time they spent in San Francisco in the summer of 1980 and had been dreaming of the day they could be back in each other's arms. Harry says,

"Your curvy body drives me crazy. Your soft skin, gorgeous eyes, and luscious lips are such a turn-on."

"Your muscular, toned body makes me tingle. I have never felt anything like this before. I just want you inside me now." They went on to have a steamy night of passion. Maria couldn't believe how much she and Harry had connected after taking their relationship to the next level. She felt that was a good decision. She knew her parents and Grandpa would totally disapprove.

They woke up the next morning, lying next to each and Harry was ready for more lovemaking. Maria said;

"Guess what I am thinking?"

"Oh Maria, you don't know how this makes me feel." They really didn't want to leave but must check out by 12 pm. They checked out and then went to hotel's Sunday brunch. They both have worked up a great appetite. After brunch, they looked at available apartments. Harry said;

"Maria, I really want us to live together, and we can have nights like last night all the time."

"I do too for sure Harry. My plan if I can find a nursing position, I am moving to Des Moines too." They drove back to Maria's house and told the family all about the weekend.

It was now July 1ˢᵗ at 6:30 am and the day Harry started his new job. Maria woke up to wish Harry good luck on his first day and to make him breakfast. Maria said,

"They will be so impressed with you. I can't wait to hear all about it. "

"Thank you, Maria. I will miss you today."

"I will miss you too, but I am studying all day. Love you, and drive carefully."

"Love you too. See you tonight."

"Ok and have a great day."

"Thank you."

Maria started studying and just couldn't stop thinking about Harry and how he made her feel. She couldn't imagine being loved so much. It was 6 pm and there came Harry.

The family gathered around Harry to find out how he liked his first day at his new job. Harry told everyone that he would be managing a department with twenty-three employees. Everyone was so welcoming, and he will be in training for the next two weeks. He admired the company and felt that it would be a good fit for him. Maria was thrilled that he was so happy.

Maria has two weeks until she takes her boards. She studied during the day so she could spend the evening with Harry. Harry was so comfortable at the Hernandez house that he had put off looking for an apartment for the time being.

It was the morning of Maria's nursing boards, and they were scheduled in an auditorium in downtown Des Moines. Maria was driving into the city with Harry. He wished her good luck on her test and told her she would ace it. Maria arrived early and waited for the doors to open. When the doors opened, she went in and registered and then took a seat. There were so many people taking the test, but they were from throughout the whole state. Maria took some deep breaths as they passed out the test. They started the test and had four hours till the lunch break. She found some questions challenging but just needed to remain calm and focused. During the lunch break, Maria went to lunch with three others, taking the test. They were all familiar with the hospitals in Des Moines and told Maria about all the hospitals. After lunch, they went back to finish their exam. Maria finished before many of the other candidates. She felt fairly confident, but you just never know the outcome until you get the results. Harry was waiting for her as she exited the building. They were going to dinner to celebrate. Throughout dinner, they talked about their future plans. Maria told Harry that she talked with some of the other candidates, and she thought she knew which hospital she was hoping she would be able to find a position as a new graduate. Harry and Maria felt that things were coming together and would work out the way they had planned.

They arrived back at Maria's house and her whole family was waiting to hear about the exam. She told them that she felt well prepared, but you just never know till the results would be back. They all told her that they would pray that she passes. Harry excused himself as he has to be up in the morning for work.

The next morning Maria called Samantha and told her about the exam. Samantha had taken her boards the previous week. They discussed where they both were going to look for a nursing position. Maria told Samantha she would apply at Iowa Methodist Medical Center, which was a teaching hospital and would be a great learning experience. Samantha told Maria that she was hoping to get into preceptor program at UCSF in San Francisco for new graduates. They went on to discuss Samantha and Stan's wedding, which would be in May of the next year. Maria would be the maid of honor and Harry the best man. They both were so excited and were waiting to hear back about state boards, both looked for their first nursing position and then of course the wedding. Maria and Samantha talked every day on the phone and both are thrilled about their futures.

Harry had decided to stay at the Hernandez house till Maria found a nursing position. Harry loved his new job and Maria loved that he came home to her every night. Grandpa was so ecstatic to have Harry back in the house. They were always talking about all the things that they have in common, and it reminded them of their time in California.

Maria applied to the new graduate program at Iowa Methodist Medical Center in Des Moines and was accepted. She would start on Monday October 5th, 1981. She had accepted a hospital float position on the evening shift, where she would work throughout the hospital. Samantha had also accepted a position at the University of California, San Francisco on the medical surgical floor for the evening shift.

Throughout the summer Maria spent a significant amount of time with her sisters and Grandpa. They went for long walks, swimming and play volleyball. She also took them all out to lunch several times during the summer. She took her sisters out shopping for new school clothes and bought herself several nursing uniforms so she would be ready to start work. Maria and Grandpa cooked dinner every night and had it ready when her parents and Harry were home from work. Maria was so happy to be back home and spend time with her family.

In early August, Maria and Harry discussed their future living arrangements. They wanted to move in together but were concerned about her parents' likely objections. They decided to seek Grandpa's approval first, hoping he could help persuade her parents that it made sense for safety reasons.

The following morning, the mail arrived early, bringing a letter from the Iowa Nursing Board for Maria. She fetched Grandpa to join her as she opened it.

"Maria, open the letter. I can't wait," Grandpa urged, his excitement palpable.

"Grandpa, I passed with good scores!" Maria exclaimed, her voice trembling with relief and joy.

"Congratulations, Maria. I knew you could do it. You are an RN now. We have an RN in our family. I am so proud of you," Grandpa beamed, his eyes twinkling with pride.

"Thank you, Grandpa." Maria then shared the news with her sisters, called Harry, her parents, and Samantha. That evening, they celebrated with a dinner ordered from a restaurant and a cake that read "Congratulations Maria Hernandez RN." The entire family was thrilled for Maria.

The next evening, Harry spoke with Grandpa about his concerns for Maria working the evening shift and driving home late at night. Grandpa agreed that it was best for Maria to live in Des Moines and suggested they share an apartment to ensure her safety. He didn't like the idea of her living alone in the big city.

On Friday night, Maria and Harry went to the movies, giving Grandpa the perfect opportunity to discuss with Ethel and Raymond the possibility of Maria and Harry moving in together. Initially resistant, Maria's parents were eventually persuaded by Grandpa's arguments that Maria would be safer living with Harry than alone.

The following evening at dinner, with only Maria, Harry, Grandpa, Ethel, and Raymond at the table, they gave Maria and Harry their blessings to move in together in Des Moines.

"Thank you, and I will take such good care of Maria. You have nothing to worry about," Harry assured them earnestly.

"We know she is in good hands with you, Harry," Raymond replied, his tone filled with trust and gratitude.

"Thank you, Mom, Dad, and Grandpa. You are the best," Maria said, her voice choked with emotion.

The next weekend, Maria and Harry went apartment hunting and settled on a place close to Maria's new job. They signed the lease and planned to move in on Tuesday, September 15th. On move-in day, Harry took the day off work to load the rental truck while Maria prepared to drive his car. Raymond, Grandpa, and both of Maria's sisters helped with the move. The family adored the modern, newly updated apartment. After unloading the last box, they all went out for a celebratory dinner at a country buffet, exhausted yet animated with lively conversation. After saying their goodbyes, Maria and Harry returned to their new apartment, eager to begin their life together.

Maria and Harry entered their apartment and were greeted by the sight of all the boxes waiting to be unpacked. The reality of their new life together filled them with a mix of excitement and overwhelming joy.

"I have my work cut out for me. I want this place organized before I start my job in two weeks."

"Don't worry honey, we can do it on the weekend where I can help."

"I will do what I can, and the rest we can do over the weekend."

They made the bed and both decided they were exhausted and were ready to sleep. Maria and Harry were both so happy, and they both fell asleep quickly. The next day, Maria organized the kitchen and went to the grocery store. She cooked a delicious dinner and then they cuddled on the couch afterwards. Over the next 2 weeks the apartment came together and looked like a model apartment.

On October 1st, Maria started her job as an RN. She was in orientation for two weeks on the day shift. She was so excited and couldn't believe the day was there. She looked so cute in her nursing uniform. Harry made them both breakfast. Her orientation was from nine to five, the same hours Harry worked, so they drove together. When Maria was exiting the car, Harry said,

"Good luck, Maria. You will impress everyone with your kindness, thoughtfulness, and your beautiful spirit. Those are some lucky patients having you for a nurse."

"Thank you, Harry, I will miss you today. Love you, Maria."

"Love you, Harry. See you here at 5:15 pm.

Harry was waiting for Maria when she left the hospital.

"Hi babe, how was your day?"

"There are ten RNs in my orientation, and everyone is so nice. Today, we went over the hospital policies and expectations, etc. Tomorrow, we start the skills lab on the mannequin, such as starting IVs, giving injections, drawing blood, placing NG and Foley catheters,"

"Sounds amazing. You will do well, Maria. You got this."

"Thank you, honey, for all the love and support. Love you, Harry."

"Love you, Maria. Where do you want to eat?"

"How about Mexican food."

"I know the perfect place around the corner." They sat and ate a delicious dinner and had a wonderful conversation. Maria was starving after her busy day at work.

They arrived back at their apartment, and Maria took a shower. Harry undressed and lay down in bed. Maria came out in a beautiful, sexy nightgown. She lay next to Harry on the bed, and they started kissing passionately and had an ultimate night of passion. Maria and Harry were so happy that they convinced Grandpa and her parents to let them live together.

Maria had completed her orientation and was starting her Monday afternoon as a 3-11 float nurse. Her first assignment was on the maternity floor, surrounded by newborns, which excited her immensely. With five patients under her care and a designated nurse available for any questions, her night progressed smoothly, filled with valuable learning experiences. Every shift brought a new assignment, sometimes returning to familiar units, other times exploring new ones. Her first week affirmed her decision to be a float nurse, convinced that this role would greatly enhance her knowledge across various specialties.

The weekend arrived, and both Maria and Harry were off work. With every other weekend free, Maria cherished these moments. Harry, sensing an opportunity for intimacy, asked, "What do you want to do this Saturday?"

"You know what I was thinking," Maria replied with a mischievous grin.

"What are you thinking?" Harry inquired, intrigued.

"I thought maybe we could slip out of our night clothes and just stay home, have a party on our couch," Maria suggested, her voice dripping with anticipation.

"Sounds good to me. Come over here, honey," Harry responded, his voice laden with desire. Their day of passion extended well into the night, leaving both feeling deeply connected.

"Harry, I can't believe how you make me feel, so wanted and loved, as if there's no one else in the world," Maria confessed, her voice soft and earnest.

"For me, there is no one else. Love you, Maria," Harry declared, his words firm and sincere.

"Love you, Harry," Maria echoed, her heart swelling with love.

As the months passed, Maria grew more adept and confident as an RN. She would return home each night and recount her experiences to Harry, while also connecting with Samantha each morning to discuss their respective shifts. They provided each other with unwavering support, more like sisters than friends. Maria had the opportunity to work in almost every unit except labor and delivery, finding a particular affinity for the ICU/CCU, where the patient load was smaller and the learning immense. She also enjoyed the unpredictability of the ER.

As the holiday season gave way to the new year, 1982 approached with Valentine's Day just around the corner. Harry planned a special trip to New York for Maria's 26th birthday, her first time on the East Coast. They took an early morning flight, landing at Kennedy International Airport by nine. After a cab ride to Central Park and a fulfilling breakfast at a nearby restaurant, they checked into the iconic Park Central Hotel, a staple of the roaring twenties.

Their days were filled with sightseeing, exploring the myriad of attractions New York had to offer. On Valentine's Day, after a special lunch celebrating Maria's birthday, they returned to their room for a brief nap, only to venture out again in the evening. At the Empire State Building, with a breathtaking view of the city below, Harry proposed.

"Maria, happy birthday, honey! I never thought I'd find someone as special as you. You are beautiful, sweet, caring, and my soulmate. I love you more than you will ever know. I want to wake up every day next to you. Life would have no meaning without you. Will you marry me, Maria?" Harry's voice trembled with emotion as he spoke.

"Yes, yes, yes! I love you so much. I can't wait to be your wife," Maria responded, tears of joy streaming down her cheeks.

The engagement ring sparkled magnificently. Maria was overjoyed, her smile beaming as they walked around the city, eventually stopping to share a piece of chocolate cake with vanilla ice cream.

"Harry, you don't know how happy you made me today. You are the love of my life, and I can't wait to be your wife," Maria said, her voice filled with happiness and love.

"Maria, I am the lucky one. I will always treasure you and do my best to make you happy," Harry replied, his voice filled with conviction and love.

"I know you will, you are my best friend, lover, and my everything, Harry," Maria concluded, her words echoing the depth of their bond as they continued their celebration into the night.

They walked back to their hotel room. Once inside you could see they both had the same thing on their mind. Maria and Harry both undressed for sleep. Maria put on a sexy nightgown, and Harry said,

"Maria, I am so happy that you like to be playful too! I just love you so much and hope you know that I do. I want to make you happy just as much as you do me."

"Please tell me anything you like. I feel safe and loved with you." They started kissing and had a steamy night of passion. Maria felt closer to Harry and wanted to show him how much she loved him. Maria never thought that sparks could fly so much, and she felt like firecrackers were going off in her head. They finally fell asleep early in the morning. They woke up in the late morning and continued their lovemaking. Maria could never imagine a better lover than Harry.

They spent two more days in New York, doing more sightseeing and eating at fancy restaurants. When they returned home, Maria couldn't wait to tell everybody her good news. Her family and friends were so excited for both of them. Maria's parents wanted to give them an Engagement party in the upcoming summer.

Spring flew by. Maria loved her job and learned so much every day. She liked working in the ICU/CCU/ER and the Maternity floor especially. She was happy that she was a float so she could learn about all the different areas that she could specialize in.

Samantha and Stan's wedding was coming up in one week. Maria had flown back to California and hosted with Samantha's Mom a bridal shower two weeks ago. There were thirty-five women at the bridal shower. It was such an opulent affair hosted at one of the downtown hotels on Union Square in San Francisco. The bridal shower was held on Friday evening and Sunday was the bachelorette party. They rented a limousine to take Samantha, her bridesmaids, and both Moms to the wine country for brunch and wine tasting for her bachelorette party. The women had such an awesome time over the weekend, one they would never forget.

Maria flew back home on Tuesday and was scheduled for work on Wednesday. She filled in Harry about the wonderful long weekend she had in California. She was exhausted from all the partying and wished she could sleep for a few days. She was back at work and felt lucky that she was assigned to the Maternity floor that evening. She had four stable patients and had a quiet evening, which didn't happen too often.

It was now Wednesday evening, the night before Harry and Maria would leave for California for Stan and Samantha's wedding. Maria was working on the Transitional step-down unit and was assigned four patients, and three were very sick. The first patient had a diagnosis of Congestive Heart Failure; his blood pressure skyrocketed, and his kidneys were shutting down with very little urine output. Maria called his physician and ended up transferring him to the ICU. Her second patient, when she did her initial assessment, had pain in his right foot, and the foot was cold with no pulses. Maria called his doctor, and he was taken to surgery for Peripheral Artery Bypass surgery for an occlusion or blockage in that leg. The ICU/CCU were full, so this patient was going to the recovery room and then would come back to TCU. The third patient was on the third-day post-op Coronary Artery Bypass and was having constant chest pain. He also had a fever, rapid heart rate, low blood pressure, and shallow, rapid breathing. Maria was worried that this patient might have sepsis, which is when harmful bacteria have entered the bloodstream and could be life-threatening. Maria called his doctor, who ordered blood cultures, and then she transferred him to the ICU, too. Her fourth patient was stable with a diagnosis of syncope, which is fainting or passing out, and she had no complaints.

Maria had so much charting to do, and when she finished, she took notes on the two patients she transferred back to the ICU. The ICU charge nurse told Maria that she had gotten both these patients here in just time. They both had tubes everywhere, and Maria was happy that they were transferred. Maria was back at TCU, and the unit secretary received a call that her patient from surgery would be back in 30 minutes. Maria had never taken care of a fresh post-op patient. Maria used the ICU flow sheet and took the patient's vital signs every 15 minutes. The surgical patient did very well and was stable. Maria's shift was almost over, and she was totally exhausted. She had another half an hour at least of charting to complete before she could leave. Maria thought she wished she was already packed, but unfortunately, that was not the case.

When Maria Opened the front door, Harry was at the door.

"I was worried if everything was okay since it was getting so late."

"I had a crazy evening at work. I had to transfer two patients to ICU and send another to surgery."

"You need to calm down Maria. You seem so anxious."

"I will make you some tea. Do you want something to eat?"

"No honey, I am not hungry, but thank you."

"I haven't packed yet."

"I know I saw that you haven't packed. Can I help you?"

"No, but thank you. I need to think about everything I need to take."

"Please let me know if I can help you with anything."

Maria finished packing, and it was almost 2 am. Maria and Harry went to sleep, and the alarm was set for 6 am. When the alarm went off, they both felt that it couldn't be the alarm already. They made it to the airport on time and made their flight to California. They both slept on the plane for almost the whole trip. The captain was on the loudspeaker saying that they were about to land and asked them to put on their seatbelts. They looked at each other and couldn't believe how well they both slept during the flight.

They deplaned, and at the arrival gate were Stan and Samantha. They were all so excited to see each other and gave each other hugs and kisses. Maria couldn't wait to tell Samantha about her last night at work. Stan and Harry, when they heard them talk about their jobs as RNs, couldn't believe the responsibility, empathy, compassion, and how it is such a rewarding career choice. They were both so very proud of all their accomplishments.

On Friday night, the rehearsal dinner took place after a wedding practice at the cathedral. Maria and Samantha, reminiscing about the fateful New Year's Eve party where they met Stan and Harry, acknowledged how their lives had been transformed from that day. They felt like sisters, soon-to-be sisters-in-law. Maria shared her joy about Samantha marrying the love of her life, and Samantha expressed her excitement about Maria and Harry's engagement.

The next morning, everyone rose early, bustling with activity from 8 a.m. A team of three stylists arrived to manage the hair and makeup for the bride, bridesmaids, and their mothers. By 11 a.m., everyone was beautifully prepared, with the wedding set to commence at 2 p.m. As Maria looked at Samantha, tears of happiness welled up, overwhelmed by the joy of the occasion. Guests began arriving at the hotel, taken to the church and back by a quaint trolley car.

At 2:10 pm, the bridesmaids gracefully made their way down the aisle, followed by Samantha, who entered the church on her father's arm. The church was filled to the brim with guests. Their vows, exchanged with deep sincerity and affection, moved many to tears, including their mothers. The priest officially presented them as Mr. and Mrs. Hayes, prompting applause and cheers from the gathered loved ones. Stan and Samantha then made their way out of the church as a married couple.

The reception was a vision of elegance with its sit-down dinner, exquisite flowers, and a band that kept the guests dancing for hours. The newlyweds planned to spend their honeymoon in Australia for two weeks. In a traditional flourish, Harry caught the garter, and Maria caught the bridal bouquet. As the couple prepared to depart for their midnight flight, they shared heartfelt goodbyes and embraces with Maria and Harry. After changing into their travel attire, Samantha and Stan left for the airport in a limousine.

Back in their hotel room, after consuming a fair amount of champagne, Maria was playful and assertive. She began to undress Harry and herself, performing a teasing strip tease. Her voice echoed loudly in the room as she repeated her words in excitement. Harry gently reminded her of their surroundings, but the night unfurled into one of deep romance. Maria lay in bed afterwards, dreaming eagerly of her own upcoming wedding day.

By the third weekend in August, it was time for Maria and Harry's engagement party. The Hernandez home was festively adorned with balloons and tables prepared for about fifty guests. Harry's parents, along with Samantha, Stan, and Samantha's grandmother, had traveled for the celebration, which lasted into the late night. Everyone marveled at how well both families meshed, having first met at Samantha and Stan's wedding.

After staying overnight at her parents' house, Maria and Harry woke to the comforting smells of brunch. Grandpa was bustling in the kitchen, preparing a feast for everyone. Harry's parents, along with Samantha, Stan, and Samantha's grandmother, joined in for the meal, enjoying a delightful afternoon together. Later, Maria and Harry drove them to the airport, exchanging warm farewells and heartfelt thanks. The weekend had been splendid, leaving everyone enriched by the joy and unity it brought.

Maria and Harry had settled into their apartment and had been so close. They did almost everything together except for work. They were so much in love with each other. They both were very playful, and on many weekend days, they preferred to stay indoors, order take-out, and watch movies while cuddling on the couch. They had also started planning their wedding, which would be on Saturday, June 23rd,1984. The wedding would be at the Church that Maria has attended since a little girl. The reception would be in a downtown hotel in their garden. They planned on inviting around 200 guests. The wedding was less than two years away. Maria and Harry were both excited and knew that there were many good things coming their way. They couldn't be happier.

Maria loved her job but decided she would like to specialize in Critical Care. She had applied for a new position in the step-down unit on the evening shift. She got the position and was to start a six-week orientation on the day shift. She was so excited to learn about this specialty. There were ten RNs in her orientation, none of whom would be in her unit. The rest of the RNs would be either in ICU or CCU. Maria loved learning about the heart. She liked interpreting Cardiac rhythm strips. The class was full of an enormous amount of information, but she thought it was presented very clearly. They learned all about the specialized equipment used in the specialty units. The two-week classroom education was over, and now it would be a four-week orientation with a preceptor on the day shift. The nurse, who was her preceptor, had worked on the unit for over 20 years. Maria asked if she could watch when different procedures were being done on the unit. Maria showed initiative, good clinical assessment skills, compassion, and love to help people. The preceptor felt Maria was a perfect fit for the unit since she was so calm. The unit was known for being chaotic, and Maria would bring some calmness to the unit. Maria was done with her orientation and would be on the evening shift next Monday.

On Monday at 2 pm, Maria was gearing up to leave for work. Filled with anticipation, she was eager to meet her new co-workers on the evening shift. Most of the RNs were young, around her age or slightly older. That evening, Maria was assigned two stable patients. She found herself frequently inquiring about the workings of the unit, trying to absorb as much information as possible. Reflecting on her first day, Maria felt confident in her decision and believed she would be content on this floor.

As June 23, 1983, rolled around, Maria realized that her wedding to Harry was exactly one year away. The proximity of the event brought a mix of excitement and nervousness. Maria, Harry, and Ethel visited the hotel to decide on the menu and wedding cake. They chose a buffet for the dinner and a lemon cake with raspberry filling, ensuring the celebration would have a touch of their favorite flavors. As the wedding approached, Maria's life became a whirlwind of activity, and she found herself spending less time with Harry due to the demands of her schedule.

In April 1984, Maria was delightfully surprised by a beautiful bridal shower organized by Samantha and her mother at her parent's house. The event was full of laughter, tears, and heartfelt conversations, leaving Maria overwhelmed with joy and gratitude for the wonderful gifts and the support of her loved ones. The excitement continued to build as Maria, along with Samantha, her sisters, and close friends from high school, planned a bachelorette party in Las Vegas. Scheduled from Thursday to Sunday, the group was set to stay at Caesars Palace, promising a weekend of unforgettable fun.

That Thursday, the excitement was palpable as everyone flew into Las Vegas and met at McCarran Airport. Their excitement was contagious; hugs and joyful cheers filled the air as they reunited. For three of them, including Maria, it was their first time in Las Vegas, and the sight of slot machines at the airport added to their astonishment. The group then piled into a limousine, which whisked them away to the hotel, passing the glittering neon signs of the Strip. After checking in and unpacking, they changed and prepared to dive into the Vegas nightlife.

Their first stop was a renowned steak and seafood restaurant, where they dined and planned out their activities for the next few days. After dinner, they returned to Caesars Palace to try their luck at the casino. Maria and several others were on a winning streak, while her sisters weren't as fortunate. Later, they visited a bar where live music set the backdrop for an impromptu dance party. When the band learned about Maria's bachelorette party, they announced it to the crowd, who applauded and cheered for the bride-to-be. The energy was infectious, and they danced until it was time to head back to their rooms, excited for what the next days would bring.

They woke up around 10 am, groggy but excited for the day. Deciding on brunch, the group was ravenous and delighted by the array of food, enjoying several Mimosas that added a cheerful buzz to their morning. Feeling stuffed and somewhat drained from the feast, they chose to spend the afternoon by the pool, laying under the sun to nap off their indulgence. As they lounged, many men glanced over, drawn by their laughter and vibrant energy. Among the admirers, two men approached and introduced themselves. While all the women were either married or in committed relationships, Kathy, a tall, blonde, and striking figure, was the exception. Finding one of the men, Rick, particularly intriguing, she invited him to join their group. Soon, Kathy and Rick wandered off to enjoy each other's company alone, spending the entire afternoon together until the pool closed.

That evening, as Friday night brought out more crowds, their adventure intensified. Their final night in Vegas was filled with laughter, dance, and memorable moments, setting the perfect tone for their departure the following Sunday. As they gathered in front of the hotel to catch a cab to the airport, they noticed Kathy was missing. Looking into the distance, they saw her bidding an emotional farewell to Rick. They then shared a cab ride to the airport, buzzing with stories from their weekend, and boarded their flights home, anticipating the upcoming wedding when they would all reunite.

Upon her return, Maria emerged from the jetway to find Harry waiting in the visitor area. Their reunion was tender, their kiss a reaffirmation of their connection. She bubbled over with stories from her weekend, and Harry listened, his joy evident in his smile, pleased that Maria and her friends had enjoyed such a fantastic time. The next adventure was his own—Harry's bachelor party in Las Vegas the following weekend. Maria, though excited for him, was also a bit anxious about what escapades might unfold.

On the following Thursday, Maria dropped Harry off at the airport. Working through the weekend, she was eager to hear about his experiences. When she picked him up on Monday, Harry shared tales of his wild weekend, including visits to a strip club that left Maria feeling a mix of amusement and relief that she'd heard enough. Despite the raucous details, she was glad Harry enjoyed his time, even as she learned about the close call two of his friends had almost missing their flight.

As the days slowly passed, anticipation built up for their own wedding. Finally, it was Friday, June 22, 1984, the evening of their rehearsal dinner. They gathered at the church first, where they practiced the ceremony, their movements and words weaving through the quiet sanctity of the space. Afterward, they moved to a nearby restaurant where laughter and light-hearted chatter filled the air. Everyone was immersed in the joy of the occasion, their hearts full of excitement and nerves for the wedding day just on the horizon.

The next morning, the hairdresser and makeup person arrived at the hotel at 8 a.m. to do Maria, Ethel, and the five bridesmaids' hair and makeup. The wedding was starting at 3 p.m. The wedding party headed to the Church in limousines around 2:30 p.m. Everyone was so excited, and Maria couldn't believe that the day was there.

Maria and her father, Raymond, positioned themselves at the entrance of the Church, ready for her grand entrance. Tears were visible on Raymond's face, a mixture of joy and nostalgia as he prepared to walk his daughter down the aisle. Maria, radiant in her exquisite wedding gown, caught Harry's gaze as she began her procession; emotion welled up in his eyes at the sight of her. The ceremony was deeply moving, accentuated by a solemn Mass where family members participated in readings, enriching the spiritual atmosphere.

The vows Maria and Harry exchanged were crafted by themselves—each word laden with love and promises for the future, stirring the hearts of all who listened. As they made their way out of the Church, a shower of rice rained down upon them, symbolizing prosperity and fertility.

The celebration then transitioned to a lush garden at a downtown hotel, where the evening light cast a warm glow over the elegantly set tables. The reception line formed quickly, with guests eager to offer their congratulations to the blissful couple. During the cocktail hour, laughter and chatter filled the air, accompanied by delicate hors d'oeuvres and sparkling champagne.

Stan, Harry's best man, raised a toast that captured the essence of the couple's journey and their future together, prompting smiles and a few teary eyes around the room. The dinner buffet opened shortly after, featuring an array of sumptuous dishes that catered to a variety of tastes.

Maria and Harry's first dance as husband and wife was a poignant moment, their love palpable in each step and turn. They then joined their parents for dances, which were heartfelt and reminiscent. The diverse music selection kept the guests on their feet, dancing joyously under the string lights that twinkled above.

A festive mood enveloped the cake-cutting ceremony, where Maria and Harry playfully smashed cake into each other's faces, eliciting roars of laughter from their friends and family. As the band played on until late in the evening, the energy remained high, with everyone reveling in the joy of the occasion.

As the clock neared 11 pm, the newlyweds slipped away to change into their travel clothes, ready to embark on their honeymoon. With heartfelt goodbyes and warm embraces, they departed for a romantic two-week getaway to Tahiti, leaving behind a night memorable for its vivid celebration of love and union.

CHAPTER 14-

Marissa was so happy to be engaged to the man of her dreams, who happened to be a doctor. Alberto had a month off till he started his internship. Marissa took a two-week vacation off from work, and they decided to travel to Southern California by car. They went to Disneyland, Knox Berry Farm, Universal Studio, and San Diego, and then drove back up the coast on Highway One. They drove by a nudist beach and decided to get out of their car. Marissa blushed seeing all the naked people on the beach. Alberto teased Marissa about joining them. They decided to forego the experience. They had awesome conversations while driving about their plans for the future. They planned on getting married after Alberto finished his residency, so they set their wedding date for Sunday, July 15th, 1984. They arrived back at Marissa's apartment after two glorious weeks away. Alberto would be staying at Marissa's for the next 10 days.

Marissa was back at work, and Alberto either cooked dinner or ordered it so that it was ready by the time she got home each night. She felt completely spoiled by the gestures, especially the flowers Alberto placed throughout the house. They would lay on the couch, cuddling after dinner and watching television. Marissa loved this life, but she knew she would soon be back in the apartment by herself. Alberto had to leave to start his internship. Although she was very excited for him, she was also sad. They shared a passionate kiss before Alberto left Marissa's apartment.

Alberto started his internship on a Monday. After one month, his days had developed a pattern. Alberto woke up at 4:30 AM, took a shower, got dressed, and headed out the door. By 5:15 AM, he was on the road, facing a half-hour drive to Stanford Hospital. Upon arrival, he printed out a list of his patients and reviewed their charts on the floor. He then checked on his patients before attending the morning report, where the previous night's team reported on the noteworthy cases.

"Morning rounds now, everyone," the charge nurse would announce as all the physicians and the charge nurse moved from room to room discussing the status of each patient.

Alberto met with his attending physician, residents, and medical students, issuing orders for his patients as needed. His pager frequently buzzed with questions from nurses, residents, and other hospital staff. Emergency Room admissions added to the day's unpredictability, with Alberto and the medical students managing all the new patient admissions. Some days were so hectic that he barely had time for charting until the end of his shift. He also gave reports to the doctors on the incoming shift.

"Every day brings a new challenge, but I'm learning so much," Alberto would say, his voice a mix of exhaustion and exhilaration.

Despite the long hours and unpredictable days, Alberto thrived and loved all that he was learning, even though some days he didn't return home until 10 PM. His passion for his work was evident, and it energized him through even the most grueling days.

Marissa was also getting accustomed to her job and liked all she was learning about running a physician's office. She loved interviewing potential new employees and had found some very qualified candidates to fill the open Nurse Practitioner position. Three physicians were going to interview the candidates. One physician in the office was always eyeing Marissa. She sometimes felt uncomfortable around him because he was always smiling at her. Dr Steve McDonald asked Marissa if she would like to go to lunch with him at the restaurant across the street. She told him innocently:

"That sounds nice." During lunch, Marissa spoke a lot about Alberto and how her fiancée is an intern at Stanford Hospital. Dr McDonald also did his internship and residency at Stanford. Steve was telling Marissa how difficult it is to date in San Francisco. Steve told Marissa,

"I am looking for someone like you, Marissa. You are so sweet, beautiful, smart, and the quintessential of a woman that any man would want by their side."

"Thank you, Dr McDonald."

"Please call me Steve, Marissa."

"Steve you will find someone. You are a smart, good looking, doctor. Any woman would love to date you."

"Marissa, if you didn't have a fiancée, I would ask you out."

"Well, we better get back to work before they come looking for us," Marissa replied.

All afternoon, Marissa was thinking about her lunch. She loved Alberto so much and asked herself why she accepted a lunch date from Steve. She was thinking, I didn't lead Dr McDonald on. Marissa was honest with him and was thinking about what she would do if he asked her out again. Marissa was quite naïve, and she did not think that when Alberto heard about the lunch, he wouldn't be happy. Marissa and Alberto have a very honest relationship. Marissa told Alberto all about Dr McDonald. Alberto trusted Marissa explicitly and thought Steve seemed like a wonderful human being and boss.

The year was going by quickly for Alberto as an intern. He was learning so much every day and was so happy being a physician. He had always wanted to help people, and this was the perfect career for him. It was challenging, but so rewarding at the same time. It also had its depressing aspects. Situations when you had done everything for a patient, and they didn't make it. Doctors and nurses also grieve when they lose a patient.

Marissa was always talking about Alberto and how in love she was with him. She couldn't wait till he had some time off to spend with her in the city. It was December 1981, and both Marissa and Alberto would have some time off during the holidays. He was going to spend the holidays at Marissa's apartment. It had been quite a while since the two of them had been able to spend time together. They spent much of Alberto's ten days off laying in each other's arms on the couch. They had a night of passion so many times.

Marissa told Alberto,

"You are amazing. I never imagined being loved and cherished so much. You are incredible, and I can't believe that you are mine."

"No, Marissa it is me who can't believe how sweet and gorgeous you are and always there for me. We are going to go on and have such a wonderful life together. I can't wait till we grow our family and can spend every day and night together. I appreciate so much how you have supported me through my schooling. I will give you a life full of surprises, love, and all the best things in life,"

"I know you will do that. You have been the best boyfriend and fiancée any woman could dream of having."

On July 1st, 1982, Alberto started as a first-year resident. He was now a little higher on the totem pole. The learning continued and Alberto was happy to think that soon he would be able to open his own practice. After residency, he would apply for a fellowship in internal medicine for 1-2 years at Stanford.

Marissa still loved her job and all the learning that she was experiencing. She went out to lunch with Steve frequently, and they had become real good friends. He loved to tease her that he still wished he could date her. Marissa told Steve she wanted to find him the perfect girlfriend. Steve always asked Marissa if she had any single friends. She said she does, but they all live in Texas.

It was July 1st, 1983, and Alberto was now Chief Resident. He was the head of all the resident doctors on staff. Being a great chief resident boils down to being a great leader and mentor. You must be fair, lead with integrity and be well respected. Alberto was excited about his new position. Marissa was very proud of all of Alberto's accomplishments.

Alberto's last year of residency was his best year ever. He thrived in his position as Chief resident. Both Marissa and Alberto liked being in charge, and both were exemplary leaders. During the last year before their wedding, they both were so busy they weren't able to spend much time together. Marissa would daydream about Alberto all the time.

Marissa was doing the final preparations for their wedding during the winter months of 1983. They were both so excited about their upcoming wedding in July 1984, which was just a few months away. They had waited a long time to be together, but soon, all their dreams would become reality.

CHAPTER 15-

Maria and Harry arrived back after their two-week honeymoon in Tahiti. They landed at the San Francisco International Airport, and reality set in that they both just had that weekend off before heading back to work on Monday.

Tahiti was magical and they stayed in an overwater honeymoon bungalow with a private waiter included. They both were spoiled over the two weeks with incredible food and frequent spa services with massages, facials, and body wraps. They also took a couple of catamaran rides during their stay. The water was so blue, clear, calm, and warm that they swam in the ocean frequently. They both have glorious tans from all the time in the sun. They loved the peace and quiet of the island. The beaches on the East Coast had black sand, and on the West Coast, they were white sand. They did some snorkeling and surfing and also took a sightseeing tour of the island, seeing all the beautiful landscapes and famous sites. It was a magnificent honeymoon, and Maria and Harry had the time of their life.

It was Saturday, and Maria and Harry were busy unpacking, doing laundry, buying groceries, and preparing to return to their working lives. They both wished they had taken another week off before returning to work, but they only had one more day of vacation left. After finishing all their chores, they had dinner together. Both were exhausted and planned to stay in bed the following day.

The day in bed on Sunday turned out to be just what they needed. They took two naps, cuddled, and gave each other back rubs throughout the day. Harry surprised Maria with some chocolate-covered strawberries for them to snack on. As they indulged, Maria and Harry reminisced about their trip to Tahiti and the wonderful time they had on their honeymoon.

"Imagine all the other places we can explore," Harry mused, his eyes sparkling with excitement. "We can travel around the world together, Maria."

Maria, who had found a newfound love for traveling but had only been to a few states in the US and Tahiti, was thrilled. "I can't wait for all our adventures, Harry. There's so much of the world we haven't seen!"

It was Monday morning, and Maria got up to make Harry breakfast before he left for work. After he left, she went back to bed to catch a little more sleep, setting her alarm for 1 PM. When the alarm went off, she got dressed in her uniform and prepared for work.

Driving to work at 2:30 PM, Maria was still feeling sleepy. As soon as she entered the hospital, she headed straight to the cafeteria for a cup of coffee to wake herself up. Walking onto her unit, she was greeted by a large sign that read "Congratulations Maria." Her coworkers had planned a potluck to celebrate her marriage, and everyone brought their favorite dish.

"I can't believe you all did this for me," Maria said, her voice choked with emotion as she surveyed the beautifully decorated nurses' lounge and the array of delicious food.

Her coworkers responded with cheers and laughter, "You deserve it, Maria!"

The unit was unusually slow that evening, which rarely happens, allowing them to properly celebrate Maria's return. Five of the nurses who had attended her wedding were recounting to everyone what a lovely event it had been.

"Harry was so handsome, and his groomsmen too!" one nurse exclaimed. "Are any of them single?"

Maria laughed, a warm glow in her cheeks. "Three of them are, actually, but they're all from California. Harry moved here from there to be near me."

Everyone listened intently, drawn in by the romance and adventure of Maria's stories. Feeling loved and appreciated by her coworkers, Maria knew she had made the right decision to accept a position on this unit.

"Thank you all for making today so special," Maria said, her eyes scanning the room filled with friendly faces. "I'm lucky to be part of such a wonderful team."

Maria arrived home around 11:45 pm. Harry was already in bed and said:

"Maria is that you. How was your evening back at work?"

"It was wonderful. They planned a potluck to congratulate me on getting married and to welcome me back to work."

"You have an awesome group of coworkers, who I can tell really like you."

"How was day back at work?"

"Mine was so hectic. There were so many things I needed to follow-up on. It is hard going back to work after such an amazing three weeks off.

"Harry, you should go to sleep; you have to get up early."

"I am going to go take a shower and watch some television and unwind for a while. I will get up with you in the morning and fix your breakfast."

"Oh honey, you should just sleep. I really appreciate it, but you need your sleep, too."

"I will see in the morning. My plan was to get up and fix you breakfast every morning before you go to work. Goodnight, Harry."

"Goodnight Maria. Love you so much, honey."

"Love you, babe. Sleep well. I hope the television on doesn't bother your sleep."

"I am so tired I think that there is nothing that could keep me awake. Enjoy your television and don't stay up too late."

"I am planning on going to sleep around 1 am. Sweet dreams, baby."

"Same to you, my dear."

Maria and Harry settled into married life with their jobs going well and both were very happy. Life was almost like a dream. Maria loved being a nurse and was learning so much every day at work. She especially loved cardiac and was so intrigued by the heart. At work on her telemetry unit, there were 20 monitors, all at the nurse's station. The Charge nurse watched the monitors and must be aware of any rhythm changes or any unusual rhythms that would require immediate intervention. Maria looked at the monitors and thought that being in charge was such a huge responsibility, but it did look like an interesting challenge.

The year 1984 passed quickly, and Maria thought that she had been working as an RN for more than three years. Maria was a smart, diligent, empathetic, quick problem solver, paid attention to detail, and was very kindhearted. She had developed great critical thinking skills and loved to problem solve. She had decided to become a preceptor for new nurses on her unit. She loved teaching and was ready to help new nurses learn the skills necessary to work on the unit. During 1985, she participated in three training programs, each 6 weeks long. She loved being a preceptor, and the new nurses loved that Maria was so patient, understanding, and helpful. Maria had found her niche and often went home and told Harry all about her being a preceptor. They didn't see each other much during the week due to their schedules. Maria had every other weekend off, and they tried to plan a night out or a weekend away during her weekend off. They were living the life, and both were so content.

It was October 1985, and Maria had been an RN for four years. She arrived at her unit to discover that her Charge Nurse had called in sick. The Director of her unit asked Maria to take charge for the night. Surprised and slightly anxious, Maria accepted, curious why she was chosen despite other nurses having more seniority.

"Why me?" Maria asked, her voice revealing her uncertainty.

"You've shown excellent leadership qualities, Maria, and you handle pressure well," the Director explained, giving her an encouraging smile.

Maria felt a mix of pride and nervousness as she nodded, taking on the role. The unit was bustling with activity, housing 20 patients that night. Maria diligently organized the assignments, took reports, and checked on all the patients. Despite the chaos of five patient transfers and five admissions, the night progressed smoothly. Maria enjoyed the challenge and began to appreciate the balance between being in charge and providing direct patient care. She started to take on the charge nurse role at least two days a week, relishing the mixture of leadership and hands-on care.

However, the demanding nature of nursing began to take a toll on her physically. Early in her shift, while assisting a coworker to lift a patient in bed, Maria felt a sharp pain in her right arm, followed by a sore neck.

"Are you okay?" her coworker asked, noticing Maria's discomfort.

"Just pulled something, I think," Maria replied, trying to dismiss the pain.

But as the night wore on, her discomfort worsened. She reported the incident to her supervisor and filled out the First Report of Injury Form. The manager of the unit, still present from the day shift, received the form.

"Go home, Maria, and take care of yourself. Hope you feel better soon," the manager said with genuine concern. "Someone from Employee Health will contact you."

"Thank you so much," Maria responded, grateful but pained.

Arriving home before Harry, Maria lay on the couch, contemplating the severity of her injury. She hoped it was just a pulled muscle. When Harry walked through the door, surprised to see her home so early, she explained the incident.

"I must have pulled something in my neck or shoulder," Maria told him, her voice laced with discomfort.

Harry immediately took care of her, preparing dinner while she rested with an ice pack on her neck. Despite the medication and rest, her pain intensified, especially at the base of her right shoulder.

The next morning, the Employee Health Nurse called to discuss the next steps. Maria scheduled an appointment with an Orthopedist/Physiatrist for further evaluation. The doctor was concerned about her increasing pain and right arm weakness.

"We'll start with some trigger point injections to alleviate your muscle pain," the doctor explained as he prepared the injections. "You'll also need to start on prednisone, pain medication, a muscle relaxer, and begin physical therapy."

He recommended she take a month off from work to recover and scheduled a follow-up appointment in four weeks. Maria left the office filled with a mix of relief and anxiety, uncertain about her immediate future in nursing but grateful for the thorough care plan.

Harry was so supportive while Maria wasn't feeling good. He fixed dinner every night and gave her neck and back rubs. He would do anything he could to help her.

The year 1986 started and Maria wondered how the year would turn out.

Maria diligently followed her doctor's orders, taking her medications and attending physical therapy three times a week, yet her pain increased, and her right arm grew weaker. At her next appointment, the doctor extended her leave from work for another month and ordered an MRI of her neck.

The MRI revealed three herniated discs pressing on her nerves. Maria was shocked by the findings, which explained the intense pain and weakness in her arm. Now barely able to lift one pound with her right arm, she continued with physical therapy, but doubts about returning to her nursing career began to cloud her thoughts. Harry was always there, offering words of encouragement when she needed them most.

"Harry, what if I can't go back to work? What if I can't even take care of our home?" she voiced her fears one evening as they sat together, his arm wrapped comfortingly around her.

"We'll get through this, no matter what it takes. You're not alone in this," Harry reassured her, kissing her forehead gently.

Her doctor then prescribed a series of three epidural injections to help alleviate her pain and arm weakness. An epidural injection involves delivering medicine into the epidural space around the spinal cord to reduce pain and inflammation.

Harry took days off to accompany Maria to her injections, allowing her to receive sedating medication before the procedures. After her first epidural, Maria experienced brief relief, but the pain soon returned, intensifying her worries as she noticed her grip weakening, with objects frequently slipping from her hand.

"I just dropped another glass today," Maria mentioned sadly after another frustrating incident, feeling the weight of her diminishing physical capabilities.

As the pain in her lower neck, right shoulder, and arm grew severe, it often brought her to tears, describing it as a sharp, burning sensation that radiated down her arm into her thumb and fingers.

On many days, she lay on the couch, alternating ice and heat on her neck, feeling spaced out and overwhelmed by her condition. Harry took care of most household chores, balancing his stressful job with caring for Maria, which only added to her feelings of helplessness.

"I hate seeing you like this. I wish I could take away your pain," Harry expressed one night as they prepared for another long attempt at sleep, which was often elusive for Maria due to her discomfort.

Time passed, and Maria remained off work, deeply missing her nursing career but recognizing the reality of her condition. She continued with her physical therapy and received several more epidural injections, gradually noticing improvements. Able to lift slightly more and adhering to a comprehensive home exercise program recommended by her therapist, she began to feel a glimmer of hope.

"You're getting stronger every day, love. I'm so proud of how hard you're working at this," Harry said one evening, noticing her increased movement as she managed to lift a small grocery bag.

Maria smiled, feeling a mix of relief and cautious optimism, "Thanks, Harry. It's a long road, but maybe, just maybe, I'll find my way back."

Maria and Samantha still talked on the phone every day. Maria looked forward to her daily call with Samantha. Samantha would tell Maria about her evenings at work, and they would discuss Maria's condition and their incredibly handsome, smart, and funny husbands. Samantha was telling Maria maybe she should think about going on the night shift for a while till she is back to herself. Maria thought that this was a great idea. It was coming on a year that she had been out of work, and if she was unable to come back to work at the one-year mark, she would be replaced permanently. Maria talked to Harry and her family about the night shift position. They were all in favor of it because there would be less lifting, and this seemed to be the answer to her dilemma.

Maria's next visit with her physician, she asked him his opinion of her returning to the night shift. Maria's right arm strength was returning, and her pain level had decreased. He thought she could try the night shift and see how she handled it. He cleared her back to work with certain restrictions. Maria called the Employee Health Nurse and her manager to tell them about her restrictions. They told Maria that they would check on this and get back to her. The week passed, and Maria was worried because she hadn't heard back from the hospital. Early one morning, the phone rang, and it was the Employee Health Nurse. She told Maria that they have a position on the night shift for 3 days a week. Maria told her that would be perfect. She was informed that she could start next Sunday night at 11 pm.

Maria was so happy that they were taking her back after her injury. She couldn't wait to see all her friends at work. She knew nurses on the night shift from giving them a change of shift reports. Also, she had done many double shifts and worked frequently on the night shift. Maria called everyone to let them know she was going back to work. She was hoping the night shift would be her answer. She would just have to wait and see how everything goes, but she was excited. Harry was happy for Maria, but had gotten used to her being home. The night shift was happy to have Maria join them. Everyone hoped that Maria would thrive on the night shift and be able to manage her condition appropriately. Only time would tell.

CHAPTER 16-

It was Sunday, July 15th, 1984, Marissa and Alberto's wedding day. Marissa had spent the previous two weeks in Dallas, where she had enjoyed a beautiful wedding shower hosted by her best friend and maid of honor, as well as her mother. The excitement of the fun-filled bachelorette party still lingered in her mind. As the big day dawned, Marissa could hardly believe it had finally arrived.

The church was bustling with guests as Marissa's bridesmaids made their way down the aisle, adorned in elegant purple gowns, holding bouquets of purple, lilac, and white flowers. When Marissa began her walk down the aisle on the arm of her father, Dave, she was radiant in her stunning wedding dress. Alberto and Dave both had tears in their eyes when they first glimpsed Marissa approaching. Over the years, Marissa and Alberto's families had grown incredibly close and were now overjoyed to witness their children unite in marriage.

Marissa and Alberto had crafted their own vows, imbued with deep emotion, sweetness, and sincerity. After traversing a long journey together, everyone in attendance felt a surge of happiness knowing the couple was about to begin their 'happily ever after.' The priest, moved by the ceremony, prompted the pivotal moment:

"You may kiss the bride."

After their tender kiss, the priest joyfully announced, "Let me introduce you to Mr. and Mrs. Bertolucci." Applause erupted from the crowd as the newlyweds walked hand in hand down the aisle and out of the church, embarking on their new life together.

As they exited, Alberto whispered to Marissa, his voice thick with emotion, "Today marks the beginning of forever for us."

Marissa, overwhelmed with joy and relief that the day had gone perfectly, replied softly, "Every step I took towards you today was a step into our future. I couldn't be happier."

Their shared glance was one of profound love and anticipation for what was to come, making the moment eternally memorable for both them and their guests.

The reception was held in their country club, which is right next to the Church. They had nearly 250 guests. They had a delicious five course sit-down dinner, with music playing softly in the background. After dinner Marissa and Alberto had their first dance. They had taken dancing lessons together and had some good moves. Most everyone got up and danced and the reception was very lively. Everyone enjoyed themselves and said that this was one of the best weddings that they have ever attended.

Marissa's friend Steve from work was there. Marissa introduced him to her single friends, who all really liked him. The day turned out to be more amazing than Marissa could ever have expected. She just married the sweetest man, who always put her first and was so smart, loving, respectful and romantic. She couldn't believe how lucky she was to be married to Alberto. The reception was winding down, and they were about ready to leave the venue. Marissa and Alberto thanked their parents, bridesmaids and groomsmen for everything and for being part of the awesome wedding. They left the wedding and headed off to the bridal suite in a local hotel.

The next morning Marissa and Alberto had breakfast with both their families. They all had a wonderful time at the wedding and were so happy that everything worked out so well. Alberto planned to surprise Marissa with their honeymoon destination. Anne and Dorothy both knew where they would be headed. They would be leaving in the morning.

Anne, Dave, Dorothy, and Tony drove their children to the airport for their flight. They would be gone for three weeks and would return to San Francisco. They were on a flight from Dallas to Dubai, which was around a fifteen-hour flight. After boarding, Alberto told Marissa:

"We are going to the Seychelles."

"Oh, I can't believe we are going there. You never cease to amaze me, my dear."

"I thought we should go somewhere we have never been. Seychelles is one of the top honeymoon destinations in the world. It has sugar-colored sand beaches, more than 100 islands, and crystal clear, pristine water. We are flying to Dubai and then onto our destination."

"I am so excited to have this alone time with you. We have waited so long to be together, and now it is finally happening."

Marissa and Alberto had a magnificent honeymoon. They had amenities such as a private pool and personal staff. They both were quite tan after spending time on their private beach. This turned out to be a fairytale honeymoon one for the books. They had the time of their lives. They were relaxed and so happy to be married. Marissa was thrilled to think that they were finally together, and Alberto would never have to leave again. They planned on living in Marissa's apartment for a while and then would think about buying a house or a condo. Their three weeks were coming to an end, but this had been a vacation of a lifetime. They flew back to Dubai and then transferred onto a plane headed for New York. They had a five-hour layover in New York and then headed back on a plane to San Francisco.

After arriving back in San Francisco, they took a cab to their apartment. They started unloading a few items from their suitcases, but they both were so tired they just went to sleep. They both slept almost 24 hours after being awake for almost two days. Upon awakening, they both felt rejuvenated. They both had six days till they had to return to work. They spent the time either in bed or on the couch in each other arms. Marissa was so thrilled, thinking that they could cuddle every night now. Alberto was very affectionate, and Marissa loved it. Soon, they would be going back to their working lives. Alberto would be doing a Fellowship for three years. Marissa was going back to her job as office manager for the group of Primary Care Physicians.

The day came when both of them had to go back to work. It was hard for both to get back into the routine. Alberto was going into a Cardiovascular Fellowship, and the training was for three years, with the last year being research. Alberto would be assigned to one cardiovascular clinic for 3-4 weeks. Alberto was thrilled to expand his horizons and delve deep into the cardiovascular system.

Marissa was happy to be going back to her job. She had learned so much and felt she would be able to help Alberto open his medical office when the time came. They both were on the day shift so that they could spend most evenings together. Alberto used to get home late one or two times a week due to his demanding days. Married life turned out to be even better than they had anticipated. They typically cooked dinner together and then spent their evenings relaxing—watching television or reading books. Despite his busy schedule, Alberto always made sure to carve out enough time to spend with Marissa.

A routine gradually developed in Marissa and Alberto's life. They worked during the week and took the weekends off. They discussed starting a family and decided to wait until Alberto had completed his Fellowship and opened his medical practice. Marissa was simply content to have him home every night. Alberto's Fellowship was scheduled to end in June of 1987, and each year during his Fellowship, he took one month off. The couple cherished these breaks, traveling the world. In June of 1985, they spent a month in Tahiti and Fiji, and in 1986, they revisited Europe.

By 1987, the final year of Alberto's Fellowship, he focused his research on dilated cardiomyopathy—an enlarged heart condition. Together, Marissa and Alberto began planning what they would need to open his practice. Alberto suggested Marissa quit her job two months before his program ended to have some time to relax before they embarked on their new venture. Following his advice, Marissa left her job in May 1987 and began researching what would be necessary to establish Alberto's practice. Once Alberto completed his Fellowship in June 1987, they found themselves both at home, not working. After three years of marriage, it was luxurious not having to wake up early and being able to spend entire days in bed if they chose. They frequently shared affectionate moments and relished this period of relaxation, knowing well that their lives were about to undergo a significant transformation. Marissa and Alberto were soon to spend nearly every hour of the day together as they worked side by side. Life seemed perfect as they anticipated the realization of their dreams.

Alberto, while lounging one afternoon, remarked to Marissa, "I can't believe how everything is falling into place for us. Soon, we'll be starting this new chapter, working together every day."

Marissa, nestling closer to him, responded warmly, "It's like we're building our future together with each decision we make. I love that we're in this together."

Alberto smiled, squeezing her hand gently, "And I wouldn't want it any other way. Here's to our dreams turning into our daily reality."

Their laughter and shared dreams filled their home, as they stood on the brink of a new beginning, both excited and ready for the challenges and joys that lay ahead.

CHAPTER 17-

It was Sunday night, and Maria had just woken up from a nap. The clock showed 9:30 pm, signaling it was time for her to change into her uniform and head back to work for the night shift. Harry was visibly worried about her, knowing she still suffered from significant neck and right arm pain. To him, it seemed a risky ordeal, but Maria felt that returning to work would offer a much-needed distraction from the constant discomfort. Harry only hoped she could manage.

As Maria entered the nurse's lounge to get the shift report, she was greeted by the warm and relieved faces of her friends from the evening shift. They crowded around her, expressing their concerns and relief.

"We've missed you around here, Maria!" one of her colleagues exclaimed, their words echoing the sentiment in the room.

"It's so good to see you back, Maria. We've all been worried," another added, her smile sincere.

Maria felt a mixture of emotions swirling inside her—gratitude for the concern, yet anxiety about diving back into the fast-paced environment. "Thanks, everyone. It's good to be back, though I'm taking it slow."

The night shift proved to be vastly different from the bustling evening shift she used to know. Instead of the constant chaos of admissions and discharges, the night was calmer, focused more on maintaining patient stability and comfort through the dark hours. Maria and her team would take vital signs, resettle patients for the night, and respond to any needs signalled through the call lights.

Around 5 am, the lab team would come for the daily blood draws, marking the start of the morning routine. "If the patient has a central line, we draw the labs from there. It's easier on them," Maria explained to a newer nurse, guiding her through the process.

The slow pace and reduced physical strain of the night shift were a blessing for Maria. "This might just be perfect for me," she thought, appreciating the hospital's willingness to accommodate her health restrictions.

After her shift ended, Maria headed straight to her physical therapy appointment, her body weary but her spirit somewhat lifted by the support of her peers and the manageable duties of her new schedule. She knew it would be a long road to full recovery, but for now, she found solace in the routine and the familiar faces of the night.

After she arrived home from physical therapy, she decided she needed to sleep during the day and before Harry came home from work so she could spend some time with him in the evening.

It was 11 am and she had picked up some breakfast at a fast- food restaurant, near her home. She ate and then felt really exhausted. She fell asleep around noon and awoke at 3 pm. She thought that she only had 3 hours of sleep but felt wide awake. She decided to start preparing dinner since Harry would be home soon.

At 5:30 Harry came walking in the door.

"How was your first night on the night shift?"

"It was great, but a little hard to get back into the routine. I really enjoyed visiting with my friends. I think the night shift will work out perfectly."

"How was your sleep?"

"I was able to get three hours of sleep this afternoon."

"You need to take a nap before you go back to work tonight. You should sleep between 8 and 9:30 p.m. at least."

"Sounds good to me. I feel bad that I am going to sleep while you are awake."

"Honey, you need to take care of yourself. There are many nights you are not working, and we can go to sleep together. I think you should take a nap every night after dinner when you work."

"Thank you so much for being so understanding and supportive. You are the best husband I could ever dream of having in my life. How did I get so lucky?"

"No, like I always say, I am the lucky one."

"We both are lucky and should cherish our relationship. We get along so well, and both are so supportive. We will go on to have a wonderful life with all the good things that life has to offer. We need to be thankful for all the graces that that we have been given in this life. I can't see my life without you. I love you more than you will ever know."

"I love you so much, Maria. Since we've finished dinner, you should go and take a nap. I will wake you up at 9:30

pm." Harry wakes Maria up, and she puts on her uniform and is out the door for her second night shift.

Maria had adjusted well to the night shift and was pleased with how well she was handling it. Typically, she would sleep for about three hours in the afternoon and then catch another 1-2 hours of rest before heading off to work. On days she worked consecutive nights, this routine made the days seem unusually long due to the segmented sleep.

Maria felt guilty knowing that her reluctance to travel or embark on weekend trips was impacting Harry. He was working tirelessly, and she knew it was unfair that they couldn't enjoy vacations together. Despite this, Harry was incredibly supportive, frequently massaging Maria's neck to ease her discomfort and always expressing his hope for her swift recovery. He had made it clear that he didn't want to consider a vacation until she felt significantly better.

In a recent development at his job, Harry had been promoted to manager of his department. Maria was immensely proud of him, and his colleagues were equally elated about his promotion. Harry cherished his role and the life they shared together; their deep bond and mutual support made them true soulmates, navigating life's challenges hand in hand.

As time sped by, Maria found herself nine months into her night shift routine. One early morning, a patient who was unsteady on her feet requested assistance to go to the bathroom. Always cautious, Maria asked another nurse to help with the transfer to ensure safety. However, as they were settling the patient back into bed, Maria felt a sharp pain in her mid-back. By the last hour of her shift, the pain had intensified dramatically. Concerned, she confided in a fellow nurse who urged her to report the incident. Following this advice, Maria informed her charge nurse, manager, and supervisor about her injury, and then headed home to await a call from the Employee Health Nurse, which came that afternoon.

Maria promptly made an appointment with her doctor for the following day. When Harry returned from work and learned of the incident, his heart sank. It pained him deeply to see Maria suffering yet again. He loved her dearly, and it was excruciating to watch his soulmate endure such constant pain. Frustration welled up inside him, not only because Maria hadn't fully recovered from her initial injury but now faced possibly another one.

"Maria, this just isn't fair to you," Harry expressed as they sat together that evening. His tone was a mix of concern and frustration.

"I know, Harry. It's just one thing after another," Maria replied, her voice tinged with exhaustion and pain.

"We'll get through this, just like everything else. Whatever it takes, I'm here for you," Harry reassured her, taking her hand gently.

Maria managed a weak smile. "I know, Harry. I'm so grateful for you. You're my rock."

As they sat in the quiet of their living room, the weight of the situation settled around them, but the strength of their bond was clear. They were in this together, come what may.

Maria had attended her doctor's appointment, where he suspected she might have a herniated disk in her mid-spine. After prescribing prednisone, he ordered an MRI to confirm his suspicions. Unfortunately, the MRI results confirmed that Maria did indeed have a herniated disk pressing on a nerve, explaining the severe mid-back pain that radiated around to her abdomen. This revelation made Maria increasingly anxious about her ability to return to her role as a hospital nurse.

Over the following months, Maria underwent several epidural injections in her mid-back and returned to physical therapy sessions two to three times a week. Despite these efforts, the pain remained significant, a constant presence in her life. Harry felt an overwhelming sense of desperation to alleviate her suffering. He frequently asked colleagues and friends for any advice or remedies that might help Maria. His profound concern for her well-being only deepened Maria's appreciation for him. She often thought to herself how fortunate she was to have such a caring, attentive partner. Harry's support made navigating her injuries more bearable.

During this challenging time, Maria maintained daily conversations with her friend Samantha, finding solace in hearing about her night shifts at the hospital. She deeply missed her own work and often wondered if she would ever return to the nursing floor.

As Maria continued with physical therapy, acupuncture, and her diligent home exercise program, her doctor eventually advised her, after about nine months of treatment, that returning to any job that involved lifting would not be advisable. This news, though somewhat anticipated, still came as a shock to Maria. Hospital nursing was all she had known, and the thought of not being able to return to it left her reeling. What could a nurse do if not nursing in a hospital?

"Don't worry about work right now, Maria. Let's just focus on getting you better," Harry comforted her one evening as they discussed her future. His voice was gentle, trying to soothe her worries.

"But Harry, what if I can't go back at all? What will I do?" Maria's voice trembled, the uncertainty weighing heavily on her.

"We'll figure it out together," Harry assured her, taking her hands in his. "You're an amazing nurse, Maria. There's so much more you can do that doesn't involve lifting. We'll explore all options."

Maria nodded, feeling a mix of gratitude and concern. "I know, Harry. It's just hard to imagine not being able to do the job I love."

"We'll make it through this, just like we've made it through everything else," Harry said, pulling her close.

When Maria returned home Harry said:

"Maria what is wrong?"

"My doctor told me today that I shouldn't return to my job because of all the heavy lifting. Your body has already endured several injuries and you don't need anymore. We will put you through Vocational Rehabilitation, which is where we will get a vocation rehab counselor who will explore options for your employment that doesn't require any lifting."

"I am sorry Maria. I know how much you liked being a hospital nurse, but hopefully, you will find a better position that is easier on your body. I am here for you. Please let me know if you want to talk or if there is anything I can do to make this transition easier."

"You know what you can do now. Lay on the couch, put your arms around me and just hold me. I will be fine, but this came as somewhat of a shock for me, and as long as I have you by my side, I can handle anything."

"Just think Maria maybe you will have a Monday through Friday job and I pray that you will be happy in your new position."

"Thank you, Harry."

Maria started her Vocational rehab about two weeks later. The counselor came to her house, and the first couple of weeks were for testing. They came up with fifteen types of RN positions that fit into her skill sets and would be a good fit for Maria. She never realized how many positions were available in the corporate world for an RN. She was more optimistic and looking forward to a new challenge. The next portion of the Vocational Rehab was to apply for positions that fit within her restrictions. Maria applied for several positions in hospitals, health plans, and offices. She landed a job as a pre-admitting nurse working in the admitting department of a hospital in Des Moines. She loved her new job, and it was so much easier on her body. She wore business clothes to work and walked all over the hospital, which was so much better for her neck and back. Maria believed all new nurses should work as a float for a year. You would never get that kind of experience in all departments without being a float. That advice she would give new nurses about floating when asked. She had so much to learn but was happy that she decided on this position. Maria was thrilled to be working Monday through Friday with weekends off.

Maria and Harry would drive to work together and sometimes go out to dinner or happy hour afterward. Harry would take Maria shopping at the mall for work clothes. He loved picking out suits and outfits for her, and she loved his taste in clothes. Sometimes, he would come home with a new outfit for her, and she would be thrilled.

Maria started thinking about having a family. Harry thought they should wait till her pain was better controlled. Maria was hoping that it wouldn't be too long from now. Maria couldn't wait to have Harry's baby, expand their family and be parents. Life was sweet and soon to be sweeter.

CHAPTER 18-

It was the fall of 1987 and Marissa and Alberto were both looking forward to the next chapter of their life. They had frequent romantic days and nights and were thrilled to be spending so much time together.

They were trying to decide if Alberto should find a medical practice to purchase or open up one from scratch. They looked all around the area for an existing practice for sale, but decided he should open a new practice. Alberto and Marissa are both smart in business, so together, they figured they could accomplish their goal.

They first developed a business plan with a mission, goals, objectives, and a timeframe. The first thing they looked at was the budget. Marissa advised Alberto that they should talk with a small business attorney for legal advice. Alberto's Mom is an attorney, and they asked her for a referral. There were so many decisions to make, and they wanted to make sure that they had all the necessary information to make good, informed decisions.

They decided on a practice name, obtained financing and a tax ID number, and set up a bank account. After speaking with the attorney, they decided to set up an LLC. They also located an accounting firm that will handle the billing. They had all the background items ready, and they were ready to find a location for his office.

They worked with a real estate agent to find the ideal location. They looked at several standalone properties but decided they wanted to find a space in an office building with other medical practices. It took a couple of months, but they found the perfect location. The space was the size they had been looking for in a newly renovated downtown office building with many physicians, attorneys, and accountants as tenants. Alberto signed a lease for 3 years with a 3-year option to renew.

Alberto and Marissa were so excited that they found the perfect space. Tony helped his son with some of the inside construction, such as putting up walls for the patient rooms, and painting. Alberto worked on getting the necessary inspections. Marissa worked on decorating the space and acquiring all the office furniture. The office was coming together well and looked elegant. Both sets of parents, Anne, Dave, Dorothy, and Tony, came to see the space. They were thrilled with what their children had accomplished. The space was beautifully decorated, and they all were so happy for Alberto and Marissa.

The next step in the process was to develop office policies, fee schedules, and employment agreements. They had to purchase a phone system, transcription equipment, a computer, and all other necessary medical equipment. Alberto worked on getting credentialed, hospital privileges, and obtaining all the necessary insurance. They discussed how many employees they would need to open the office. They developed job descriptions, salaries, and benefits. Marissa initially interviewed the candidates and then referred them to Alberto for final approval. They had two office staff members in place and then developed their marketing strategy. They hired an office RN and an office coordinator. The office hours were going to be 9 am-5 pm Monday through Thursday and 9 am – 1 pm on Fridays. The practice opened its doors on March 1, 1988.

Marissa and Alberto worked so well together. The staff loved working for this employer. They both felt they had found the most awesome job. The nurse, Carol, had worked in a cardiac unit in a local hospital, so she had great experience and wanted to do something in an office setting for a change of pace. Marissa and Carol became good friends. As time progressed, more and more patients started coming to the office. Alberto was an internal medicine physician with a cardiac specialty. The patients that came to the office were quite impressed with Alberto and his staff, and many had their family members also change to this practice. Alberto felt that without Marissa's help, the office wouldn't have run as smoothly. She was on top of everything and had learned so much working for her previous employer and had gained invaluable experience. Alberto would take Marissa and his two employees out to lunch frequently. He was such a kind boss, and they all loved working for him.

Alberto and Carol would discuss patients at times, and Marissa was amazed at how much she was learning just by listening to them talk. She sometimes wished she had gone into the medical profession, but was very happy being the office manager.

Alberto's practice grew and thrived. He was happy working with his wife. They went to work together and usually came home together unless Alberto had to see a patient in the hospital. One thing about having your own business is that it does take a lot of time, but it is well worth it.

They had a routine down and were living their best life. Alberto didn't have anyone to cover for him, so he took calls every night and weekend. He had a friend from medical school who also opened a solo practice, so they took calls for each other when away or on vacation. The one thing Marissa was getting used to was if one of Alberto's patients was hospitalized, he could get called at any time and would need to go to the hospital sometimes. This didn't happen too often, but it did happen. That was the life of being married to a doctor. Their job wasn't an 8-hour job, and some nights, he could be gone most of the night. Marissa worried so much about him when he didn't get any sleep. She told Alberto that he should recruit another physician for his practice or find someone he could share evening and weekend calls. Marissa felt Alberto was wearing himself out by being on call 24 hours a day seven days a week.

There were three new physicians on his floor, one of whom was also in internal medicine with a cardiac specialty. They have become close and go to lunch frequently. They have decided to share calls every other night and every other weekend. The nights they were on call might be busier, but they would have more evenings and weekends off. Marissa was so happy to hear this and spoke to the office manager to work out the details.

Over the next two years, Alberto's practice expanded, and he hired a nurse practitioner in 1990. He had so many patients that he could hardly handle them all. The nurse practitioner was a wonderful addition to his office. She examined many of the internal medicine patients, and Alberto examined mainly the cardiology patients. Everything was working out the way Marissa and Alberto planned, and they couldn't be happier.

CHAPTER 19 -

Maria and Harry enjoyed driving to work together. He would drop her off in the morning and pick her up in the afternoon. Maria felt blessed to still be able to work and manage her injuries. She found her job very interesting and had learned a tremendous amount. She handled pre-admission authorizations, ensuring that patients were appropriate for hospital admission. She also served as a resource for the admitting department for any questions they might have during the day. She realized that this position was so much better for her neck and back than bedside nursing. She loved working Monday through Friday with weekends and holidays off. Maria and Harry often went out to dinner after work and sometimes to a movie. They were so much in love, both so kind and thoughtful, and knew each other so well that they could finish each other's sentences. They were living such an awesome life and were thinking about when they should buy a house and then, after the house, consider starting a family. Harry wanted Maria to wait to have children until her back was better. Maria, however, was worried that she was getting older and didn't want to wait too long.

Maria and Samantha still talked every day on the phone. Samantha was still working on the medical-surgical floor, and her back had been hurting lately, especially at night. She reflected on what Maria had gone through with her back and neck. Samantha had worked nine years on the medical-surgical floor and had gained significant knowledge but was ready for a change. She was considering getting out of bedside nursing and doing something more like Maria's position. She searched all over the city and found a position as a Utilization Review Nurse in a downtown office, Monday through Friday, for a major insurance company. Samantha was happy to be taking a different direction in her career. She liked her new position and loved that there was less stress than hospital nursing. She told Maria that they worked hard because the requests kept coming and coming, and it was quite challenging, but she thought she had found her niche and really liked doing this kind of work.

Maria and Harry frequently went to Maria's parents' house to check on her parents and grandpa. Her Grandpa had been having chest pain, and Maria was worried about him. Every time she was there, she took his vital signs and assessed him. His cardiologist was running some further tests. He had angina—severe pain in the chest, arms, and neck caused by inadequate blood supply to the heart—and had nitroglycerin to take if he experienced any chest pain. Despite his condition, Grandpa still loved cooking and doing things around the house and yard. Everyone was telling Grandpa to slow down.

"Grandpa, you really need to take it easier," Maria would say, her voice laced with concern each visit.

"Don't worry so much, Maria. I know my limits," Grandpa would reply stubbornly, his voice firm yet gentle, showing a mix of reassurance and independence.

One evening in the spring of 1991, Maria and Harry were lying on the couch watching TV when they received a frantic call from Ethel. She told them that Grandpa had a severe episode of chest pain where the nitroglycerin hadn't helped. They had called an ambulance, and Grandpa was now in the Emergency Room. Harry and Maria drove to the hospital, arriving there in about 45 minutes. Ethel was at the bedside, and they let Maria and Harry into the room. The nurse informed them that the doctor would be in shortly.

Maria glanced at the monitor and noticed ST elevation and some abnormal beats, clear signs of trouble. Soon, the doctor came in and told them that Grandpa's cardiac enzymes were elevated, indicating he had suffered an anterior myocardial infarction (heart attack). They were giving him medications for pain, oxygen, and aspirin. They planned to admit him to the Cardiac Care Unit. He was awake and alert, bewildered by what had happened.

"I don't understand. I felt fine this morning," Grandpa murmured, his voice tinged with confusion and fear.

"It's going to be alright; the doctors are doing everything they can," Maria reassured him, squeezing his hand gently.

Maria decided to wait at the hospital with her mom. Harry stayed until Grandpa was settled into his room and then said goodnight to Grandpa, Ethel, and Maria. He drove home while Ethel and Maria went to look for the visitor lounge. The lounge was large, occupied by two groups of people who had blankets and food, looking as if they had been there for a while. Ethel and Maria walked around the hospital searching for vending machines to get a snack. The lounge offered pillows, warm blankets, and coffee. Maria and Ethel visited Grandpa one more time before trying to catch some sleep. They asked the night nurse about his condition.

"He's stable now, resting comfortably," the nurse reassured them.

Feeling a bit relieved, they decided since it was 1 am, they would try to get some shut-eye. They wrapped themselves up in warm blankets and managed to sleep for about three hours before noise in the corridor woke them. They called the nurses' station for an update, and were informed that Grandpa was comfortable with no further pain and was sleeping well. They decided to go back to sleep for a little while until the hustle and bustle of the day shift began.

It was 6:30 am and the sun was shining through the window; everyone in the visitor lounge was awake. Ethel and Maria, anxious for more information, awaited Grandpa's physician. Around 8 am, the cardiologist arrived and reassured them that Joe had been stable throughout the night. They were planning to take him for a cardiac catheterization on Thursday for diagnostic and therapeutic purposes. Maria and Ethel visited Grandpa several times during the day for a few minutes at a time but wanted him to rest well. Harry returned to the hospital that afternoon after work, relieved to find that Grandpa had been stable. Maria decided to go home with Harry and would return to work for the next couple of days, planning to come back on Thursday, the day of Grandpa's cardiac testing. Ethel also decided to go home to get some sleep.

It was Thursday, and Grandpa had remained stable. Maria and Ethel met early in the morning in the lounge. His doctor came to talk to them and discussed Grandpa's upcoming procedure. They both gave Grandpa a kiss and wished him the best before he was wheeled to the heart lab. He was gone from the room for about 2 hours. After the procedure, his physician came to talk to Maria and Ethel.

"He did well, and we were able to get a clear look at what's going on. We'll discuss the next steps shortly," the doctor explained, offering them a small smile of reassurance.

"We found a 95% blockage of his LAD (left anterior descending artery) and we were able to open it up via Angioplasty, which is a balloon that is inflated and pushes the plaque out. Your Dad should be able to be discharged most likely tomorrow. We will need to adjust some of his medications before he can leave."

"Thank you so much Dr Finnegan. It looks like he got here just in time." Maria states.

"Yes, Joe is a very lucky man."

"Mom the LAD is the largest artery in the heart."

"Wow, Dad is very lucky he came to the hospital when he did." Joe ended up being discharged the next day. Maria and Harry decided to spend the weekend at her parent's house to make sure everything was going well with Grandpa. Maria checked his vital signs several times during the weekend, and everything looked stable. When Maria and Harry leave Sunday night, Maria said:

"Call me if you have any questions. Love you, Grandpa and Mom. Grandpa, please try to take it easy and don't push yourself. Stress isn't good for you, so please try and relax."

"I will Maria. Don't worry, everything will be fine."

"Love you guys, and please say bye to Dad for us when he gets home from work."

"We will, and you drive carefully. Let us know when you get home." Per Ethel.

"We will. Goodnight."

"Goodnight, Maria and Harry." Exclaimed Grandpa and Ethel.

As the months of 1991 passed, Maria and Harry settled into a comforting routine and were thrilled to be able to spend so much time together. They were not just spouses but best friends, genuinely content with their lives. Maria often reflected on her blessings: wonderful, loving parents, an incredible grandpa, and the best husband a wife could dream of having. She felt her life was nearly perfect.

One day at work, Maria received a call that disrupted her peaceful musings. It was from her parent's neighbor, a close friend of hers.

"Maria, I'm sorry to bother you, but your parent's housekeeper came knocking on our door. They were supposed to clean your parent's house this morning, but your grandpa isn't answering the door. Your mom isn't answering the phone number she gave them as an emergency contact either."

"Oh, thank you for letting me know. I'll leave work right away and check on him. It's unusual for Grandpa not to answer; he always lets the housecleaners in."

With a sense of urgency, Maria spoke to her supervisor and left work. Her heart raced as anxiety gripped her; Grandpa was always meticulous about such matters. Driving was not her usual routine, but today she had taken the car because Harry was tied up with a meeting after work. Luckily, the traffic was light, and she made it in less than forty minutes.

She knocked on her parent's front door, but there was no response. With a deep sense of foreboding, she unlocked the door and called out for her grandpa as she entered. The silence that greeted her intensified her worry. Not finding him in the front part of the house, she proceeded to the back where his bedroom was located. Taking a deep breath to steady her nerves, she opened the door.

Maria's fears were confirmed when she saw Grandpa lying in bed, his face pallid and his breathing rapid and shallow, accompanied by loud, audible wheezes. He was alert and responsive to commands, which was a small relief.

"Grandpa, you're looking very pale, and your breathing doesn't sound right," Maria said as she helped him sit up more comfortably with a wedge pillow behind his back. This seemed to ease his breathing slightly.

She quickly took her stethoscope and listened to his lungs; both sides seemed congested with decreased sounds in the lower portions and moist sounds in the upper lobes. It was clear to her experienced ear that he likely had pneumonia.

"Grandpa, it looks like your cold has turned into something more serious. I'm calling an ambulance right now. You need to be seen in the Emergency Room immediately," Maria said, her voice a mixture of professionalism and concern.

Grandpa, understanding the severity of the situation, nodded his agreement, trusting Maria's judgment. As she dialed for the ambulance, her hands trembled slightly, a mix of fear and determination etched on her face.

Maria quickly opened the front door and rushed back to assist Grandpa as the paramedics arrived. They immediately administered oxygen and monitored his vital signs. Maria briefed them on his condition, and they swiftly set up an intravenous line, preparing to transport him to the hospital.

"I'll see you in the ER, Grandpa. I love you very much," Maria said, her voice laden with concern. After the paramedics took Grandpa, she called her mom, Ethel, and Harry to update them. Ethel was already on her way to the hospital, and Maria promised Harry she would call him with updates after the doctors assessed Grandpa in the ER.

Upon arriving at the hospital, Maria found that her mom hadn't arrived yet. She inquired at the reception desk and was escorted to Grandpa's room. He was now on oxygen, his breathing slightly eased but still labored. As they brought in the X-ray machine, Maria stepped outside the room for a moment, observing through the window that his heart monitor displayed a fast heart rate along with signs of distress. Once the chest X-ray was completed, the ER physician approached Maria, knowing her medical background.

"Your Grandpa has double pneumonia affecting both lungs," the doctor explained, showing her the X-ray. "His heart monitor shows sinus tachycardia—it's fast but regular—with many premature ventricular contractions. We're starting him on intravenous antibiotics and steroids to help him breathe easier."

"Thank you, Dr. Smith," Maria responded, absorbing the gravity of the situation just as Ethel rushed into the room. Ethel kissed her father on the cheek, turning to Maria with a worried expression.

"The doctor just left," Maria informed her mom. "Grandpa has pneumonia in both lungs, a fever, and a fast heart rate. They've begun treatment. Now, all we can do is wait and see how he responds."

"What happened that made you check on him today?" Ethel asked, puzzled.

"Mom, Elsie's mother called me at work because the housecleaners were concerned when Grandpa didn't answer the door. They tried to reach you without success. I came over as soon as I could and found him in bed, breathing fast and shallow. I immediately called for an ambulance," Maria recounted.

"Oh, our next-door neighbor probably saved his life. They are really wonderful neighbors," Ethel sighed, relief and worry mingling in her voice. "Thank you, Maria, for coming so quickly."

"Mom, you don't need to thank me. I would do anything for you, Dad, or Grandpa," Maria assured her, her voice thick with emotion. "I sure hope and pray that Grandpa recovers. I'm going to call Harry now and update him."

After speaking with Harry, Maria used the restroom and unexpectedly ran into him in the waiting room, where he was speaking with her dad. She updated Harry on Grandpa's condition, grateful for his support during such a stressful time.

"Hi Dad, Grandpa has pneumonia in both lungs. They are admitting him to the Intensive Care Unit."

"Oh no, he seemed fine last night. He had a bad cold, but I am so shocked."

"Dad, sometimes it happens this way. All we can do is pray for Grandpa."

Ethel, Raymond, Maria and Harry were all in the ICU waiting room. Ethel had called Emily and Edith and informed them about Grandpa. They both were living in San Diego California. Maria told them she would call them back when they had further information. The attending physician came out and talked to the four of them. He asked how aggressive they wanted to be with Joe. All of a sudden, the physician got called back to the unit. Maria tried to explain to her family what the doctor was asking them. She explained that the doctor wants to know the patient's and family's wishes for treatment. He had been gone for a long time, and Maria was getting worried.

Maria looked at the door to the unit and saw the doctor heading their way. They were the only ones in the ICU lounge.

"There was just an issue with Joe. His heart and breathing just stopped. We tried to restart his heart and did everything we could for him, but unfortunately, he didn't make it. I am so sorry. My condolences to you and your family."

"Can we go see him?"

"Of course. I will have his nurse come out and get you. Again, my condolences to you and your family. Let us know if there is anything we can do and if you have any further questions."

"Thank you."

They were all in shock. Maria, Ethel, and Harry all started crying. They were all thinking about how this happened. Harry hugged Maria tight, and Raymond hugged Ethel. The tears were pouring down, and they had no idea what to think. The nurse had the room closed off and told them that they could take the time they needed. The four of them remained with Grandpa for a while. They all said their goodbyes. Raymond and Harry went back to the waiting room. Maria helped her mom with the forms that needed to be signed. Maria said her goodbye, and Ethel remained in the room for a while. When Ethel said her final goodbye, the four of them left the hospital together. They were all in disbelief at what just occurred. It happened so fast, and nobody had expected this outcome. They all looked dazed and confused. They were all thinking about where they would go from here. Maria told her family how much she loved them and:

"Grandpa didn't suffer; we can all be comforted in this thought. "

"Your right Maria, but it is such a shock." Ethel states.

"I wish I could take the pain away from all of us."

They all headed to their own cars, left the hospital parking lot, and drove home. When they got home, they checked to make sure everyone arrived home safely. Life, as they knew it, had changed tonight. Grandpa has been an integral part of all their lives. Now, they must go through the grieving process and come to terms with what just happened. You never know what will happen in this life. At least they all had each other for support.

Maria and Harry got home and look at each other, staring off into space. They both were so connected to Grandpa, and both felt so lost. Maria says:

"We did everything we could for Grandpa, but I wish I didn't feel guilty that I should have gone over there sooner and checked on him."

"Maria, there was no reason for you to go to your parent's house as he just had a bad cold. Don't blame yourself as you were an amazing granddaughter, who was so loved and please just try to remember the good times. I am totally broken, too, as he was the grandfather that I never had. I was always amazed at how we had the same interests. I wish I could take away the pain from you, me, and your whole family."

"Thank you so much, Harry. You are loving, wonderful, supportive and I know I will need you to get over this."

"Maria I am always there for you whatever you need. If in the middle of the night you need to talk just, please let me know. You are my priority. I love you so much and it really breaks my heart to see you so sad."

"Thank you, Harry. The same goes for you. I know you were very close to grandpa, so if you ever need to talk you let me know too. I love you so much. I think I want to get some sleep"

"Me too. Love you"

"Love you."

The next day, Maria helped her mom plan the services. Maria and Ethel both wanted to speak at the funeral. Grandpa had so many friends that he made during his time in Iowa. He also had so many friends from California and relatives. Edith and Emily arrived back in Iowa. Maria hadn't seen her sisters in a while but wished the reunion was under different circumstances.

Joe's service is planned for five days from that day. There were many out-of-town friends and family coming, and they wanted to give them time for whoever wanted to attend. Maria found herself crying at frequent intervals. She was still in shock and disbelief. Maria learned the stages of grief in nursing school. She was wondering how long she would cry at any given moment.

The Church was completely full for Joe's services. Maria knew her Grandpa was loved by so many, but the outpouring of love for him was overwhelming. After the services, they asked everyone is invited to join them at their house in 2 hours. They also said that anyone could come to the cemetery if they wished. The caterers were at the house getting everything ready. Most of the guests showed up at the Hernandez house. There was so much reminiscing, love, support, and memories brought up throughout the evening. It turned out to be a special memorial for a very special man.

After the services, as everyone resumed their normal lives, the reality of her grandfather's absence hit Maria hard. She took another week off work to gather her strength, feeling emotionally and physically drained. During this time, she took many naps and spent hours reflecting on her life. Grief is profoundly personal, and Maria found herself intermittently crying when memories of her grandfather surfaced unexpectedly. He had always been her steadfast supporter, cheering her on in every endeavor. She reminisced about the years they cared for her grandmother together, growing closer with each day. She was grateful he had moved back to Iowa to be close to family. She fondly recalled how he surprised her with a car and how warmly he had treated Harry, even convincing her parents to let her move in with him. His encouragement was a pivotal reason she pursued nursing—a career that had brought her much fulfillment. Maria returned to work the following week, carrying the memory of her grandfather close to her heart.

Throughout 1992, Maria often found herself in tears, understanding that the pain of loss lingers because love does not end. She and Harry gradually returned to their routine, the normalcy a bittersweet comfort. Maria continued her daily conversations with Samantha, who was now expecting her first child, a girl. Maria was thrilled for her friend and hoped that she too would soon be pregnant so their children could grow up close in age. She was eagerly looking forward to attending Samantha's baby shower in a few weeks.

Maria and Harry decided to try for a baby, believing there was no better time than the present. They were uncertain about whether to stay in Iowa or move back to California, a decision they had postponed since they had initially stayed for her grandfather. They opted against buying a house for the time being, waiting to see how their plans unfolded. Each month that Maria wasn't pregnant brought disappointment, but she remained hopeful about the future.

The winter of 1992 was particularly harsh, with widespread illnesses including severe colds, flu, and pneumonia affecting the community. One particularly rough day, half of Harry's office was out sick. Despite feeling unwell himself with a persistent sore throat that wouldn't abate, Harry, ever the dedicated manager, chose to continue working. Maria, concerned, urged him to see a doctor and get a throat culture, but Harry reassured her he was fine and didn't need medical attention. His condition worsened, however, developing into a cough and sudden fever. Maria, increasingly worried, insisted:

"Harry, we are going to Urgent Care now. It's clear you're sicker than you've let on. You don't need to protect me; let's get you checked out."

Reluctantly, Harry agreed, fetching his coat with a weak smile. "Okay, if you say so. I trust you, love."

Their drive to the urgent care was tense, with Maria's concern growing as Harry's coughs echoed in the car. The looming worry about his health cast a shadow over their spirits, reminding Maria of how quickly situations can change.

The urgent care was part of the hospital complex where Maria's current job was located. The nurse started asking Harry numerous questions. Harry told her that he had had a bad sore throat for days. He told her that some of his co-workers had strep throat. He said that his throat felt raw and itchy. He also told her his tonsils looked red and swollen, and his neck looked swollen. She told him the neck is probably your lymph nodes, which swell up to fight infections. He told her that he was here today because he had a fever of 103 degrees, which came on suddenly. He also told the nurse that he had a cough and his chest hurt.

"One other thing I noticed just today is that I am not urinating very much at all."

The nurse asked Harry if he was on any medications Harry informed the nurse that he took nothing but Tylenol. She told him she was going to take his vital signs. "His blood pressure was low, and his heart rate was fast. She told him she was going to do a throat culture and the doctor would be in soon. The doctor came in and ordered a Chest X-ray and lab work. After the results were available the doctor came in and told Maria and Harry:

"You have pneumonia (inflammation of the sacs of the lungs), lung abscess (dying of a portion of the lung), and streptococcus glomerulonephritis (a rare kidney disease caused by the streptococcus bacteria). Your labs are abnormal, especially your kidney function. We need you to go to the Emergency Room now. I will let them know you are coming and give them your history."

'Thank you, Dr Fleming," Harry and Maria stated.

The Emergency room wasn't too far away, but Maria insisted on getting him into a wheelchair to transport him there. Harry thought that she was making a big deal about the situation. The nurse was waiting for them and took them back to a room. Maria went out of the room to fill out the paperwork and insurance information. When she returned to the room Harry was on the heart monitor and getting blood gas to measure his oxygen level. Harry's heart rate increased up to 170-190 beats per minute, which was fast and abnormal. They were giving him some medication through his intravenous line to slow down his heart rate. Maria was looking at all the things transpiring with Harry, and now she was starting to really worry. Harry never let on that he wasn't feeling good until he spiked a fever and started coughing.

Harry remained in the ER for hours. They called in a Renal Specialist (kidney doctor) to evaluate him. The specialist thought that Harry may have developed an acute kidney failure. Maria thought Harry was a healthy man in his thirties. How did this happen? All from an untreated probable strep throat infection. Maria was very worried. They admitted Harry to the Intermediate Step-down unit, where they could keep a close eye on him. This was the same type of unit that Maria did her patient care experience in the hospital. The transport team came to the ER and transferred

Harry to his room. He had a private room, so Maria was able to stay with him in the room. Maria introduced herself to his nurse and asked if she could have a cot and stay with her husband. The nurse said she would admit Harry and then went to ask her charge nurse. His nurse came back and said all was clear for Maria to stay. Maria thanked his nurse. She told Harry:

"I am going down to the cafeteria and get something to eat before it closes. I will be right back."

"Ok darling, you know where to find me. Love you"

"Love you, babe." Maria looked for the nearest phone to call Stan and Samantha, as well as Harry's parents. She didn't want to cause undue worry but felt they needed to be informed about the situation, especially since Harry's parents were physicians and would want to know about their son immediately. Maria reached Harry's mom and shared everything the doctors had told her. She mentioned that she would call his admitting physician for further clarification. Harry's mom thanked Maria for notifying them so quickly. Maria then called Samantha to inform her and spoke with Stan about his brother's condition, promising to call them back the next day.

After the calls, Maria headed to the cafeteria, grabbed a turkey sandwich, ate it quickly, and returned to Harry's room. Harry was settled in, and the lab technician was there to draw more blood. His nurse, who was very kind and reminded Maria of herself, checked in and asked Harry if he was hungry, offering to get him a sandwich or whatever was available at that late hour. Housekeeping brought in a cot for

Maria as it was close to the change of shift and a new nurse would soon arrive.

The night nurse entered and introduced herself to both Harry and Maria. She commented that Maria looked familiar and mentioned that she worked in case management and was the admitting nurse. She took Harry's vital signs and completed her assessment. She asked if they needed anything before turning off the lights to let them rest.

Before they knew it, Harry and Maria had fallen asleep and were awakened at 5 am by the lab technician who came to draw more blood. They fell back asleep until the day nurse introduced herself. She informed them that several doctors would be visiting that day, including Harry's primary care physician, a cardiologist, and a kidney specialist. The primary care physician was the first to arrive, explaining that since Harry's heart had moments of rapid beating, he had arranged for a cardiologist to evaluate him. He also mentioned that a kidney specialist would give their opinion.

Doctors came and went throughout the day, conducting exams, ordering tests, and prescribing medications. Maria noticed that Harry's breathing became increasingly rapid and shallow. He was spiking a fever and had minimal urine output despite taking fluids orally and through his IV. The nurse administered Tylenol to manage his fever. As Harry's condition appeared to deteriorate, Maria grew more concerned by the minute.

The kidney specialist arrived and mentioned that they were closely monitoring Harry's labs. He warned that they might need to start dialysis soon to compensate for his kidneys' diminished function. As the evening progressed, the nurse observed Harry's breathing becoming even more labored, and despite being on oxygen, it seemed insufficient. He also began to accumulate fluid in his extremities, causing noticeable swelling in his feet and hands. Concerned, the nurse called his physician, and they decided to transfer him to the Intensive Care Unit for closer monitoring.

In the ICU, Maria was required to stay in the lounge while additional lines were set up for Harry. Once settled, they allowed her to visit him. Harry, looking confused and weary, asked why he had been moved. Maria explained that it was so the medical staff could keep a better eye on him. She then stepped out to call Harry's parents and Samantha and Stan, informing them of the situation. They all booked flights to Des Moines for the following morning, and Maria's parents agreed to pick them up from the airport.

As Harry's condition worsened, more equipment was attached to him every hour, and a drip was started to help maintain his blood pressure. After Harry fell asleep, Maria returned to the lounge to catch some rest before his family arrived. She asked the nurse to notify her when he woke up.

Maria slept in the lounge until 5 am and then waited a while before going back to see Harry. By 7 am, she returned to his room. Harry appeared somewhat disoriented and asked if she could take him out for a McDonald's milkshake. Maria stayed briefly but left as the nurses needed to attend to him; she returned only after they called her back.

Around 5 pm, Harry's parents, along with Stan and Samantha, arrived. The reunions were emotional; Maria and Samantha cried as they hadn't seen each other in some time. Harry's parents were deeply concerned and spoke with the physicians about his condition. A dialysis access line was inserted in preparation for starting dialysis. They decided to stay with Maria's parents or at their apartment to rest.

Harry's condition in the ICU continued to deteriorate; he became less stable and less responsive. Medication was continuously adjusted to manage his blood pressure, and despite starting dialysis, which improved his mental clarity somewhat, his lung function continued to decline. Everyone, except for Maria's parents who were going back and forth, stayed in the visitor lounge, unwilling to leave. Maria was grateful for Samantha's presence, who had left her newborn daughter with her mother to support her. The gravity of the situation kept them all praying and hoping for Harry's recovery.

Maria told Harry:

"Harry, I love you so much. I can't believe what a wonderful life we've had so far. You need to fight to stay with me and your family. You can do it. We have so much of life to still live. You are my everything, honey; I love you more than you will ever know."

Harry's heart rate was slow, and the medical team decided to insert a temporary pacemaker to control it. Each day brought more medical lines and interventions. Maria updated her parents on Harry's worsening condition, and Stan's parents did the same for him. Things were looking grim; all they could do was pray and urge the doctors to try anything that might help. The entire hospital staff had grown close to the family and shared their hopes for a positive outcome.

As the days passed, Harry did not respond to the treatments. Maria was haunted by how such a tragedy could befall a healthy man in his thirties. Harry's parents were deeply worried, sensing that Harry's body was shutting down. One afternoon, Maria heard the urgent call over the intercom, "Respiratory to ICU, stat." Her heart sank with the realization that the call was for Harry. She was right. Despite repeated efforts to restart his heart and the administration of numerous medications, Harry's heart stopped, and they could not revive him. The ICU staff, deeply affected, continued their attempts to save him, but it was not to be. This was profoundly upsetting for everyone involved. Harry's nurse, in tears, thought of his wonderful family and his devoted wife. It was a scene of profound sadness, uncommon for someone so young.

Surrounded by both families and Samantha, Maria broke down and wept uncontrollably. She mourned, "This isn't how it was supposed to end." In just eighteen months, she had lost both her grandfather and her husband—the two most important men in her life, aside from her father. Overwhelmed by grief, she questioned how she could continue. "Life can be so sweet and yet so cruel," she sobbed, surrounded by her loved ones who tried to offer comfort. The reality of facing life without Harry was daunting, and in that moment, the support of her family was her only solace.

CHAPTER 20-

Maria was so distraught that she quit her job and moved back in with her parents. After the service for her husband, she felt like she couldn't go on. Her parents were deeply worried about her. She talked to Samantha every day, who tried to comfort her sister and best friend, but no words could console Maria. Samantha attempted to persuade Maria to move back to California and get a job with her company. If there were no positions available there, there were many other Utilization Review companies in her building. Maria could apply to Samantha's company and others in the building. She was likely to get a job with one of them. Her two sisters were also trying to convince Maria to move to San Diego, where they both lived. Maria had moved to Iowa to keep her grandpa company and ensure he thrived there. Eventually, Maria decided she would move back to California, specifically to the San Francisco Bay Area near Samantha, Stan, and Francisca. Stan and Samantha lived in Burlingame, a suburb of San Francisco.

Maria drove to California with her parents, with a U-Haul trailing behind her car. They drove slowly, so it took them four days. When they arrived at Stan and Samantha's house, they all started crying. Maria was thrilled to meet baby girl Francisca, who was adorable and very talkative. Maria thought to herself, sadly, "It's too bad I didn't get pregnant when Harry and I were trying. Then I would have a part of

Harry forever." The thought saddened her even more, realizing it wasn't meant to be.

The next day, Maria's parents had a flight back home. Driving them to the San Francisco airport, Maria cried, thinking about how she would be away from her parents. "I've been in Iowa for so many years," she said tearfully to her parents as they unloaded their bags. "I'm going to miss you and everyone so much." Despite the tears, she was relieved to think that she would be around her best friend, Samantha, Stan, and Francisca.

Maria looked around for a nice apartment in Burlingame while staying with Samantha and her family. Francisca, at eighteen months old with such a bright personality, cheered up Maria. "You're such a little sunshine, aren't you?" Maria would say, lifting Francisca into her arms, feeling a momentary escape from her sorrows. Being back around Samantha brought some solace, yet Maria found herself unable to understand how a healthy man like Harry could get so sick so fast. "I'm still in denial, aren't I?" she confessed one evening to Samantha, who listened sympathetically. Maria knew deep down that she would never fully get over losing Harry, but she hoped that in time, the pain would become more bearable. Harry would always be in her heart.

Stan and Samantha had helped Maria move into her apartment. Samantha stayed over Friday and Saturday nights to help Maria decorate and fix up her new space. It reminded them of when they had first moved into their college dorms, bringing back fond memories of their days in college. Samantha had to leave on Sunday evening because she had work the next morning.

Ethel called Maria to let her know that a letter had arrived from one of the companies where she had applied for a UR job. She asked her mom to please open the letter. It stated that Maria had been accepted for the position of Utilization Review Nurse. This was the company that had interviewed her several times by phone while she was still in Iowa. They assumed that with her experience as a float nurse and working in the critical care units, she would have all the background necessary to excel in her position. They also liked that she had experience discussing situations with physicians and some charge nurse experience.

Maria first called Samantha to share the wonderful news. "I got the job, Sam!" she exclaimed, her voice brimming with excitement. She then called her sisters and friends back home to tell them as well. She was going to start her new job in three weeks, and they had told her she would have a two-month orientation.

Maria often babysat Francisca when Samantha and Stan were working. She adored being around Francisca and had so much fun with her. However, she frequently found herself daydreaming about what it would have been like if she had been able to get pregnant when she and Harry were trying. She tried to push those thoughts out of her mind because they just made her sad.

Maria went shopping for some new clothes to wear to work. She needed business attire such as suits, pantsuits, and dresses. She loved to shop and found five outfits at one store and two more at another. She was excited to work in a business environment. "You're going to love it," Samantha had told her. "The day goes by so fast because the requests for authorizations just keep coming in. There's a lot to learn, but you'll be on top of the latest medical advances."

Maria started her new job that day. She and Samantha drove to work together. Everyone at her job was so nice and friendly. The company was quite large, and they went around introducing Maria to the managers of the different departments. She wasn't good at remembering names and was so relieved they had given her a list of all the employees and their extensions. Today was orientation for all the new employees from every department. They went through all the company's policies, rules, and regulations. Most of the talks were interesting, but some were a bit dull. Maria was the only new employee from her department.

As they walked through the halls, Samantha whispered, "You're going to do great here. Just give it some time, and soon it'll feel like you've been here forever." Maria nodded, feeling a mix of nervousness and excitement at this new chapter in her life.

The next day, Maria learned about the computer and how to access all the essential information required for her job. She found her orientation very interesting but felt overwhelmed by the sheer amount of information she needed to absorb. As they settled into their routines, Samantha and Maria often discussed their jobs, and Maria gleaned an enormous amount from Samantha. They both held identical positions at different companies, but on the same floor. They drove to work together and came home together, alternating who drove each week. There was a large lunchroom on their floor, and they usually had lunch together. They were not just best friends; they were sisters and sisters-in-law.

Maria's life seemed stable as she established her new existence in California. Yet, she often found herself reflecting on her previous life in California, many years ago. Thoughts of Alberto and that incredible day on the beach occasionally surfaced. She hadn't thought about him in a long time and felt guilty for these reminiscences as she missed Harry intensely.

"Sam, do you ever feel guilty for thinking about the past?" Maria asked one day during lunch, her voice tinged with a mix of nostalgia and sorrow.

"Sometimes, yes," Samantha replied, understanding her conflict. "But it's part of who we are, and it's okay to remember and honor those parts of our lives."

Maria nodded, appreciating Samantha's reassurance but still struggling with her emotions. "I just want these thoughts to go away sometimes, so I can focus on building my new life here, without feeling like I'm betraying Harry."

"It's not a betrayal, Maria. It's a part of healing and moving forward, even though it hurts," Samantha said gently, offering a supportive smile.

Maria sighed, looking out the window of the lunchroom, feeling the weight of her memories and the challenge of moving forward. She knew she needed to find a way to live with her past and embrace her future, whatever it might hold.

CHAPTER 21-

Marissa and Alberto had the picture, perfect life. Things were running smoothly since Alberto hired a nurse practitioner in his office. Also, he shared calls with another physician, and life had become less hectic for Alberto. Marissa loved running the office, and she did an amazing job, per Alberto. The office staff loved their jobs, and everyone worked well together. Alberto and Marissa ordered lunch for the staff or would take them out to lunch frequently. Marisa and Alberto thought they were living their dream.

Alberto and Marissa frequently went out to dinner after work. One night, as they discussed their future over a meal, they decided that it was time to start looking at houses to purchase their first home. Having paid off a significant portion of their student loans, they felt financially prepared to take this step toward home ownership. They debated whether to live in the city or the suburbs, ultimately deciding to look in San Francisco since Alberto's practice was located there, making it more convenient. They planned to explore options in the Marina District, Pacific Heights, and the Sunset District.

During one of these dinners, Alberto said to Marissa:

"We are situated financially and have the office running well now. I think we should start our family now. I know you wanted to start it after we were married. You patiently waited for me to finish school and for us to get married. Then you waited for me to set up my office and get established before having children. I want you to know how much I love you for all the support you have given me through all of this. It must not have been easy for you, Marissa. I love you more than you will ever know."

"Thank you, Alberto. At times it was difficult, but I just kept focusing on the prize, which is all of our dreams. I still pinch myself at times, thinking how lucky I was to meet you in Mexico during that awesome holiday season. I know we will have an amazing family and go onto to have a wonderful life. I can't wait to start a family and we can start right away. I love you so much Alberto."

Marissa and Alberto frequently tried to have a baby. Months went by without Marissa getting pregnant, and she started to get discouraged. One day, Marisa felt a bit nauseous and tired. She missed her period and decided she would go to her doctor, and it turned out she was pregnant. She couldn't wait to tell Alberto. She was going to tell him tonight at home. She was so excited at work. Alberto says to Marissa:

"Marissa, you seem to be in such a good mood today.'"

"The sunshine just makes me happy. There is no fog, and this makes me think of summer. I am going to the bank to make our deposit now."

"Be careful, Marissa"

"I will. Don't worry, the bank is across the street." Marissa waited for the light to change, and with no cars in sight, she began crossing the street. Suddenly, a car sped around the corner and struck her with tremendous force. She was hurled through the air and landed several yards away. Onlookers on the sidewalk witnessed the horrific accident and rushed to assist her. Marissa appeared unresponsive, not reacting to sound, her breathing shallow though her pulse was strong. One of the bystanders quickly called 911.

The police arrived at the scene swiftly, followed by the fire department and paramedics. Meanwhile, Alberto, hearing the commotion, looked out the window onto the street below. To his dismay, he saw someone lying in the road and feared it might be Marissa, who had mentioned heading that way. Panic gripped him as he ran out into the street and found his beautiful, sweet wife lying motionless on the ground. His heart plummeted.

"Marissa! Can you hear me?" he called desperately, but she did not respond.

The paramedics quickly set up an IV, attached her to a heart monitor, performed an EKG, and administered oxygen. They prepared to transport her to St. Francis Hospital, where Alberto had privileges and was well-known. As they loaded Marissa into the ambulance, Alberto's fear and anxiety overwhelmed him.

Rushing back to his office, Alberto's face was pale, his steps hurried. He burst into the office, where Carol, his nurse, immediately noticed his distress.

"Alberto, what's wrong?" Carol asked with concern.

"It's Marissa... she's been hit by a car. They're taking her to St. Francis now," he managed to say, his voice breaking.

"Oh no, I'm so sorry, Alberto. Do you need me to do anything?" Carol responded, her tone full of sympathy.

"Yes, please handle things here. I have to go to the hospital," Alberto replied, trying to maintain composure.

"Of course, Alberto. We'll take care of everything here. Go take care of Marissa," Carol reassured him, offering a supportive touch on his shoulder as he turned to leave, rushing to be by his wife's side at the hospital.

"We will take care of everything; please just call us with an update. Our prayers and thoughts are with you and Marissa,"

"Thank you so much, Carol." Alberto flew out of his office to his car. He drove to the hospital, parking in the physician's lot, and Marissa was already in the ER. Alberto knew the ER doctor very well." He told Alberto:

"Your wife's vital signs are stable, but her breathing is shallow, and she isn't responding to any verbal commands. We are going to take her for CT brain." They took Marissa right away for the CT scan.

Alberto went to call her parents, Anne and Dave. He told them what happened, and Marissa's current status. They decided they would just go to the airport and get on the next flight. Alberto told them to let him know when they arrived, and he or his parents would pick them up from the airport. They thanked Alberto for letting them know so quickly. Alberto also called his parents to let them know what had happened. They told Alberto to keep them updated and that they would pick up Anne and Dave from the airport. He also called his office and gave Carol an update, and told her to call with any questions.

Marissa was back in her room. They waited a little while, and the results of the CT scan were back. It showed severe brain edema (swelling) and decreased white and grey matter differentiation. They were putting her on anti-seizure medication to prevent seizures, diuretics, and steroids to decrease the swelling in her brain. They would transfer Marissa to the ICU shortly. Alberto was numb and thought about the accident. He wondered if anyone got the information from the person who caused this terrible accident. He thought all he could do at that moment was focus on Marissa and pray for her recovery.

Marissa was in ICU, and they were worried about her oxygen level. She was breathing very shallowly, her oxygen levels were falling dramatically, and they had no choice but to intubate (insert a tube down the trachea to help the patient breathe) her. Alberto was just distraught as this wasn't a good sign, and Marissa was just getting worse. The Neurologist and Alberto discussed different possible treatment options for the brain swelling, which was most likely why she remained unresponsive. They monitored her with Intracranial pressure monitoring (ICP), which monitors for increased intracranial pressure, and EEG monitoring, which monitors for seizures and is sensitive to changes in her brain function. If the medications didn't decrease the swelling, they would have to take her to surgery.

It was now around three in the morning and Alberto went to the physician's lounge to get some rest. He asked Marissa's nurse to call him if there were any changes. Alberto managed to sleep until eight thirty. He cleaned up and went back to the ICU to see how things had gone overnight. Marissa was critical but stable. She remained unresponsive to stimuli. Alberto talked to Marissa.

"You are an amazing, wonderful wife. I love you so much. We have so much to live and experience in life. You will get better, and I will take care of you. I am your protector and will be by your side forever, until our last day on earth. You are my soulmate and my everything. I love you more than you will ever know." After visiting for a while, Alberto decided to go to the cafeteria and get some breakfast. He ate a little but realized it was hard for him to eat because his stomach was just turning in knots. He kept thinking about the person who hit his wife. Had the police caught them for excessive speed, negligence, and did they even stop at the scene?

Coincidentally, the phone rang and Alberto received a call from a detective from the San Francisco Police Department. He wanted to meet with Alberto if he had some time. The detective said he could come to the hospital. Alberto agreed, and they decided to meet at the front entrance of the hospital at two that afternoon. At two, Alberto was at the front entrance, and the detective, Jerry, introduced himself. He asked Alberto how Marissa was doing. Alberto gave him an update on her condition. Jerry told Alberto that the person who hit his wife had fled the scene. There were several witnesses who had provided information on the make and model of the car, but they were unable to get the license plate. They were looking for the car now. They had several people on the case. Jerry handed Alberto his business card and told him that he would be in touch. He told him to call if he had any questions. Jerry assured Alberto they would catch the person who could leave the scene and just let his wife lay there. Jerry walked away, and Alberto was left dumbfounded by the news.

Dorothy had just called, informing them that they were picking up Anne and Dave at the airport in a few minutes. They would all proceed to the hospital. Dorothy would call Alberto when they arrived at the hospital. Alberto went back to the ICU and checked on Marissa. She was unchanged and stable. He talked to her, gave her a kiss on her cheek, and held her hand, hoping desperately that she might squeeze his hand in response. There was no response to verbal commands, but the best thing he could do was talk to Marissa, as it was believed that persons in a coma could hear what was spoken to them. Alberto's phone rang, and it was his mom. He said he would go to the atrium to meet them.

Alberto saw his parents and Anne and Dave. They all hugged, kissed, and Anne and Dorothy were crying. They had become such close friends over the years and wished they didn't have to meet under these circumstances. Alberto gave them all an update on Marissa's condition. She had been holding her own, and he told them that she wasn't responding yet, but that could happen with brain swelling. She had a breathing tube and other lines. He said he was going in there to check if they could go in. They allowed two people at a time into the ICU. Alberto told Anne and Dave that he would check out her room to see if they could go see Marissa. He told them he would be right back. Alberto came back and told them that the three of them could go in, and she was in room three. Anne thought her daughter looked very pale. Alberto introduced Marissa's parents to her nurse and then he left the room so they could visit. He went back to the lounge to see his parents. Marissa's parents were at the bedside for a long time as they didn't want to leave their daughter. Alberto tried his best to explain the situation to alleviate their fears. Poor Anne just kept crying and saying:

"My only baby, how did this happen." Dorothy and Tony went in with Alberto to see Marissa for a short time. Dorothy came out with tears rolling down her cheek. They all stayed in the ICU lounge for a while and then decided to go to the cafeteria to get something to eat. Anne and Dave wanted to stay at the hospital during the night and sleep in the lounge. Dorothy and Tony tried to convince them to stay at their house, and they would bring them back in the morning. Anne and Dave decided to stay at the hospital. Alberto's parents went back to their house for the night.

The next morning, Dorothy and Tony came back to the hospital. Anne, Dave, and Alberto were able to get some sleep in the lounge. The days passed, and Anne and Dave would sometimes go over to Dorothy and Tony's house to sleep, and other times, they would stay in the ICU lounge. It was just so sad to see Marissa unchanged and remaining unresponsive. The doctors saw some changes and thought Marissa might be pregnant. They did a pregnancy test and found out she was pregnant. They all found out that Marissa was pregnant, and they were all in shock. They all thought about how that could happen. Alberto believed that since she was pregnant, she would fight with all her might to come back to them. As the days rolled along, there wasn't much change. She couldn't breathe on her own and was still unresponsive. Alberto was so weary and couldn't think about returning to his office and seeing patients. All their lives were on hold.

Regarding the person who hit Marissa, the police were able to locate the car and the owner. He was charged with a felony hit and run and drunk and reckless driving. Everyone was happy someone was in custody, but that didn't change the situation. They were glad that he was off the streets and couldn't do this to another family. Whenever he had his day in court the whole family planned on being there.

They had all decided to go to the hospital cafeteria for dinner. As they sat there eating, the intercom blared, "Pulmonary therapist to ICU stat." Alberto's heart sank. Although he knew the unit housed sixteen patients, he was deeply worried that the call might concern Marissa. After sitting for a few minutes, trying to engage in conversation and eat, he excused himself from the table and ran upstairs. Upon arrival, he saw that it was indeed Marissa's room. From the doorway, he observed a flat line on the heart monitor and watched as they shocked her heart several times. They continued with CPR and started several drips to help her heart. Alberto stood by the door, praying. He wanted to rush in and assist, but knew he had to leave it to the medical team. As minutes passed, the heart monitor showed no activity. The medical team persistently tried to restore a normal rhythm. After an hour of effort, the attending physician called off the code. Alberto entered the room and saw his beautiful, sweet wife lying there lifelessly. Shock overwhelmed him, as he had never anticipated such a tragedy. They were expecting a baby; they had so much life ahead. How could life be so cruel? Alberto remained in the room with Marissa for an hour, walking around like a zombie, trying to figure out the next steps. He had informed several family members about losses before, but never his own.

Alberto returned to the cafeteria, where the others were still engrossed in deep conversation. He appeared pale and anxious. They all looked up and asked, "Alberto, what is wrong?" He started crying, the distress evident on his face. "I don't know how to tell you this. My sweet wife, whom we all loved so dearly, has taken a turn for the worst. Her heart stopped, and despite all efforts, they couldn't restart it. I'm so sorry to bring this news to you. I am so, so sorry." Alberto, Dorothy, and Anne began to cry. They all embraced each other in a group hug. Anne and Dave then went upstairs to see their daughter one last time. Alberto had to return upstairs as well to complete some paperwork and answer some questions. Dorothy and Tony offered to drive Marissa's parents back to their house, and Alberto said he would head to his parents' house shortly after.

Anne and Dave were in utter shock. They had lost their only daughter, who had been their whole life. How could they continue without her? Dorothy and Tony felt deeply for Alberto but also for her parents. Dorothy said to Tony, "Alberto is such a compassionate man, who loved Marissa dearly. How will he survive without his dear wife? We have to be there for all three of them. They will need our help in the coming months." Tony agreed, "Dorothy, they will need our support. This is such a sad, unexpected outcome. You never know what the future will bring. We must live each day to the fullest."

Alberto left the hospital and drove to his parents' house. The five of them sat in shock and disbelief, crying at times. Dave turned to Anne and Alberto and began to speak.

"We have to think about where we will have Marissa's services. Do we want to have it here or go back to Texas. Alberto what do you think?"

"She has so many friends in Texas. I would love for her to stay here, but she is from Texas, and whatever you and Anne think is right, I will go along with it. I just can't believe we are having this discussion. Your daughter was so sweet and liked by so many people. I am in shock, as I know all of us are. I am so, so sorry."

They planned Marissa's memorial for five days in Texas at the Church she grew up in. They all six flew back to Texas together. Dorothy, Tony, and Alberto helped Anne and Dave as much as possible to get ready for the Memorial. Many people flew out from California for the services. Everybody in Alberto's office came to the services. The Church was crowded with so many of her friends. It was a beautiful memorial, and many people spoke about how caring and wonderful Marissa was and how nice she was to everyone. There were so many tears during the remembrance. The family was going to the cemetery, and they announced all were welcome to come by their house at five this evening for a celebration for Marissa.

There were so many people who came to the house. It was a nice gathering, and Anne and Dave were happy so many people came. Dorothy, Tony, and Alberto helped out immensely. Alberto knew many of her friends that he had been introduced to when they visited Texas several times. They all felt this was a beautiful celebration for a lovely daughter and sweet, adorable wife taken way too soon.

Tony, Alberto, and Dorothy stayed in Texas for a few days after the memorial to help Anne and Dave do the clean-up and just be there for support. They really appreciated the amazing friendship between the families. Alberto and his parents were back in California. His parents needed to get back to work. Alberto decided to go back to work, too.

It was nice to be back in the office. Alberto was glad to see Carol and everyone else. He thanked them all for coming to Marissa's memorial. He was going to call an agency for a temporary office manager. The office seemed to be running smoothly, with Carol taking on more responsibility. It was hard for Alberto as he missed Marissa, something fierce at home and enormously in the office. She was so organized and made life for Alberto so easy at work. The temporary fill-in office manager was good, but she wasn't Marissa. He was spoiled by Marissa. He could never stop thinking about her and how much he loved her. It is really difficult to lose your spouse as you lose part of yourself. Everything changed, and for Alberto, that included his work life too.

Alberto's lease had been set to expire in six months, and he grappled with the decision of whether to keep his office open and renew it. He often consulted his parents, seeking their opinions. He shared with them how challenging it had been to run the office without Marissa. During a visit to see Dorothy and Tony, Marissa's parents came over, and Alberto looked forward to their company. They had a heartfelt visit during which Alberto confided that he was contemplating closing his office. It was hard for them to give advice, but they listened attentively and provided thoughtful feedback.

Ultimately, Alberto decided not to renew his lease and closed his office. He felt terrible that his employees would lose their jobs, but they understood the difficulties he faced in maintaining the office atmosphere without Marissa. He provided them with an extremely generous severance package and assured them of his intention to remain in touch. Following this, Alberto found himself unemployed for several months, pondering his next career steps.

Alberto had a friend who had recently been hired as a medical director for an insurance company and spoke highly of the role. Intrigued, Alberto learned of an opening for a medical director at a downtown company seeking someone with a background in internal medicine and cardiology. Alberto fit the criteria perfectly. Encouraged by his friend, he applied for the position. Within less than a week, he received a call for an interview. After undergoing three interviews, where his character and expertise were clearly appreciated, he was offered the job and started two weeks later. He was eager to embark on this new chapter, looking forward to expanding his horizons and delving into a new facet of the medical field.

During his orientation week, Alberto engaged with the whole company and met all the department heads. He also spent time with another medical director who helped him acclimate to the new environment. He got to know the nurses, who shared their experiences and backgrounds. The nurse sitting right next to him, Samantha, was particularly helpful. She offered assistance with any computer issues or other queries he might have. They spoke often, and although Samantha thought his name rang a bell, she couldn't quite place where she had heard it before. His name, Dr. Alberto Bertolucci, was well-received, and he quickly became known as a pleasant and easy-going colleague among the nursing staff.

Samantha and Maria had lunch every day in the cafeteria on their floor. Sometimes they brought their food, and other days they purchased it from the restaurant. Samantha told Maria about the new, young medical director who had been recently hired. She mentioned she was going to ask him to join them for lunch. Maria agreed, saying it would be nice. The next day, Samantha asked Alberto to join them. He said he was free for lunch and appreciated the invite.

Maria was already seated at the table when Samantha and Alberto walked in. Alberto bought Samantha her lunch, and they walked to the table where Maria was seated. Samantha introduced them: "Maria, this is our new medical director, Dr. Alberto Bertolucci." Alberto said: "It's so nice to meet you, Maria." "Thank you. It's very nice to meet you too." They started talking, and Maria couldn't help but wonder if this was the same Alberto from the beach so many years ago. Her heart began pounding, and she could tell her face was flushed. Samantha could tell something was up with Maria. Maria said to Alberto: "Please don't take this the wrong way, but were you at the beach in July of 1974 and met a girl named Maria from Iowa?" "Yes, I was there." "I am Maria." "OMG, I can't believe that is you." Samantha, this is Alberto that I talked to you about forever and ever." "Oh Maria, no wonder I thought his name sounded familiar." Maria and Alberto started talking. She explained that the reason she didn't come to the beach the next day was that their family's car broke down that morning. She was so upset. He told her he came to the beach every day hoping she would be there. She explained that she stayed at her grandparents' house to help her grandfather take care of her grandmother with dementia. She told him she met Samantha there, as she was next door taking care of her grandfather too. They became best of friends. Alberto told Maria that he tried to find her. He called every high school in Iowa with a Lincoln high school. Then he asked if they had a Valedictorian named Maria Hernandez. Then he tried to find a listing for her parents, but that was unsuccessful too.

Alberto and Maria were both so happy and ecstatic about this coincidental meeting. They both expressed how amazing it was to meet again. Alberto asked Maria: "Are you married or involved with anyone?" "No, I am a recent widow," Maria exclaimed. "OMG, I am a widower too. Would you like to go out after work and catch up on our lives?" "Absolutely, I can't wait. See you at five at the ground floor lobby." "Sounds perfect." Samantha had driven them that day. Maria told Alberto that she would need a ride home. He said that would be no problem. All three of them went back to work for the afternoon. Maria couldn't wait to tell her mom, and she called her to share the great news. Ethel was very happy for her daughter. Maria had difficulty concentrating and just thought about how lucky she was that Samantha had asked Alberto to lunch. It was getting close to five, and Maria was getting excited. Alberto was also looking forward to seeing Maria. He thought she was so beautiful and sweet, just as he remembered. He still felt a connection to her, just like that day at the beach. There was a definite spark between them.

It was five in the evening, and they were both downstairs in the lobby. Alberto asked Maria if she would like to go for drinks and then for dinner. Maria said: "That sounds wonderful. I almost feel like I am dreaming, but you are real, Alberto." "Yes, I feel that way too, Maria." They crossed the street, and Alberto took Maria's hand. Maria found Alberto so good looking and such a gentleman. They decided where to go for drinks. Maria told Alberto that she had gone back home to Iowa and lived there for years after her grandmother passed. She had become very close to her grandfather, and they both went back to Iowa to live. She and Samantha went to nursing school together in Iowa. They graduated from nursing school the same year that Alberto graduated from medical school. Both Alberto and Maria were married in 1984. There seemed to be many similarities in their lives. The more they talked, the more they couldn't believe how similar their lives were. They decided to get dinner. They had a delicious dinner then decided to go to the bar for a nightcap. Maria and Alberto had so much to talk about they didn't want the night to end. They were drinking slowly but were just happy to hear about each other's lives. The bartender called last call, they didn't order anything, but continued talking until the restaurant closed. They were the last ones out of the restaurant.

Maria told Alberto that she lived in Burlingame. He told her she could stay at his place, and he would sleep on the couch. She told him she would need a change of clothes, or she would be the talk of the building. She suggested that he could stay at her place, and they could go by his place in the morning so he could change his clothes. Alberto thought this was a good idea.

They got to Maria's apartment, and they didn't want to go to sleep, but they wanted to continue talking. They started thinking it was Thursday night and they both had to work in the morning. Alberto kissed Maria and said they should go to sleep. Alberto was going to sleep on the couch, but then Maria told Alberto that he should sleep in the bed as long as all they did was cuddle. They cuddled and kissed and neither one could believe how this chance encounter may change both their lives forever.

The alarm went off and it seemed so early. Maria got up and made coffee and got ready for work. Alberto was still sleeping, and Maria said:

"Darling, you need to wake up. Here is some coffee."

"Thank you. Do you want to spend the weekend together, Maria?"

"Oh, that would be awesome. Do you want to meet after work? If you want, we can come here, and I will cook dinner."

"That sounds great. I will be thinking about you all day.
"

"I feel lucky that we have reconnected. I used to dream about you, and now you are my reality. You are so good-looking, Alberto. You must have all the women after you"

"You know Maria, after I lost my wife, I thought I would never be attracted to another woman until I saw you sitting in the cafeteria. The sparks flew, and I feel so close to you, although it has only been a day. I see the possibility of a future that I never thought I would have. I hope I am not scaring you by coming off like this, but I just want to express to you how I feel. "

"No, Alberto, I love hearing this, and I feel the same way. After my husband passed, I thought I would never be attracted to another man. Then I saw you, and firecrackers went off in my head and in my heart. I am so attracted to you and never thought this would be possible. I want to be around you all the time. I know that might sound too forward, but that is how I am feeling. I can't wait to introduce you to my family."

They drove to Alberto's condo, and he changed his clothes and got some clothes and things for the weekend. Then they went on to work. Alberto walked into his office, and behind him came Samantha. Alberto said to her:

"Thank you, Samantha, for asking me to go for lunch. I am so happy that Maria is your best friend. We had an awesome night. If it weren't for you, Maria and I might never have connected."

Maria was in such a good mood today, and she couldn't wait to speak to Samantha at lunch. They went to lunch as usual, and Maria told Samantha all about her night. She was so excited for both of them. Samantha said:

"Alberto is a doll and such a sweetheart. Just the way he treats us, nurses. I can see that any woman would be happy to be with him. Maria, I am so thrilled for you. You have gone through so much, and you deserve to be happy."

"Thank you, Samantha"

Friday night Maria cooked them a delicious dinner. Alberto said:

"Besides all your other great qualities, you are a wonderful cook too. I am so lucky"

"No, Alberto I am the one who is lucky. You are a charming, smart, very good-looking physician, and you are every girl's dream. I am not sure what I did to deserve you, but I feel like the luckiest woman on earth."After dinner, they cuddled on the couch and watched some TV. Alberto was kissing Maria, and she was just in heaven. They went to a movie on Saturday night. Alberto stayed at Maria's apartment all weekend. Things were going so amazingly well. Both of them were just thrilled to be in each other's company. It is now Sunday evening, Maria didn't want Alberto to go back home, but he needed to get ready for work on Monday. She would next be able to see him at lunch tomorrow. It sounded so far away. She has definitely fallen for Alberto and fast. He asked her

"Do you want to get some clothes for work? you can come stay at my house tonight."

"Oh, Alberto that sounds great. Just give me a few minutes and I will be ready."

Maria loved Alberto's San Francisco condo. She was happy to be there. Maria said:

"I need to take a shower. "

"Help yourself. I have two bathrooms. Take your choice. I would do some laundry and then order dinner."

"Sounds wonderful, babe." Maria came out of the shower with her wet hair and dressed in a silky long nightgown. Alberto said:

"You look amazing in whatever you have on Maria. You are gorgeous, sweetie."

"Thanks, Alberto."They ordered dinner, and then they lay on the couch and watched a movie. Alberto went to take a shower. Maria put his second load of laundry in the dryer. Now Alberto came out of the shower with his shirt unbuttoned and showing his sexy muscles and six-pack abdominals. Maria said:

"Boy are you something to look at with all those muscles. Do you spend hours in the gym? You could definitely be on the cover of any magazine. I never thought anyone as amazing as you would want to spend time around me. You are the total package and more."

"I have some exercise equipment in my exercise room. I should exercise more, but I try to at least three times a week. Maria, you know I love spending time around you, but you know we aren't getting much sleep."

"I think I am just living on the high of being with you," Maria called Samantha to let her know that she was at Alberto's and wouldn't be driving with her to work the next day. They would see each other at lunch the next day. Alberto had called his parents to let them know the amazing news. They couldn't wait to meet Maria. They asked Alberto if they would like to come to dinner on Friday night. He told them he would ask Maria and get back to them. Maria said she would love to meet his parents on Friday.

They had spent every night that week together, either at Maria's or Alberto's place. Samantha had asked Maria and Alberto to come over on Sunday and meet Stan and Francisca. Alberto said that he would love to go to Samantha's on Sunday. It was Friday evening, and Maria and Alberto were going to his parents' house for dinner. Maria had brought flowers for his mom and was excited to meet them. Maria loved their house and his parents. Dorothy and Tony were so impressed with Maria. She seemed so sweet and beautiful on the inside and out. They were really happy for their son and Maria. They told Maria to come back anytime. Maria thanked them for such wonderful hospitality. Alberto and Maria went back to her house for the weekend.

On Saturday, they woke up late and had coffee. They both expressed that they were afraid that they were dreaming and that they would wake from the dream. They felt this was almost too good to be true, but it was real. They both realized how lucky they were to be living this amazing life. There was one thing on both their minds. They both were thinking about taking the relationship to the next level. Alberto wanted Maria to make the first move on this issue. He wanted to take things at her pace. He loved her so much and wanted her to feel comfortable and he was respectful of her wishes. Maria loved Alberto and was ready to show him. Maria said to Alberto:

"You know, I was thinking maybe we could take things to the next level. I know I said I only want to cuddle, but you are driving me crazy, and I want more, Alberto,"

"Oh, Maria, those are the words I was hoping to hear, but I would have waited as long as you wanted. Are you sure this is what you want?

"Yes Alberto, I am sure."

"I am going to the store and will pick up some Chinese food for us to eat."

"Sounds good, babe." Alberto got the food and two dozen roses and returned to Maria's. They ate the Chinese food, and Alberto said: "Maria, why don't you slip into one of your short, silky nightgowns. I am going to change too." He went in and put rose petals all over her bed. Alberto came out with no shirt on, and Maria was about to melt, thinking this gorgeous, intelligent man wanted to spend his life with her. She knew he could have almost any woman he wanted, and he had chosen her. She had some difficult years, but God had really blessed her lately.

Alberto brought the rest of the flowers to Maria. She said: "How thoughtful of you. Thank you so much." They started kissing on the couch. Alberto ran his hands tenderly all over her body. Maria's body tingled everywhere. They stayed on the couch for about an hour. Then Alberto carried Maria to her bedroom. She saw all the rose petals over the bed. Maria said: "Alberto, you are so romantic." He took off her panties and started massaging her all over. They spent all evening in bed making love. Alberto said to Maria: "I love you, Maria." "Oh, Alberto, I love you too." They both were so in love and couldn't believe they had such strong feelings so quickly for each other. The relationship was meant to be. This is what storybooks and fairytales are made of, but this was real. They were going to have to go to sleep soon as tomorrow was Sunday and they had plans. Alberto said: "Maybe one more time." Maria said: "You are so amazing in this bed. You can take someone to places that they have never been, and never dreamed existed. You are incredible, Alberto." They went on to make love one more time and both fell asleep in each other's arms.

They woke up Sunday around nine am, both naked, lying in each other's arms. Alberto started kissing Maria passionately and they made love again. They got up to shower together and they loved soaping each other's body. Alberto dried Maria's hair and rubbed lotion on her whole body. Maria put lotion on Alberto's back and started giving him a back massage. They both got dressed and were ready to leave for the day. They headed to Samantha's house and had a gift basket for them.

They arrived at Samantha and Stan's condo. Alberto and Stan hit it off and had so many things in common. Alberto loved Franscica and loved being around children. She took him to her playhouse, and he played with her for quite some time. Maria thought, besides all his amazing qualities, Alberto was great with children. She thought what an amazing father he would make. She loved him even that much more. How could someone be this awesome? Maria was so in love with Alberto, she never expected to love someone so fiercely in such a short time. She had no doubt in her mind that she wanted to spend the rest of her life with him. Maria was so happy that he got along so well with her best friend, her husband, and their child. They all had a wonderful lunch and just an awesome time. Maria and

Alberto were ready to leave and Franscica ran to Alberto and tugged on his pant leg and said: "No, no, no" She didn't want them to leave. Samantha picked up her daughter and said: "We will see them soon." They all said their goodbyes and thank yous.

Maria and Alberto returned to Maria's apartment. What a weekend this turned out to be. More amazing than you could ever dream possible. They decided they would stay at Alberto's through Thursday night. Maria needed to bring clothes for the whole work week. She packed her things, and they drove to Alberto's condo.

Alberto and Maria were getting to know each other better and they were learning about their lives and previous spouses. Alberto told Maria that Marissa was pregnant when she passed, and he wasn't even sure if she knew. Maria said: "Oh, I am so sorry to hear something like this. Besides losing your wife you lost your unborn child. How awful for you and her family." "Marissa was my office manager, and we were like together twenty-four hours a day." "Oh, how terrible. She sounds like a special person, so sweet and caring."

"You actually remind me of her in so many ways. I know she would want me to go on and find love again, and she would be happy about our relationship." Maria and Alberto had so many things in common that they could relate to each other so well. Maria had already shared a lot about Harry. Explained that he was Stan's younger brother and that Maria and Samantha met the brothers in California on New Year's Eve. She told Alberto that Harry helped her care for her grandmother. He told them that her grandfather loved

Harry and they became best friends. The week passed quickly, and Maria really liked being at Alberto's condo. They went and spent the weekend at Maria's so she could get caught up on things she needed to do. Alberto was always so thoughtful, thinking about Maria's needs before his own. He did whatever he could to make her life better. He was such a wonderful man, and Maria couldn't wait for her family to meet him. Maria wanted to take Alberto to Iowa to meet her parents and to San Diego to meet her sisters. She mentioned that Memorial Day was coming up and it was a three-day weekend, and she asked Alberto if he would like to go to Iowa then. He thought it was a great idea. Maria made the reservations, and the trip was set for three weeks later. Her parents were so excited to meet Alberto and to see Maria.

Maria and Alberto had been spending weeknights at Alberto's and weekends at Maria's house. They realized they had spent every evening and weekend together since the day they went to lunch. They were so in love with each other. You could see it in their eyes, smiles, and they both had a radiant glow. Life couldn't be any better for them.

On weekends, they would relax and often go to Alberto's parents' house for dinner. Sometimes they would come to Alberto's, and Maria would cook. Maria won the hearts of Alberto's parents. They could see why their son was so impressed with Maria the day they first met on the beach so long ago. Alberto's parents felt things like this only happened in fairytales. Life had been so cruel to both Maria and Alberto, but now they were only living something that usually only happens in a dream.

Maria and Alberto were at the airport waiting to board the plane for Des Moines. It was Friday of a long weekend, so the airport was crowded. The flight was on time, so they arrived as scheduled. Ethel and Raymond were thrilled to meet Alberto and to see their daughter. They drove to their house, and Maria showed Alberto her room. Ethel asked them if they were hungry. Both were hungry. She had prepared spaghetti, meatballs, and garlic bread on the stove. Ethel brought out the food and put it on the table with some wine. They all sat around the table and had a stimulating conversation. The weekend went by quickly, and Maria showed Alberto the town she grew up in and introduced him to many of her friends. Alberto made a great impression on Maria's parents.

It was Monday evening, and they were back from their trip. Alberto had missed being close to Maria at night. He had slept in the back bedroom at Maria's parents' house. They didn't want to be disrespectful, so Maria slept in her room by herself. Alberto asked Maria:

"I want to ask you, if you would like to move in with me here in my condo. I just don't want to spend another night away from you."

"Oh, Alberto OMG my answer is yes and yes. I will need to give my thirty-day notice, so I should be able to be out at the end of June, or I can move into your place sooner. Alberto said to Maria:

"We will look at the calendar and see what weekend will be the best to move you Maybe Samantha and Stan can help too." Alberto was in Maria's bedroom and said:

"Maria, come here," Alberto called from her room, his voice a mix of anticipation and warmth. She entered to find him reclined on the bed without his shirt, an inviting smile on his face. He swiftly lifted her, placing her gently on the bed. With deft movements, he unzipped her pants and unbuttoned her blouse, his touches exploring her body with a blend of passion and tenderness. Maria responded with equal fervor, kissing Alberto fervently, their actions mirroring a dance of deep intimacy. She marveled at his prowess and the careful attention he paid to what she enjoyed, urging him to be less gentle and more assertive, a change she found thrilling.

Alberto's respect for her desires made her feel comfortable and cherished, allowing her to express her true self. That night, their intimacy was profound and filled with exploration.

By the third weekend in June, they had decided it was time for Maria to move into Alberto's condo. The early June weekends were spent packing her apartment, with Alberto taking on much of the work. He considered the idea of buying a house together, wanting only the best for Maria. His career as a physician had taught him much about financial stability, and together with Maria's own financial acumen, they formed an impressive team.

Samantha and Stan lent their hands to help with the move. Alberto had rented a U-Haul, and Stan brought his truck to transport some of the larger furniture pieces. They started early in the morning and by eight in the evening, they were done. Exhausted but satisfied, they shared pizzas that Maria had ordered, their appetites fueled by the day's labor.

After thanking Samantha and Stan for their indispensable help, Maria and Alberto collapsed into sleep, utterly spent.

Living together brought Maria and Alberto even closer. Their commute was shorter, giving them more time together, and each day deepened their understanding of each other. Maria knew without a doubt she wanted to spend her life with Alberto. Their relationship was everything she had dreamed of and more, a sentiment Alberto shared wholeheartedly. They often visited Samantha, Stan, and Franscica, enjoying the family atmosphere and discussing future plans for their own family.

However, a few months into their living together, Maria started feeling unusual—she missed her period and experienced morning nausea. Despite being on the pill, she confided in Samantha, who suggested a pregnancy test. The test turned out positive. Overwhelmed with happiness yet tinged with disbelief, Maria worried about Alberto's reaction. She secured a doctor's appointment the next day, which confirmed her pregnancy. That evening, as they lay on the couch, she decided to share the news.

"I have something to tell you," Maria began, her voice shaky with nerves.

"What is it, sweetie?" Alberto responded, his tone full of curiosity and concern.

"It's a surprise, something very unexpected," Maria continued, her heart racing.

"Well, now you really have my curiosity," Alberto said, his eyes locking with hers.

"I hope it makes you happy," Maria whispered, taking a deep breath.

"What are you trying to tell me, Maria?" Alberto prompted gently.

"Honey, I am pregnant," Maria finally revealed, her voice a mix of joy and anxiety.

"OMG, Maria, you are? That is so exciting! How are you feeling?" Alberto exclaimed, his face lighting up with joy.

"I'm fine, just a bit nauseous," Maria replied, relief washing over her as she saw his enthusiastic response.

"I can't believe this. This is wonderful news," Alberto said, pulling her closer.

"So, you are good with this?" Maria needed to hear it, to confirm his feelings.

"Absolutely, I love you so much, and I want to be with you forever and eternity. You are my soul mate, my everything. My dear Maria, we were blessed to reconnect, and now we are blessed with a child. I am so excited and can't wait to be a father. You will make an awesome mother. Life has been really good to us lately, and this is just another blessing," Alberto affirmed, his words brimming with love and excitement.

They embraced tightly, overwhelmed by the turn their lives had taken. Together, they looked forward to the future with anticipation and boundless love, their dreams merging into a shared reality.

"Thank you, Alberto. I feel better now. I am so happy and glad that you feel that way, too. You are my everything, and

I am so excited about this new chapter in our lives. I want you to know I want to spend the rest of my life with you and become your wife. I never thought a love as great as ours was possible. I thought it was only in fairytales, but this is real."

Maria and Alberto started kissing and had such a night of passion that went on till sunrise. Luckily, it was Sunday morning, and they planned on staying in bed all day. They both had trouble keeping their hands off each other. Alberto told Maria that they needed some sleep. They could pick this up when they wake up. Maria agreed and felt she had never been so frisky. Alberto liked that Maria had become kind of wild, and he felt that she was just comfortable with him and being herself.

Alberto and Maria went to the Tonga Room at the Fairmont Hotel to celebrate the news of the pregnancy. Alberto adored Polynesian food, as did Maria. They savored a four-course dinner, the flavors reminiscent of their memories of Hawaii. After dinner, dancing commenced, and the atmosphere was electric. As the music played, encompassing all genres, the band started performing "I Will Always Love You" by Whitney Houston—Maria's favorite song. They danced together, and as the song concluded, the band announced, "Is there a Maria Hernandez here? Please come up here." Maria walked up, and Alberto, full of love and anticipation, got down on one knee and proposed:

"Maria, you are my everything. I love you more than life itself. I want you forever and eternity. I can't live my life without you. Will you do me the honor of becoming my wife? Will you marry me?"

"Yes, yes, yes!" Maria exclaimed as Alberto slipped the engagement ring onto her finger. The crowd around them erupted in applause, shouting "Congratulations!" They returned to their table, and Maria, overwhelmed with joy and surprise, said:

"You really surprised me, but I am very happy, honey. You are the sweetest, most kind and good-looking man I could ever imagine being in my life. The ring is stunning. OMG, I can't believe it. I feel like the luckiest woman on earth."

"I can't wait until we are married. I wanted to ask you, do you want a big wedding or a small cheerful ceremony with family and a few friends? You can think about it. I'm just excited with the baby coming and all," Alberto responded, his eyes gleaming with excitement.

"You know, sweetie, since this is both our second marriage, I am thinking that we can just elope. We can go to Vegas next weekend, and then I can be your wife. What do you think of that idea?" Maria suggested, her voice tinged with excitement and a bit of mischief.

"That's a great idea. I just don't want to take anything away from you, if you want a wedding with your family and friends," Alberto replied, his tone understanding and supportive.

"I am fine with just you and me being there," Maria assured him.

"Okay, I will make the reservations for Las Vegas for next weekend," Alberto confirmed, his smile wide with anticipation.

"I am really excited, sweetie," Maria beamed.

"I am glad. We are keeping the secret from everyone, right?" Alberto whispered.

"Yes, from everyone. We can tell everyone our news when we get back from Vegas," Maria agreed, already bubbling with the thrill of their little secret.

Maria was excited all week, finding it hard not to tell Samantha, but she had promised Alberto she wouldn't tell anyone. She couldn't wear her engagement ring, or else they would piece it together. She did mention to Samantha that they were going to Vegas for the weekend.

On Friday evening, Maria and Alberto arrived at the Las Vegas airport. They took a limousine to Caesar's Hotel, where Alberto efficiently handled the check-in. They rode the elevator to the top floor, their honeymoon suite sprawling and luxuriously appointed, setting the stage for their excitement about the next day. They dined out, then enjoyed some gambling, both winning at the slot machines. Eventually, they returned to their room, their thoughts aligned perfectly.

"I just can't keep my hands off you, my dear," Maria confessed as they entered their suite.

"That's okay. I love that you feel that way. It turns me on," Alberto replied, his desire palpable.

"You are so incredible, Alberto," Maria murmured, her admiration for him deepening.

"You are amazing, Maria. I can't believe how lucky we were to reconnect," Alberto acknowledged, pulling her close for another passionate night.

The following morning, filled with eager anticipation, Maria and Alberto found themselves in a cab heading to the iconic Little White Wedding Chapel. This venue, steeped in history and glamour, had witnessed the unions of countless celebrities, adding a touch of stardust to their special day.

As they were called forward, the excitement was palpable. Standing hand in hand, they exchanged vows with heartfelt sincerity, promising to cherish each other forever. The officiant's voice rang clear, "Ladies and gentlemen, I present to you Mr. and Mrs. Bertolucci." At that moment, Maria and Alberto stepped into a new chapter of their lives as husband and wife. Surrounded by the enchanting ambiance of the chapel, they sealed their vows with a kiss, a symbol of their unbreakable bond.

In the land of dreams, America, where anything is possible, Maria and Alberto proved that dreams do indeed come true. Their love, a testament to the enduring power of faith and passion, was perfectly captured by the words of Robert Browning: "Grow old along with me! The best is yet to be."